The Garden of Lost Secrets

KERRY BARRETT

ONE PLACE. MANY STORIES

HQ
An imprint of HarperCollins*Publishers* Ltd
1 London Bridge Street
London SE1 9GF

www.harpercollins.co.uk

HarperCollins*Publishers*
Macken House, 39/40 Mayor Street Upper,
Dublin 1 D01 C9W8

This paperback edition 2024

1

First published in Great Britain by
HQ, an imprint of HarperCollins*Publishers* Ltd 2024

ISBN: 9780008603175

MIX
Paper | Supporting
responsible forestry
FSC
www.fsc.org   **FSC™ C007454**

This book contains FSC™ certified paper and other controlled
sources to ensure responsible forest management.

For more information visit: www.harpercollins.co.uk/green

Printed and Bound in the UK using
100% Renewable Electricity at CPI Group (UK) Ltd

Prologue

The Americans had arrived and everyone in our little town was in a state of frenzied excitement.

They'd been whizzing along the lanes for hours, their noisy jeeps looking odd against the old-fashioned stone cottages.

'They're going to build a new air base,' my friend Patty told me, even though I knew. We all knew. We'd been talking about their arrival for weeks and weeks.

'It's not a new air base,' I said with the lofty air of someone who'd overheard a conversation that may or may have not been true. 'They're just taking over Eaton and making it bigger.'

'I've heard they have their own dances,' Patty said, clutching my arm. 'Remember my cousin, Lizzie? She lives in Bristol now and there are lots of GIs there already. They have dances on their base, and . . .' She breathed out in joy. 'And they have their own picture house, and they show films on a Friday night.'

I stared at her, dumbstruck with astonishment. 'Is that right?'

'That's what Lizzie said.'

We were perched on a wall at the back of my house where we

1

had a good view of the troops arriving. They'd been speeding along until now but somewhere up ahead – where the big farm was – a sheep had wandered across the lane and the procession of jeeps and trucks had slowed down.

'Pretend we're not looking,' I hissed to Patty as a jeep pulled up right next to us. 'Let's just make out like we're chatting to one another, and we don't even know they're there.'

Patty nodded vehemently.

'And anyway, I said to my mother that wouldn't do . . .' she said loudly, waving her hands around animatedly.

I watched the jeep out of the corner of my eye. Inside were four GIs who looked, well, disappointingly normal.

Along the road, the sheep was shooed back into the field and the procession started up again.

'I thought they'd look more like cowboys,' I said, adjusting how I was sitting on the wall because it was digging into me through my woolly stockings.

'Or like Clark Gable.' Patty pretended to swoon, and I laughed.

'They just look like our boys,' I said as another jeep swept past us along the lane. 'I really thought they'd be more . . .'

'Exotic?'

'Exactly.'

We both giggled.

'I can't believe I have to go back to school after Christmas and miss all the fun.'

'There won't be any fun.' Patty folded her arms. 'It's going to be hard work. My mum's used to just having your mother to look after, but now she's going to have a house full of men.'

I threw my head back in despair. 'And me hundreds of miles away. It's not fair.'

'Life's not fair, Gloria,' said Patty, sounding so much like my mother – deliberately – that I hooted with laughter.

'There's a war on, you know,' I added, doing my best to imitate Patty's mum, Fran, who I adored.

We both collapsed into giggles once more.

Reluctantly, I stretched my legs out in front of me, feeling the icy wind through my thin skirt, and jumped off the wall.

'I need to go,' I said. 'If I don't pass my exams then I'll have to go back to school for another year and I really don't want to.'

'Still planning to do your bit for the war effort?' Patty said.

I rolled my eyes. 'I am longing to do my bit,' I groaned. 'But how can I leave my mother?'

Patty looked sympathetic. 'She's getting better.'

'She is,' I said uncertainly. 'I suppose.'

'I'm going to join the Land Army,' Patty said, even though she'd told me that about twenty times already. 'Come with me?'

I screwed my nose up. 'I don't want to dig fields or make pots of tea,' I said. 'I want to be a spy, sneaking behind enemy lines to bamboozle the Nazis.'

'Bamboozle?' Patty said. 'How are you going to do that?'

I raised an eyebrow in what I thought was a mysterious manner. 'I will confuse them with my excellent French,' I said. I really did speak good French because I'd learned from my grandmother who was from Paris.

'Oh really?' Patty said.

'*Peut-être.*'

'Well, *bon chance* with that.' Patty stuck her tongue out at me and slid off the wall too. 'I'll see you tomorrow.'

'*A demain,*' I said, waving at her over my shoulder.

With the Americans all having passed, I thought about clambering over the wall into the grounds of my house but the drop was much higher on the other side, and if my mother saw me I would be in trouble. In fact, I thought, she frightened me more than the idea of falling. So I began walking towards home along the road our visitors had whizzed along, though I was going in the opposite direction. I'd only gone a little way when another convoy came along trundling past me to the junction in the road. There were fewer jeeps this time – just one or two, followed by a

3

couple of trucks. As they passed me, I could see inside where there were more soldiers, all with darker skin. I stood and watched as they went by and turned left at the junction instead of right on to the road that led to RAF Eaton.

Our house had been allocated to be used as accommodation for some of the American officers. The top brass, we'd been told. And we'd been told the rest of the GIs were going to be staying over at the air base. But if that was true, then these latest arrivals had gone the wrong way.

For a brief moment, I considered chasing after them to tell them they were lost. But then I shrugged, my mind already on my arithmetic homework. They'd work it out soon enough.

Chapter 1

The house had a drive. Not a patch of paving stones in front of the house, that a normal-size car didn't quite fit on, like our house in London had. This drive was more like a private road with gravel that crunched beneath the wheels of our car and made Marco tut because he didn't like anything that could damage the paintwork.

The entrance to the house was marked with two pillars built from the same honey-coloured stone as all the buildings nearby, and a strange, small, square brick-built sentry post.

'In the summer, we can hold events in the garden and sell ice cream from that funny wee building,' Marco said, slowing down to stop the gravel flying up. 'It'll be perfect.'

I looked out of the window at the tangled mess of undergrowth, fallen trees and muddy paths and tried to look enthusiastic.

'Definitely,' I said.

Marco pulled up outside the house, next to a dirty black SUV, and we got out of the car, stretching after the long drive.

'Here we are then,' he said. He put his arm round me. 'A new start.'

'An exciting new start,' I agreed. Firmly. Almost as though I was trying to persuade myself.

'Mr and Mrs Costello?' A man in a three-piece suit got out of the SUV, grinning broadly but unconvincingly.

'That's us,' I said. 'Philippa and Marco.'

'Graham Hodgson.' He reached out and shook my hand. 'Hodgson and Dobbs estate agents.' He turned to Marco and shook his hand too.

'*Ciao*,' he said. 'Welcome to Honeyford House. *Benvenuto!*'

Marco pushed his dark curly hair off his forehead and smiled at him. 'Hiya,' he said in his broadest, west-of-Scotland accent. 'Good to meet you, Graham.'

Graham looked startled for a moment and then recovered his composure. 'Did you come far?'

'South London,' I said. 'The removal van should be here any minute.'

'I have some keys for you.' Graham dropped them into my hand. 'Let me show you around.'

'We've been here lots of times . . .' I started to say, but Graham was already walking up the steps to the big front door. 'Looks like we're getting a tour,' I said to Marco, wandering over to where he was standing on the gravelly drive that surrounded the house, looking out over the garden.

He turned to me and put his arm round my shoulders, pulling me close and kissing my temple.

'This was a good decision,' he mumbled into my hair. 'It's just what we need. Something new to focus on. The beginning of the rest of our lives.'

I leaned into him for a second, enjoying the closeness after all the time we'd spent far apart. Then I took his hand. 'Come on. Graham wants to show us round.'

Hand in hand, we crunched across the gravel to the front of the house, then we went up the stairs, where we paused for a moment at the top and looked up at the house.

'I can't believe it's all ours,' Marco said.

'Well, it's the bank's,' I pointed out. 'If we're being picky.'

'Always the accountant.'

'I thought you were chefs?' Graham said. 'My colleague said you're planning to open a restaurant?'

'I'm the chef. Philippa is the business brain.' Marco grinned. 'But yes, we are planning to open a restaurant and rooms.'

'And maybe a wedding venue,' I added. 'We've got big plans.'

Graham raised an eyebrow. 'Good luck with that,' he said in a tone that suggested we were going to need it.

He pushed open the door and in we went.

Inside Honeyford House, there were eight bedrooms, a professional kitchen, a dining room, a largish ballroom, and a separate staff area with its own kitchen, bedroom and living room.

And it was absolutely and completely falling down around our ears.

We stood in the large foyer, watching the dust dancing in the winter sunlight that was coming in through a broken window.

'Shit,' said Marco, echoing my thoughts. 'It's much worse than I remember.'

'Lots of it is just cosmetic,' I said, trying to stay positive. 'The survey said it was sound, don't forget. Two surveys in fact.' I looked round, my enthusiasm wavering and added, rather weakly: 'It just needs a good clean.'

'I would recommend getting those stairs looked at, before you use them,' Graham said, wrinkling his nose up. 'They don't look very safe to me. It's just the two of you, isn't it? No kids?'

Marco found my hand again in the dim light. 'No,' he said. 'No kids.'

Chapter 2

Four months later

'It's not a difficult job,' the builder said, looking up at the roof. 'But we're going to have to take off most of the tiles and start again. So it will take a while.'

'When you say most of the tiles . . .' Marco screwed his face up and the builder, a lovely man named Harvey who'd been working on the renovation on Honeyford House for us, slapped him on the back sympathetically.

'I do really mean most,' he said. 'It's not all of them. It's just a bit fiddly.'

'I can't believe how unlucky we've been,' I said.

We'd had a leak, thanks to a few damaged roof tiles. And when Harvey had gone up to look at the damage, he'd discovered some of the roof struts were beginning to sag. Which was the problem, he had told us.

Harvey shrugged. 'Could say you were lucky. Because the struts are all right for now, but a bad winter and the whole roof could have come down.'

'Could we sue the company that did our survey?' Marco said hopefully.

8

'It was in the survey,' Harvey said, looking at Marco as if he was an idiot. 'You knew this repair would have to be done at some stage. This has just brought it forward.'

He pointed up at the ceiling. 'Those struts are too weak to take the new tiles. And if you want solar panels, too then we need to do this now. Or the solar panels will fall through the ceiling as soon as they're put up. So that means we need to take all the tiles off, replace the wood and then put the new tiles on.' He made a face. 'In fact, it's not just the damaged bit that needs replacing. Most of the tiles are worn. Probably best to replace them now rather than having to do it all again in a year or two.'

Marco groaned. 'Really?'

'False economy to wait, mate. You'd end up paying for more repairs every time it rains.'

Harvey pulled a scrap of paper out of his pocket and started drawing a diagram to explain why the roof above what was going to be the restaurant would keep letting in water if we didn't act.

Marco watched intently, asking questions about the bones of the house that I didn't understand and wasn't convinced he did either.

But I had a more pressing query.

'How long is a while?'

Harvey grimaced. 'Couple of months?'

'Okay,' I said. 'Right. We can work with that.'

Marco had gone a bit pale but I was not about to give up. We were absolutely going to make this work.

'What if we get screens to hide the damage from the leak?' I suggested. The restaurant was a beautiful addition on the side of the original Honeyford House, built from the same warm Cotswold stone with large, leaded windows that twinkled in the sun and were a bugger to keep clean. I called it an orangery even though I wasn't completely sure that's what it was.

We were standing outside, at the far end of the building where Harvey had climbed up to inspect the roof tiles, and now I went to the windows and peered in.

'The worst damage is to the ceiling and the wall there,' I said. We'd had a spring storm a few nights ago and come downstairs in the morning to a huge puddle of water, a hole in the ceiling and water running down the walls closest to the original house. 'So, we could screen it off, and use the rest of the restaurant.'

But Marco shook his head. 'We'd lose a lot of tables, though. And what if there's another leak somewhere else?'

I looked at Harvey. 'Could that happen?'

He narrowed his eyes and looked up at the roof. 'Probably not,' he said. My heart lifted a little bit. 'The problem's with the original part of the roof, not the new conservatory.'

'It's an orangery,' I said.

'Is it?' Harvey looked unconvinced.

I ignored him. 'So, we could get some screens,' I said to Marco, who had wandered across the terrace and was looking out over the view. 'What do you think, Marco?'

'I've got an idea,' he said.

I went to where he was standing. 'What's your idea?

'We could make the most of this,' he said, waving his hand and taking in the land that surrounded us.

The countryside around Honeyford House was breath-taking; there was no doubt. The house itself sat on a small hill, with a garden that sloped gently down to a small river. The river itself snaked through the fields to the town of Honeyford with its little humpbacked bridge, the ford that no one used except tourists and occasional, impatient lorries, and its golden stone buildings that glowed in the evening sunshine. From where we stood, we could see the fields falling away from us, like a patchwork quilt in every shade of green, the spire of the church in the town, and a few cottages on the outskirts of Honeyford.

'What do you mean?'

'We can put tables on the terrace for the summer. Expand the restaurant outdoors. I don't just mean for nice days, I mean for every day. Like I did at the pub in London during Covid.'

'This terrace?' I looked round at the weeds growing through the gravel, and then down at the overgrown garden.

'Yes, this terrace,' Marco said with mock frustration. 'I know it's not ideal, but I can hire some tables and chairs. Bit of power washing up here. You love power washing.'

I nodded, pleased he wasn't letting this hiccup interfere with our plans. It felt very important that we made this new life a success. 'That's true, I do love power washing.'

'See!' He looked excited. 'We can do it, Phil.'

'We'll have to clear the garden,' I said. 'We can't have guests looking out over waist-high grass and brambles.'

'We could ask Harvey to help.' He turned round to look at Harvey, who was halfway up his ladder, looking at a window frame.'

'Do not ask Harvey,' I said hurriedly. 'I'm not paying for anything else.'

Marco grinned. 'We can do some outdoor dining, and some inside. It's better than losing tables.'

'I know,' I said, taking his hand, relieved he was being so proactive. 'And we've come such a long way, we can't stop now.'

Since we'd moved in, we'd totally cleaned and redecorated the entrance hall – all by ourselves – and had the stairs repaired – by Harvey, thank goodness because our DIY skills only stretched so far. Marco had updated the kitchen and together we'd created a bar area, with comfy sofas and great views.

We'd decided not to worry about the guest rooms this year – we'd tackle those after Christmas – or our own part of the house, which had once been the servants' quarters. So our own kitchen was a 1990s dream, decked out in tiles with pictures of little sheaves of wheat and cupboard doors that were hanging off. And our bathroom was worse – pink sink, pink bath, pink toilet. Even the floor was pink. It felt like being back in the womb. But our priority had been getting the restaurant up and running so the rest of the house had to wait. Marco was a great chef, and we were confident that the momentum of the restaurant would carry us through to becoming an upmarket B&B and eventually let us rip out that pink bath.

This latest mishap was disappointing, but not insurmountable. At least I hoped it wasn't. And yes, it would make a bigger dent in our budget than we'd planned. But I was a whizz with an Excel spreadsheet. I could sort that out.

I looked over the garden. 'We could probably hire one of those lawnmowers you sit on,' I said.

'Is that a yes?' Marco looked eager. 'We'll try expanding outdoors?'

Of course it was a yes. 'Let's give it a go.'

He put his arm round me and squeezed me tight. 'It's not ideal, but we'll make it work.'

'Story of our lives,' I said, only half-joking.

I looked round at the terrace. 'How many tables do you think?'

'Four tables of four, perhaps?' Marco scanned the space. 'We might get a smaller one in over there, too.'

'We'll need good lighting.'

'We will.' He screwed his nose up. 'And perhaps some sort of shelter? If we're unlucky and we get a rotten summer, then it'll ruin everything.'

I gave him a rueful smile. 'Knowing our track record with luck, I'd say we should definitely plan for the wettest summer since records began. And also gales. Perhaps even snow.'

'We could put up a sort of awning?' Marco said, puffing his chest out. 'Or I could build something. A pergola.'

'Or, we could just buy some big umbrellas.'

'What if they blow away in the gales we're expecting?'

'What if this is a listed building and we're not allowed to build stuff without permission?'

'Ah, shit,' Marco said. 'Do you think a pergola would need planning permission?'

'No idea. I could phone the council and ask.'

'Yes please.'

Harvey clambered down the ladder and came over. 'I'll write you up an estimate,' he said. 'At least I'll try. I've got this new software that's meant to make my finances more straightforward, but it's taking me twice as long to do anything at the moment.'

'QuickTax?' I said.

He made a face. 'That's the one.'

'I can help you with that, if you'd like? Go through it all with you?'

Harvey frowned. 'I thought you'd left accountancy.'

'Oh, you can never really leave,' I joked. 'Honestly, it's fine. I've been doing the books for Mick at the village shop too, because his accountant left him in the lurch.'

'You wouldn't mind?'

'Course not.'

Harvey looked delighted. 'Make it all make sense and I'll knock twenty per cent off the bill.'

'God, you don't have to do . . . Ouch.' I trailed off as Marco gave me a poke in the ribs and gave me a tiny shake of his head. 'It's a deal.'

'Speaking of Mick, I've got some paperwork for him, so I'll wander down there now, if you're all done, Harvey?'

Harvey nodded. 'I'll call you about the software.'

'Great.'

We waved him off as he gathered his bag and headed towards his van.

'You really think we can break even, if we put enough tables outside?' I said.

Marco looked thoughtful. 'If I'm clever with the menus and you can help serve to save the cost of one member of staff, then I think so. Just about.'

I put my arms round him. 'It's just another hiccup.'

Marco rested his head on my chin. 'We should be used to them by now, eh?'

'We should.'

We stayed that way for a little while and then he said: 'Did you say you were going to the shop?'

'Yes.'

'Get a bottle of wine, while we can still afford to drink.'

'Come with me and we can go to the pub?'

But Marco shook his head. 'Nah,' he said. 'I'm going to google pergolas and awnings.'

'Don't watch that *Chateau* programme again,' I groaned. 'You know it makes you think you can build anything out of a couple of offcuts and an old jam jar. Remember what happened with the shed in London?'

'Trust me,' Marco said.

'I absolutely don't.'

I found the paperwork I needed for Mick, then I picked up my bag and my phone, and set off down the road to the town. It was a beautiful spring day – the rainstorms that had leaked into the restaurant had cleared and everything looked like it had been washed clean. I breathed in deeply, enjoying the fresh air. It felt like a new beginning, I thought. Which was just what we needed – it was why we'd come to the Cotswolds in the first place. We needed a new start after the perfect storm of huge life-changing events that had left us a little shell-shocked, and desperate to move on.

First of all, we'd spent years trying – and failing – to have a baby. It had been almost five years now since my last miscarriage. Five years of heartache as we realised that with us both heading into our mid-forties, babies weren't really an option for us anymore.

And then my mother died, and my relationship with her had been, well, complicated was an understatement, so I felt odd about grieving, prickly and out of sorts.

Shortly after that, I'd been made redundant. I'd been in my job a good few years – staying way longer than I'd ever intended so I'd get the maximum maternity leave, except of course, I'd never needed it. But it meant I got a nice payout. Meanwhile, Marco was struggling with the pub after lockdown and all that, and he and his business partner had an offer to sell, but he was worried about what to do next if they agreed a deal.

And then we'd been to a friend's fiftieth birthday party in Cheltenham and on the way home, we'd stopped in Honeyford for lunch, and we'd seen the house and we'd realised that perhaps it was the change of direction we'd been looking for.

So here we were. And the gnawing emptiness inside of me was getting smaller every day. Or at least, that was what I told Marco.

And myself.

I wandered along the main road of the village. It really was a million miles away from South London – though I'd liked it there, too. The street was wide with strips of grass separating the road from the pavement and the shops on either side. The buildings were all the same tawny Cotswold stone, with leaded windows like the ones at Honeyford House and the shops were a mixture of little local businesses and the occasional high-end brand.

The high street wound down to the river, where the hump-backed bridge – and the ford – crossed the water. But I was approaching from the top end. On the corner of a side street was Honeyford Essentials – a cute store that sold everything from milk and bread, to booze and crisps, as well as light bulbs, newspapers and headache tablets. It was open late, and early, and I spent almost as much time in there as I spent at home.

'Hi, Mick,' I said, as I entered, waving at the owner, who was chatting to a woman at the counter.

He made an exaggerated play of checking his watch. 'It's five o'clock,' he said. 'Frankly it could be either wine or milk at this time of day.'

'Rude,' I said mildly. 'I'm here to return your paperwork.'

He laughed. 'Then I apologise,' he said. 'And I'm so grateful for your help.'

I smiled at him. 'I'm also here for wine.' I took two bottles of white from the fridge.

I put the bottles on the counter and pulled the folder of paperwork out of my bag. 'Here you are. It's all done.'

Mick took the folder and stared at me in wonder. 'Have those bottles on the house,' he said.

'Are you sure?'

'Absolutely.'

'Then thank you,' I said with a smile. 'It's been one of those days.'

'Problems with the renovations?' he asked. He turned to the woman. 'Philippa and her husband bought Honeyford House.'

The woman looked delighted. 'Wonderful! I've been watching the renovations every time I drive by. I was so pleased it sold – a house like that shouldn't be standing empty.'

'We're pleased too,' I said.

'I think I've seen your husband around,' the woman went on. 'Dark curly hair?'

'That's him.' I smiled at her. 'He's a chef – we're supposed to be opening a restaurant at Honeyford.'

'Supposed to be?' the woman asked. She was a little older than me – perhaps early fifties, and though she was dressed in fitness gear and looked athletic, she also had large dark circles under her eyes.

'The roof is leaking so part of the dining room's out of action,' I said with a groan. 'Harvey's sorting it but it's going to take a while and it means we can't fill the restaurant, and that means making less money, obviously.'

The woman was looking thoughtful. 'What about the terrace?'

I was surprised she seemed to know the house so well.

'That's Marco's plan,' I said. 'He wants to put up an awning or a pergola or something for shelter and offer outdoor dining.'

The woman was frowning. 'You might need planning permission for that.'

'That's my worry.'

'Vanessa works at the museum now, but she used to work for the council,' Mick said. 'In the planning department.'

'Oh, brilliant, that's so useful,' I said. Then, remembering my manners, I added: 'It's lovely to meet you, Vanessa.'

Vanessa shook my outstretched hand. 'And you,' she said. 'I might be able to help you if you like? With your plans.'

'Really?'

She nodded. 'I need to dash off now – Alex will be wanting his dinner and he's got football tonight so he can't wait – but I'm around tomorrow. Would you like me to pop round and we can go over your ideas together?'

'Would you?' I was almost weak with gratitude. People were so nice here.

'Of course.' Vanessa grinned at me. 'It'll be lovely to get to have a nosy inside Honeyford House, too. See what you've done.'

'You might be horrified,' I said, only half-joking. 'We've not done much yet. Our bit of the house is monstrous.'

She chuckled. 'I bet I've seen worse.'

I wasn't sure about that, but we swapped numbers and arranged that she'd come round in the morning, and then she headed off.

'What a nice woman,' I said.

Mick nodded. 'She's a trouper,' he said approvingly. 'She's not long taken in her grandson.'

'She's a granny?' I was astonished.

'Yes, Alex is twelve.'

'Where are his parents?'

Mick shrugged. 'His mum lives in Oxford, I think. But she's got some issues. I don't know all the details.'

'Vanessa just took him in?' I felt a rush of pity for the little boy – and admiration for Vanessa.

Mick sighed. 'Didn't think twice about it, by all accounts. She's done her best for that lad. That's why she left the council, actually, because she couldn't commute anymore and be around for him, so she works locally now.'

'Didn't think twice,' I repeated softly to myself. 'Alex is lucky to have her,' I said more loudly.

'I think they're lucky to have one another.'

True to her word, Vanessa arrived the following day, just as she'd promised. I was in our living room looking at Harvey's accounts when I heard the doorbell clanging and Marco calling out from the back of the house. I pressed save and went outside to say hello.

Marco was in full flow when I arrived, with Vanessa listening intently.

'An awning wouldn't work because you'd have to attach it to the house, but a pergola could be fine. If it's not attached in any way,' she was saying.

Marco shook his head. 'We could keep it completely separate.'

'And it won't be brick?'

'I was thinking wood, with perhaps a plastic roof?'

I screwed my nose up. 'Plastic? Hello, Vanessa.'

She nodded a greeting at me, and I studied her. She looked more groomed today. She was wearing flared jeans and a faded Fleetwood Mac T-shirt, and she had makeup on, and she most definitely didn't look like a granny.

'Plastic would work,' she said to Marco. 'The key is to keep it a temporary structure, makes life easier. Though obviously that's not as pretty.'

'We can use transparent plastic and put fairy lights up,' Marco assured me. 'Maybe some of those fake flowers like the Instagrammers use. It'll look great.'

I smiled at Vanessa. 'Marco's so much better at this stuff than I am. I have no vision.'

Marco draped his arm round my shoulders. 'But you have the business brain, my darling.'

'Let's hope so.' I rubbed my nose. 'What do you think, Vanessa? Is a pergola a go-er?'

Vanessa made a face. 'Should be. But this is a conservation area, so I'm reluctant to say it's one hundred per cent going to be all right without double-checking.'

'If you had to say one way or the other?' Marco said.

'Gun to my head?' She looked up at where the pergola would be, almost like she could see it already. 'I'll email one of my former colleagues and get them to say one or the other for definite, but I'd say start measuring up.'

I felt Marco slump in relief. 'Thank you,' he almost whispered looking slightly tearful. He was a slave to his emotions, my husband. He said it was the Italian in him, but as his whole family were the most stoic people I knew, I thought it was just the way he was made. I rather liked it. Now he shook his curly head and forced a smile. 'If you'll excuse me, I've got something to sort out in the kitchen.'

He hurried off and Vanessa gave me a curious look. 'Is he all right?'

'He's fine.' I grinned at her. 'Thank you so much for coming. If we can do some outdoor dining until the roof is fixed, it'll make such a difference.'

'Happy to help.' She looked up at the house, taking it in.

'Want the tour?' I could see she was keen to see inside.

'Am I being really obvious? I'd love to see what you've done so far.'

I laughed. 'Come on, then.'

I took her round the kitchen where Marco had recovered his equilibrium and was writing trial menus, and then the restaurant where I showed her the damage caused by the leak. She was so interested and chatty, asking about our plans, and what Harvey was up to. It was a pleasure to show her round and I felt a surge of pride as I took her upstairs and talked her through what we wanted to do with the bedrooms.

'You like it here,' she said.

I leaned against the doorframe and thought about it. 'I do.'

'You sound surprised.'

'I am a bit.' I sighed. 'It wasn't what we had planned, but I'm glad we're here now.'

'Life has a habit of changing our plans,' Vanessa said with a grin.

'Do you have time for a cup of tea?'

'I'd love one.'

We went down the back stairs into our part of the house, with me apologising for the dated décor and Vanessa waving aside my protests.

'You're going to make it beautiful,' she said.

'Mick told me you had to leave the council. Are you missing it?' I asked, as I filled the kettle.

She gave me a mischievous glance. 'It wasn't what I'd planned,' she said.

'Because of Alex?'

'That's right – Mick filled you in, did he?'

'Just briefly.' I didn't want her to think we'd been gossiping about her.

'Alex lives with me now, so I'm back to being a taxi service and supervising homework.'

'Must take some getting used to,' I said.

'It does.'

I looked down at the mugs of brewing tea. 'I was in care for a little while,' I said. 'My mum couldn't always look after me.' I glanced over my shoulder at Vanessa. 'It's a really good thing you're doing.'

Vanessa took a deep breath. 'Tilly – that's my daughter – she has made some . . .' She paused, searching for the word. 'She has made some bad decisions. She can't have Alex with her. So I've got him.'

I felt a sudden and unexpected jolt of envy that Alex had the security of a loving grandmother to care for him when his mother couldn't, followed almost immediately by a sense of shame for feeling that way.

'Milk and sugar?' I asked brightly, trying to distract myself from my horrible thoughts.

'Just milk please.'

I poured the milk and passed her the mug, and we went into the lounge to sit down.

'It's lovely having Alex with me,' Vanessa said. 'But it's been a big change.'

'I'm not surprised. How long has he been living with you?'

'Just about six months full-time.'

'Is he with you permanently?'

She grimaced. 'Social services say not, but . . .'

For a horrible moment I thought she was going to cry.

'Don't talk about it if it upsets you,' I said hurriedly. 'I was being nosy, sorry.'

But Vanessa took a mouthful of tea and said: 'Alex's father is not a nice man. And Tilly knows he is dangerous, but she continues to choose him. And as long as she sees him, she can't have Alex with her.'

'It's not always straightforward,' I said, even though it seemed very straightforward to me. For the millionth time I thought about how unfair it was that some people didn't want the children they'd been blessed with, while I . . . well, nothing was straightforward really, was it?

'It's not,' Vanessa said. 'She's as much as a victim in this as Alex is I suppose. She has a lot of demons and Alex's father is very manipulative.'

I drank some tea. 'It can't have been easy for you.'

She gave me a small smile. 'No.'

There was a short, slightly awkward silence, then as though she'd found something safe to talk about, Vanessa sat up and her expression brightened.

'I work at the Honeyford Museum now,' she said.

'I've walked past lots of times but haven't got round to visiting the museum yet.'

She smiled. 'It's very small. But I could have a look and see if there are any old photographs of the house.'

'I'd love that.'

She nodded. 'It's got a lot of history, this house. Not all of it good.'

I shivered, even though it wasn't cold. 'I can't wait to hear all about it.'

Chapter 3

Gloria
Spring 1943

School was over for me. All my classmates had gone to train as nurses, or to drive jeeps, or any one of a hundred jobs that sounded more exciting than what I was doing. Which was absolutely nothing.

'But your house has been full of GIs for months,' my friend Cynthia had said as we'd parted after our final day at school. 'That's thrilling in itself.'

Cynthia was terribly clever at reading maps, could drive a car even though she was only 17, and she wanted to fly aeroplanes. I had no doubt at all that she'd do as she planned. I'd given her a weak smile. 'Thrilling,' I'd said.

The trouble was, my father was dead. He had been killed almost before the war had really got going, and my mother had been absolutely furious about it.

When the telegram had first arrived, and I'd come home from school for the funeral, she'd been in a rage. Smashing plates. Drinking endless bottles of gin and then throwing the glasses at the wall. Staggering out into the garden and screaming into the sky. And then sobbing her heart out.

Once those strange, bleak early days after his death had passed, I'd been relieved to go back to school and have an escape from all the grief. I was sad about my father too, of course, but in a kind of distant way because really, I'd never had much to do with him. That sounded awful. I had loved him. But both my parents regarded me with what I always thought of as fond bewilderment as though I was an amusing stranger who'd wandered into their house.

Once Daddy died, though, I felt the weight of responsibility heavy on my shoulders. I knew I had to look after my mother and help her through her sadness.

At home I'd watched my mother like a hawk, keeping an eye on the level of the gin bottle on the sideboard and making sure she was all right. It was three years now since my father had died, and a month since I'd been home from school for good. It seemed that most of the time Mother would go along quite nicely. Until something would happen – my father's birthday, a song on the wireless that reminded her of him – and she would tumble down into that dark anger once more. I'd usually tried to come home from school on Daddy's birthday, just so I was there to support her.

When the bad days hit, she would be angry and melancholic in turn. And today was a bad day because it was my parents' wedding anniversary. And worse – I'd forgotten so I'd not even prepared myself for the sadness.

So now, I was in the garden, and behind me in the house I could hear Mother shrieking about how she'd told Daddy not to go, how he'd done his bit in the last war, and she'd told him not to join up. Thankfully, Fran, Patty's mother, was here and I could hear her talking in a calm, low voice.

'Hiding?' said a voice. I was sitting on the wall of the terrace, looking out over the garden. But now I turned to see one of the American officers. He was an older man, with a bushy moustache speckled with grey. Handsome, I thought. He had faded blue eyes that were watching me with kindness.

'Not hiding,' I said. I thought about how to explain. 'Bracing myself.'

'Your mom?' he said, tilting his head towards the house, where the sound of my mother's raised voice drifted.

I nodded.

'What'd you do?'

I smiled a little smile. 'Nothing. She's not angry with me.'

'Who's she angry with?'

'The war.'

The officer patted the stone wall next to where I sat. 'May I?'

'Course.'

He sat down next to me letting his legs dangle over the edge like mine. I thought that was funny. He took out a cigarette and lit it and I thought that even though he was old, he was much more like the movie star type of American Patty and I had been expecting.

'I'm Waldo,' he said.

'Gloria.'

He nodded at me in greeting. I didn't know if Waldo was his first name or last name, but I didn't want to ask.

'You lost your dad?' he said.

Taken aback by his direct question, I swallowed. 'Yes. In 1940.'

He nodded. 'Not surprised she's angry.'

'She's fine most of the time now,' I said. 'But it's their wedding anniversary today.'

'That's tough.'

'Yes.'

He looked at me. 'You miss him? Your dad?'

'Sometimes.'

He smiled at me. 'I lost my dad when I was about your age. How old are you?'

'Seventeen.'

'I was fifteen when my dad died.'

'That's tough,' I said, echoing his own words.

25

'It was.' He blew some smoke rings up into the sky. 'More than thirty years ago. But I still miss him sometimes too.'

I felt very close to tears suddenly. 'I miss him today,' I said in a small voice.

'Yep.'

He nudged my shoulder with his, letting me know he understood, and we sat there in silence for a moment.

'You done with school?'

'Yes.'

'So what's next? Going to join up?'

I shook my head. 'I don't think so.' Behind me, something smashed. Mother had thrown a lot of crockery when Daddy first died, but not so much nowadays so I thought it had probably been an accident. But I still winced. Waldo's eyes flashed with understanding.

'Don't want to leave your mom?'

'Not yet.'

The sound of an engine starting up made Waldo look round. He ground out his cigarette and flicked his butt off the terrace.

'They'll be looking for me shortly.'

He jumped down off the wall and dusted off his hands.

'When my dad died, my mom took on a project,' he said. 'Kept herself busy.'

'Project?'

'She organised the Fourth of July celebrations in our town.' He smiled. 'She still does it now. Maybe your mom just needs a distraction?'

'Huh,' I said. 'A distraction.'

'Maybe.' He grinned at me, and I wondered if his moustache tickled his lips. 'I'm sure you can come up with something.'

He crunched off across the gravel and I sat on the wall and looked down towards Honeyford, thinking about what he'd said.

A project? I liked the idea. I liked solving problems and my mother's grief was the biggest problem I had. Perhaps she did need something to do, something that would keep her busy.

And perhaps I needed a distraction too, because the truth was, I was bored and lonely and I was missing Patty, who'd been as good as her word and joined the Land Army.

My grandmother – my Mamie, my mother's mother – didn't like the countryside so she never left London if she could help it despite us begging her to come to live with us. When the Blitz had been happening, I'd written to her almost every day because I was so worried about her. Now I only wrote every now and then because I was finding I had less and less to tell her.

I kicked my heels against the wall and thought about Waldo's mother organising the Fourth of July celebrations. Honeyford was sadly lacking in Fourth of July parties but surely there was something I could find for Mother to do.

Full of determination suddenly, I jumped off the wall. I'd go for a walk into the village and see if inspiration struck.

Our garden was big. Too big, really. We'd had gardeners when I was younger but of course since the war, they'd all gone. Now the lawn was overgrown and tatty. When Mother was on an even keel she pottered round the borders, and occasionally she'd find someone willing to cut the grass. I quite liked it like this though. It felt better.

I marched across the lawn, enjoying the feeling of the long grass tickling my shins, then walked through the trees at the side of the lawn and came out on to the long driveway. At the end, where the gates were, was an American jeep with a GI inside. He was in the driver's seat, but he was lying back, looking half asleep. He had fair hair and a chiselled jawline. A little bit further on were two other airmen, who were busy building what seemed to be a sort of sentry box. They were using red bricks, which looked odd next to the honey-coloured stone of the gates and the wall around the garden. My father would have been furious if he were here to see it. He had been very proud of our Cotswold stone home.

As I approached, my feet crunching on the gravel, the GI in the jeep must have heard me coming. He jumped out and saluted me.

'Hello, miss,' he said.

I waved at him. 'Hello.' Then I turned my attention to the men who were laying the bricks. 'What are you building?'

One of the men straightened up, holding a brick in his hand. He grinned at me and I grinned back. He was about my age, I thought. Perhaps a little older. And he was dark-skinned, as was the other GI helping him. Most of the GIs we saw round Honeyford were white. I never really saw much of the Black GIs.

'Is it for a guard?' I asked.

The GI nodded. 'That's the plan.'

'So you can keep an eye on who's coming and going to my house?'

The fair-haired man stepped forward, so he was in between me and the GI holding the brick. 'We need to keep you safe, miss.' Then he turned. 'Get back to work, boy,' he said, his tone much harsher than the polite voice he'd used to speak to me. 'We don't have time for your dawdling.'

I didn't like the nasty edge to what he said, and the way he called the man "boy" made me bristle, though I didn't really know why.

I watched the GI holding the brick, wanting to catch his eye and share a moment of "who does he think he is" as I'd always done at school if a teacher spoke unnecessarily harshly. But he dropped his gaze and immediately crouched down to carry on laying bricks.

I watched him for a second, then to my surprise, the fair-haired man took my elbow and steered me away from the gates, out on to the pavement.

'I'm very sorry about that, miss. You shouldn't have been put in that position.'

I stared at him. 'What position?'

'I shouldn't have allowed you to get close enough to speak with the other men there.' His voice was heavy and drawling, and made me think of the last days of summer. 'I apologise. They're a little workshy, and take any chance they get to slack off.'

28

He gave a little chuckle. 'That's why this building work is taking so long, I imagine.'

'Don't you think they'd get along quicker if you gave them a hand?' I said.

'Well, I'm not sure about that, miss. I'm overseeing the work. I need to keep an eye on them.'

'You do?'

He lifted his chin. 'Yes, miss. They ain't always trustworthy, that's the truth. It's a sad truth but that's just how it is. And that's why I shouldn't have let you speak with them.'

I studied him. He was quite handsome with his all-American cropped hairstyle and his white teeth. But his eyes weren't sparkling like Waldo's were. Instead, they were cold and I didn't like the way he looked at the men he was watching over.

'What's your name?' I asked.

'Corporal Cole Perkins.'

I smiled. 'I'm Gloria Henry,' I said. 'I live here.' I gave him a beaming smile. 'And I can speak to whomever I like in my own garden.'

Annoyance flashed across his handsome face and then he recovered his composure. 'Pleasure to make your acquaintance, Miss Henry. I'm just looking out for you, is all.'

'Well,' I said. 'There's absolutely no need.'

'Corporal Perkins?' The GI who'd smiled at me stood there, looking at his feet. 'We're going to need more cement, sir.'

'Already?'

'Yes, sir.'

'I need to get back to work,' Corporal Perkins said to me. 'Have a good day, miss.'

I gave him a polite nod goodbye as he went back through the gates, tutting about how the men were using too much cement, too quickly. The other GI stood there for a second, then just before he turned to follow the corporal, he lifted his gaze and met my curious stare. Then he winked at me.

Amused, and surprised, I wasn't quick enough to respond before he vanished back into the garden and out of sight.

But I found myself hoping I'd see him again soon.

Chapter 4

Gloria

I wasn't sure exactly where I was heading, but as I spent most of my time reading, tearing through every book I could get my hands on, I thought I would start off at the library, to see if there was anything new I could borrow, while I thought about how to occupy Mother.

I spent a very satisfying half hour in the library, browsing my favourite spy novels and detective stories. I chose a few, and had a chat with the librarian, Mrs Poole, and then I wandered outside again. I knew I should go home because it was getting late and my mother would be expecting me for dinner, but I still hadn't come up with any good ideas so instead, I walked very slowly through the village, in the opposite direction to my house, waiting for inspiration to strike.

At the end of the street was the post office and outside was a jeep with four GIs inside. Two of them jumped out and took a bag of mail into the post office, while the others sat in the jeep and smoked. As I approached, I recognised one as Corporal Perkins – the chap I'd met earlier, who'd been supervising the men building the sentry box at home.

'Hello again, Miss Henry,' he called through the open window.

'Hello,' I said.

'Miss Henry lives in Honeyford House,' Corporal Perkins said. 'Miss Henry, this is Corporal Taylor.'

Taylor smiled at me. He had dark hair and sleepy eyes. 'Nice to meet you, Miss Henry.'

'Headed home now?' asked Corporal Perkins.

I glanced at my wristwatch. 'I suppose so.'

'We could give you a ride, if you want to wait? The others are just collecting our mail, and dropping off some letters.'

I thought about walking back up the hill and smiled. 'If you're sure that would be all right?'

'Absolutely it is,' said Perkins, smiling. He looked a lot friendlier than he had done earlier. 'Hop in.'

Feeling rather daring, I waited while Taylor got out of the jeep, and let me sit down. He got in the back seat.

'Did you finish the sentry box?' I asked Perkins.

He made a face. 'Not as quickly as I'd have liked. But it's getting there.'

I thought again they'd have got it done faster if he'd helped, but I didn't say that. Instead, I just nodded.

'So where are the others?' I asked.

Perkins gestured over his shoulder with his thumb.

'Getting mail,' he said. 'I told you.'

I smiled, arranging my library books in my lap where I sat. 'Not those others, the other others. The ones who were building the sentry box.'

He frowned at me.

'Now, Miss Henry, you don't need to be concerning yourself with their whereabouts,' he said. 'All you have to do is trust me when I say those men will not be bothering you again, and once again, I am very sorry about them engaging with you.'

It was my time to frown. 'They didn't bother me,' I said, scratching my head. 'Not one jot.'

'One jot,' said Taylor from the back seat in a vague approxima-
tion of my English accent. 'Not one jot.'

I turned round and fixed him with my most withering look
and he dropped his gaze, satisfyingly chastened.

'Sorry,' he muttered. 'That was rude.'

'It was a bit,' I said. I turned my attention back to Perkins.
'You don't need to make such a fuss about the others. They were
perfectly polite.'

'Perfectly . . .' Taylor began.

'Don't,' I warned, and he shut his mouth.

Perkins looked amused. 'You just need to be careful is all,' he
said.

'Of what?'

He sighed. 'I can see you're a young woman who knows her own
mind but I'm assuming you've never visited the United States?'

'I've only ever been to France.'

'Well, things are a little different back home.'

'How so?' I asked. 'No,' I said to Taylor, seeing him open his
mouth again. 'Don't mimic me.'

But Taylor shook his head. 'I was just going to point out that Perkins
here don't speak for all of us,' he said. 'Not all of the United States.'

Perkins gave Taylor a fierce glance. I had absolutely no idea
what was going on between the two men but I felt the tension
crackling between them and I was relieved when the other airmen
came out of the post office.

'Hey, Perkins. There's a dance,' one began to say, but he stopped
short to see me sitting in the jeep.

'This is Miss Henry from Honeyford House,' Perkins said.
'We're giving her a ride home. You boys behave yourselves now.'

The men both nodded politely to me and bundled into the
back of the jeep.

'There's a dance,' I said in delight. 'Of course!'

Perkins started the engine and pulled away. 'What's this about
a dance?' he asked me.

'We have the summer fair during the day then the dance in the evening,' I said. 'It used to happen every year on the green.' I gestured behind me to the village green in front of the church. 'But we've not had it since the war started. I'd heard people saying it was going to happen this year but I didn't know it had been decided. I wonder if there's a committee organising it . . .'

It was the perfect project for my mother to take on. She knew everyone and she had a knack of getting people to do exactly what she wanted them to do. I was pleased.

'You going?' Taylor asked, over his shoulder.

I screwed my nose up. 'I don't have a lot of friends in the village because I went away to school. Except Patty and she's joined up.'

'You're not going to the dance?' Perkins glanced round at me and winked. I felt my cheeks flush. 'Shame.'

'I'm not really a dancer,' I said.

'You should come,' said Taylor. 'It'll be fun. I bet you don't get a lot of fun round here.'

I thought about being offended at that, but actually he was right.

'Not much,' I admitted.

'Then come,' he urged.

'I won't know anyone.'

'You'll know us,' said Perkins.

I laughed. 'I'll think about it.'

'That's a start,' he said.

We motored on up the hill. Up ahead I could see the sentry box standing straight at the side of the road.

'Goodness, they did a lot,' I said. 'They worked hard.'

'Well, that's a first,' said Perkins. 'Huh, guys?'

The other airmen muttered in agreement, except Taylor who snorted.

Perkins turned into the driveway of Honeyford House. 'Miss Henry,' he began.

'Lord, please call me Gloria,' I said.

34

'Gloria, you know we have two bases, right? One for the men like us, and one for the others.'

I did know that. I thought back to the first day when Patty and I had watched them arrive and how the men went in opposite directions. The officers were at my house, the white airmen were stationed on the air base along the river, and the other airmen – the Black ones – they were living in different accommodation, which was much more basic. It was clear there was a hierarchy among the Americans. Of course there was. There was a hierarchy everywhere; I knew that. And nowhere more than in the armed forces with ranks and whatnot. But this was different. More complicated.

'I know that,' I said.

Perkins stopped the jeep. 'Gloria, it's hard for you British folk to understand but those other men are different from us, so it makes sense that we stay separate.' He sighed. 'Separate but equal.'

Taylor snorted again and Perkins glowered at him.

'Separate schools?' I said, because I did read the newspapers and I wasn't a complete ignoramus. 'Separate churches?'

He nodded. 'Separate bases,' he said. 'And different jobs to do.'

'In what way?'

'Well, the airmen you saw today, they do a lot of physical work.'

'They worked on the air base, I heard,' I said. 'Getting it ready.'

'That's correct.'

'Like I said, Gloria, they're different from us.'

'Ignorant,' said one of the other airmen in the back seat, but Taylor wasn't having that.

'No,' he said firmly. 'Not so educated. But that ain't their fault, is it?'

'Ain't it?' said Perkins.

There was a moment as the men looked at one another and then Taylor clambered out of the jeep. 'I'm going to walk from here,' he said. 'Nice to meet you, Miss Henry.'

He walked off across the gravel. Perkins watched him for a moment, then he turned back to me.

'Different from us,' he said. 'Not so brave.'

'Really?' I was surprised by that. 'How so?'

'We're all in combat roles, but they're not front-line,' he explained.

'They don't fight?' I asked.

'Their skills are better used elsewhere.'

'Right,' I said. I felt a little uncomfortable. I gathered my library books into my arms and prepared to get out of the car.

'It's the law,' Perkins said, with a shrug.

'It's American law,' I pointed out.

'That's right. And on our air bases those laws apply.'

But when you're off the base, I thought to myself, *it's English laws that you need to obey.*

'Thank you so much for the lift,' I said.

'I'm not saying it's right or wrong,' Perkins said, putting his hand on my arm to stop me leaving. 'It's just the way it is. So just take care, Gloria.'

'I'll do that,' I said.

But I was really only telling him what he wanted to hear.

I walked back into the house, wondering what sort of mood my mother might be in, and I was astonished to hear laughter and the chink of glasses coming from the lounge. Gingerly, I stuck my head round the door and saw, to my absolute delight, my grandfather – my mother's father – standing beside the fireplace, a glass of whisky in hand. Mother was sitting on the sofa, clutching what I thought was yet another gin, and Fran was hovering nearby.

'Grandpa,' I shouted, barrelling towards him.

'Gloria, my darling girl,' he said, wrapping me in his arms. 'How the devil are you?'

'Bored out of my mind,' I said. 'Take me back to London with you?'

He put his hands on my face and looked at me. 'I would if I could – you know that.'

36

I sighed. 'Patty's gone to be a land girl.'

'I'm sure you can find a way to make yourself useful,' Grandpa said. 'Make tea for the Home Guard.'

I snorted and my mother laughed.

'Oh, Daddy, you do talk nonsense,' she said fondly. 'Gloria's fine here with me, aren't you, darling?'

I eyed her for a moment searching for any trace of her earlier rage and was relieved to see nothing, so I judged her able to laugh again. I threw myself on to the sofa next to her. 'I am dying of boredom,' I said overdramatically, and she laughed again, patting my leg in affection.

Seizing the moment, I said: 'Do you know the summer fair is definitely happening?'

My mother took the bait. 'It is? That's wonderful news.'

'As long as there are enough people to help organise it of course,' I said, casually. 'Because I imagine lots of the folk who helped before the war aren't around now.'

Fran caught my eye and I saw understanding dawn on her face.

'That's true,' she said. 'Mrs Malone always did most of it, but she's in Wales now. They'll be looking for people to volunteer I expect.'

'Better than making tea for the Home Guard,' my grandfather said. 'Wouldn't you say so, Rose?'

My mother nodded, looking thoughtful. 'Yes,' she said. 'Sounds rather fun.'

I leaned back against a cushion, pleased with myself.

'Is that the GIs' dinner I can smell?' I asked hopefully as a delicious meaty scent wafted past my nostrils and my stomach rumbled loudly.

'Grandpa brought us a chicken,' Mother said. 'Fran's roasting it for dinner.'

'Oh yum,' I said, delighted. 'How long will it be?'

Mother looked at me. 'You should get changed before we eat, darling. Where on earth have you been? You look all windswept.'

'The library,' I said, deciding not to mention my trip in the jeep.

Mother rolled her eyes. 'I'm going for a little lie-down before dinner.'

She blew Grandpa a kiss, and wafted out of the room, followed by Fran.

Grandpa came to sit next to me.

'Which books did you borrow?' he asked, picking them up from the sofa where I'd thrown them. '*The 39 Steps* again?'

'It's my favourite,' I said, unapologetically. 'It's good research for when I can become a spy.' I gave him a sideways glace. 'Like you.'

'I'm not a spy, Gloria,' Grandpa said.

I grinned. 'That's exactly what a spy would say.'

He chuckled and I was pleased.

'How is your mother doing?' he said in a low voice. 'Still up and down?'

'Not so bad,' I said honestly. 'More ups than down. I do really think she's getting better. Bad this morning though.'

Grandpa nodded. 'Wedding anniversary,' he said.

'Yes,' I was pleased he'd remembered.

'What was all that about the summer fair?'

'A project,' I said. 'To give Mother something to do.'

Grandpa ruffled my hair like I was a little girl and I ducked away from him even though I quite liked it.

'You're not just a hat stand, Gloria,' he said. 'Smart thinking.'

'Are you staying?'

'Only for one night.'

'Are you here for work?' I asked. Grandpa worked for the government in the War Office. He said it was terribly dull and mostly filling in forms. But I had an inkling he was much more important than he made out.

'I'm here to see some American general,' he said. 'Awful chap with a dreadful accent, but I have to admit, he really knows his stuff.'

'I met some more Americans today,' I told him.

Grandpa smiled. 'They're proving to be rather useful to us, I believe. They're working hard.'

'They're building a sentry box at the entrance to the drive, did you see?'

'I did.' Grandpa made a face. 'It's not quite in keeping with the rest of the house. Your father would hate it.'

'That's exactly what I thought.'

He laughed. 'For that reason, I rather like it.' Grandpa had enjoyed tormenting my father by pretending he didn't like him, but we'd all known he was just being silly. And after my father's funeral I'd caught sight of his stricken face when he thought no one was looking.

'Grandpa, the Americans I met today were Black. Well, some of them. They're the ones who were building the sentry box.'

Grandpa nodded and I carried on.

'The man they were with was called Corporal Perkins, and he was just telling them what to do. He wasn't working with them – he was just sitting in the jeep, watching them and bossing them around.'

Grandpa tutted. He hated laziness.

'I saw him later on in the village, and I asked about the other men.' I chewed my lip, remembering what Perkins had said. 'He told me they were different. Separate but equal. But I have to say, the way he talked to the men – and the way he talked about them – didn't sound very equal.'

'Hmm,' Grandpa said. 'It's a complicated business, Gloria. Americans have laws about this sort of thing.'

'We don't. And there was another man there, Taylor. He said it wasn't all over America.'

'No,' Grandpa said. 'Like I say, it's complicated.' He sighed. 'Trust me, that's something we talked about before they arrived.'

'Really?'

'Oh yes, absolutely. It's a tricky business.'

'But surely they just have to obey our laws when they're in England?'

'Not on their air bases.'

I rubbed my nose. 'That's what Perkins said.'

'Perkins was right.'

'What did you talk about? Before the Americans arrived?'

Grandpa got up and went to the drinks trolley. He opened the whisky bottle and poured himself a stiff measure.

'We thought the British public – like you – wouldn't like to see a segregated foreign force arriving on our shores,' he said. 'We didn't want to encourage people to adopt the American attitudes towards the Black soldiers and airmen.'

'But?' I said. I could read my grandfather like a book – I knew there was a "but" coming.

Grandpa sat down again. 'But?'

'It sounded like you hadn't finished.'

He looked at me. 'But . . .' he said. 'The Americans are an important ally.'

'We need to keep them sweet,' I said, understanding.

'Indeed.' Grandpa nodded. 'We decided that while we couldn't expect the British people to go along with segregation, it would be better for everyone if we avoided the locals becoming too friendly with the Black troops.'

'Better for everyone?' I said.

'Exactly.'

'Except for those troops, that is.'

Grandpa looked half cross, half amused. 'I'm sure they get along just fine,' he said.

'Perkins said they don't fight.'

'I wouldn't know about that.'

'And that they weren't brave.'

'Perkins had a lot to say for himself.' Grandpa patted my knee and then tipped his head back and sniffed the air appreciatively. 'I don't know about you, Gloria, but I'm getting hungry and that chicken smells very good indeed. Didn't your mother want you to get changed before we eat?'

So the conversation was over.

'She did,' I said. 'I'll be back in a minute.'

I picked up my library books and headed to the door.

'Gloria,' Grandpa said. 'Remember what I said? Don't get too friendly with them.'

'Righto,' I said cheerfully.

'Gloria,' he said again, his tone more sombre. 'I know what you're like. Telling you not to do something is always a guarantee you'll do it. But this time I mean it. Don't get too friendly.'

I looked at him for a moment and then I turned away. 'I'll go and get changed,' I said.

Chapter 5

Philippa

I was up a ladder in the restaurant, peering at bits of peeling wallpaper when the doorbell rang.

'Marco!' I bellowed. 'Door!'

There was no response. I wondered if he was out looking at the garden – he'd been talking about getting started on clearing it as soon as we could.

Reluctantly I climbed down the stepladder and went to answer the door, in a bit of a grump.

Vanessa stood on the doorstep. She was wearing aviator sunglasses and a floaty maxi dress and I immediately felt self-conscious and completely uncool.

'I've brought good news,' she said without waiting for me to say "hello". 'I spoke to my friend from work and she says she'll fast-track your planning application.'

'Really?' I said. 'That's wonderful, thank you.'

Vanessa took off her sunglasses and looked past me into the dim hall. 'How's it going?' she asked.

'Want to come in and see?'

'Definitely.'

I led her into the restaurant.

'We've done very little,' I said, spreading my arms out wide. 'Harvey's waiting for tiles or something.'

'Always waiting for something, is Harvey,' she said, glancing round as Marco came into the room.

'Hello, Vanessa,' he said.

Vanessa gave him a broad smile. 'I came to share the news that your planning application is being fast-tracked.'

'Because of you?' Marco looked delighted.

'Well, I put in a good word.'

Marco let out a little shout of triumph. 'Thanks so much,' he said.

'Yes, thank you,' I said. 'We owe you one.'

'How about I cook you dinner?' Marco said. 'The kitchen's just sitting there and it's ready to go – I'm itching to try it out. Are you free on Saturday?'

Vanessa nodded. 'I'd have to get a sitter. Alex is fine by himself for a while now but I'd not leave him alone all evening.'

'Of course, you've got your grandson to think about,' Marco said. 'Bring him too. Come a bit earlier. Say six o'clock?'

'Sounds good,' said Vanessa.

'Perfect,' I agreed, though it was a bit of a fib. I felt slightly odd about meeting Vanessa's grandson though I wasn't sure why exactly. Perhaps it was because he'd had someone to pick up the pieces when his mother had let him down, something I'd always longed for. Or perhaps it was because Vanessa was getting a second chance to be a parent when I'd never had a first. Or perhaps I was just drowning in self-pity? I slapped on a smile. 'Can't wait.'

On Saturday I was a bundle of nerves. I'd changed my outfit three times and laid the table twice and there was still an hour to go before Vanessa and Alex arrived.

'Why are you getting yourself in a tizz?' Marco said. 'It's just lasagne.'

'I know, but she's so glam and she's been really kind to us. I want it to be nice.'

I'd laid the table in a bit of the restaurant where there was no water damage. It was beside the window so we could appreciate the views out to the garden where to my surprise, bluebells had sprung up in all the shady parts of the lawn. It actually looked rather pretty – if a bit neglected.

Now I looked out of the window and smiled. 'It's like the forest round Sleeping Beauty's castle,' I said, nodding towards the brambles and long grass.'

'More like the red weed from *War of the Worlds*,' Marco said. He came up behind me and put his arms round me, and I leaned back against him. 'Is it Alex?' he said. 'That's got you in a tizz?'

'No,' I said quickly. 'Perhaps.'

'Want to talk about it?'

I sighed. 'I'm being horrible, Marco. Don't indulge me.'

Marco took me by the shoulders and turned me round to face him.

'I still feel funny about being round kids sometimes. Remember the counsellor said it might take us by surprise when we thought we were fine.'

'I do remember that,' I said. 'But that's not it.' I screwed my face up, trying to explain but Marco, bless him, understood. 'It's not just that.'

'Is it because she's looking after her grandson?' he said. 'Because he's got family to care for him.' He paused. 'And you didn't.'

I pinched my lips together. 'I did,' I muttered. 'I did have some family.'

'You had a rough time growing up, Phil. It's understandable you have mixed emotions about it all.'

'I feel . . .' I began. I sighed. 'I feel jealous. Is that awful?'

'Not at all.'

'But Alex is just a little boy, who's lucky enough to have a

44

grandma who loves him. How can I be jealous of him? I've not even met him.'

'Because it's not about that little boy,' Marco said. 'It's about the little girl who you were. The little girl who grew up with a mum who couldn't really care for her properly.'

'Yes,' I said cautiously, feeling – ridiculously – disloyal to my mum. 'I suppose.'

'And that little girl who had a safety net that was taken away, is envious of Alex whose safety net is still there.'

I rubbed my nose. 'Yes,' I said again.

Growing up, there had only ever been my mother and me. Just the two of us against the world. But for as long as I remembered, my mum had suffered with poor mental health. She was a hoarder, so our house was always chaotic and sometimes frightening. She didn't always manage to get out of bed, or remember to feed me, or wash my clothes and so I'd learned to look after myself from a very young age. Too young, really.

My mother had no family – I'd never met my grandparents, who'd died before I was born, nor my father, who my mother refused to talk about. But she did have a cousin called Rick, who was kind. And when things were bad, I went to stay with Rick and his wife, Ellie. I loved them so much. For a while, they kept a bedroom for me in their flat and if Mum was having a bad patch, I'd go and stay. My bedroom had clean pink sheets on the bed and a shelf full of Ellie's old books. Books she'd kept since she was a little girl and looked after, and had thought I would like. And on the floor was a fluffy white rug that I could scrunch my toes into when I got out of bed. I even had pyjamas and a dressing gown to wear when I was there.

And then Rick got a job in Canada. I thought he and Ellie might ask my mum if I could go with them. I wasn't supposed to know their plans, of course, but I heard conversations. I planned my new life in my head imagining myself as Anne of Green Gables, which was the only thing I knew about Canada.

45

But they never asked. Or perhaps they did and Mum said no. But either way, Rick and Ellie emigrated when I was eleven. They had their own kids, and they kept in touch regularly at first, and then less so. They hadn't come to my mother's funeral.

But Alex had a granny. A glamorous, loving granny.

'It's not your fault,' Marco said, watching me closely. 'You're bound to feel a bit weird just because of your background. But I bet once they're here and you've met Alex, you'll feel totally normal.'

'I hope so.'

He was right actually. Vanessa arrived – looking amazing obviously, in shiny leggings an oversized white shirt, and leopard-print Converse. I looked down at my own maxi dress – chosen because it was similar to what Vanessa had worn the other day – in dismay. But I perked up when she presented me with a bottle of wine, and a delicious-looking cheesecake that of course she had made herself.

And there was Alex, standing beside his granny, looking up at the large front door. He was tallish for 12, I thought, with scruffy dark hair and curious eyes, and a football under his arm.

'Is this all your house?' he said.

'Alex,' Vanessa said. 'Say hello first.'

'Hello,' he said. 'Is this all your house.'

'Hello,' I replied. 'Yes and no. It's going to be a restaurant and a hotel, and we only live in a bit of it.'

'Decent,' he said approvingly, and I was pleased. Marco gave me an "I told you so" look over the top of his head.

It was a lovely evening in the end. Vanessa was good company, filling us in on all the gossip from Honeyford, and Alex was bright and funny.

It was only April but the sun had been out all day, and so after dinner Marco put on one of his new patio heaters and we went outside with our drinks.

'Fancy a kickabout then?' Marco said.

'Ah now that's exactly what he was hoping for.' Vanessa ruffled her grandson's hair affectionately. 'I am endlessly disappointing to him when it comes to football.'

'Granny will not play,' Alex said, curling his lip in disgust.

Marco laughed. 'Come on then, Alex. Let's see what you're made of.'

He led Alex down the steps from the terrace to the small patch of lawn that wasn't completely overgrown. I watched as Marco found two stones to mark a goal and they began to play.

My heart felt tight, like it was swollen with unshed tears. Marco loved kids so much. He adored his nephews and nieces. He loved our friends' children. He would have been a great dad.

I swigged a large mouthful of my wine.

'Alex is a lovely boy,' I said truthfully. 'He's lucky to have you.'

Vanessa watched her grandson laughing as Marco failed to make a save. She smiled, but it was a sad smile. 'I worry that I failed Tilly as a mother,' she said slowly. 'I chose the wrong man and now she's done the same.'

'Is your husband . . .?'

'Oh, he's not dead,' Vanessa said. 'He lives in Manchester. He's got two kids younger than Alex with his new wife and is, by all accounts, a reformed character.' She raised an eyebrow. 'But Tilly grew up watching him break my heart over and over, and me taking him back over and over. It's not a good example to set.'

'I'm sure you did your best,' I said.

'Well, now I can make amends by looking after Alex.'

'That's a nice way of thinking about it.'

Vanessa was watching the football on the lawn.

'Marco's very good with him,' she said.

'He likes children.' I stood up. 'More drinks?'

I topped up her glass, hoping she wouldn't ask the inevitable next question. And perhaps there was something in my tone, or perhaps Vanessa was savvy enough to know that a forty-something couple who liked kids but had none of their own might not want to talk about why that might be. Either way, she didn't ask.

But Alex did.

When he and Marco came back up to the terrace, a little muddy, a little sweaty, and chatting like old friends, he looked round and, like he'd only just noticed he was the only child present, said: 'Where are your kids?'

I felt the question like a sharp scratch. Marco caught my eye. 'We don't have any kids, pal.'

Alex frowned. 'How come?'

'We just don't,' said Marco. 'Right, who's for cheesecake?'

Chapter 6

Gloria

I had to admit, Grandpa was right. I did not like being told not to do something. Sometimes – often – I deliberately did the things I'd been forbidden from doing.

But I didn't set out to meet the airmen again. Not really.

Well, perhaps a little bit.

It was a lovely day. Grandpa had gone to meet his American chap and my mother was in much better spirits. She'd gone from yesterday's melancholy to being, well, chipper, and to my absolute delight, she'd announced she was intending to help out with the summer fair and the dance. In fact, she'd already telephoned Margery at the post office and made arrangements.

'I've got a meeting about the fair,' she told me in the morning. 'Do you want to come?'

'Not really,' I said.

'Really?' She looked a little disappointed. 'I thought you were bored.'

'Not that bored.'

'What else are you going to do today?'

I shrugged. 'Go for a walk in the garden, perhaps?'

'Read your book in the garden you mean?'

'Maybe.'

She kissed me on the cheek, admitting defeat. 'I'll volunteer you for a stall.'

'The book stall?'

She regarded me for a long moment. 'Sometimes I wonder if you're actually my daughter at all,' she said. 'Yes, fine, the book stall.'

She checked her hair in the mirror and then set off towards the gate. I watched her go, wondering idly if the airmen were back to finish the sentry box. There was no harm in taking a walk. In fact, being in the garden would do me good. Fresh air and all that. And if I were to walk past the gate, then so be it.

I went to fetch a cardigan, noticing with some resignation that it was beginning to fray, just like all my clothes. Neither my mother nor I were particularly good at making do and mending, though Fran tried to teach me how to sew. But it was the only cardi I could find and though the sun was shining, there was a breeze, so I pulled it on regardless and headed outdoors.

At first, I walked in the opposite direction to the gate, telling myself I might not even go that way. I went down the sloping lawn and off to the left, where my father had wanted to put a tennis court, even though I was hopeless at ball sports and my mother really only liked games she could play without changing her outfit. Like petanque, or croquet.

Or bridge.

The sun was warm and it was a nice day to be out. I wandered along, thinking about the book stall at the summer fair. I should have gone with Mother, I thought. But I wanted her to make it her own before I got involved. Next time I'd tag along because it would be nice to have something to do, rather than rattling around in the house all day by myself.

The far side of the garden, close to the lane that ran along the back of the house, had been given over to an enormous vegetable patch where we grew enough produce to feed half the village. Well, we didn't grow it. One of the local farmers – a friendly chap called Mr Wilson – oversaw it and his land girls did the work. We barely saw them as they came and went through the back gate, though my mother liked to tell people she was doing her bit and Digging for Victory.

Past the vegetables was my favourite part of the garden. Right at the bottom there were two oak trees. They provided shade on a sunny day and shelter when it rained. Bluebells grew underneath in the spring and there was a hollow in the trunk of the larger tree that provided the perfect place to sit and read. When I'd been little I would pretend it was where fairies and elves lived, and now I was older, I would escape there. It was a good place because though when I was sitting in the hollow I was hidden from view, more or less, I could see the house from there and it had sight of the gate.

And the sentry box.

I settled down and pulled my book out of my pocket, telling myself I was reading but actually keeping one eye on what was happening by the gate.

Over by the wall I could see the same two airmen who'd been there before and Corporal Perkins. Again, the two men were doing the work and Perkins was leaning against the wall, smoking, his head turned towards the sun. I wondered if he was from a part of America where it got very warm in the summer and felt a glimmer of sympathy at him having to cope with English weather. It had been a long and dreary winter and I thought it would be hard to have coped with the relentless grey skies if you were used to sunshine all year round.

I could hear their voices occasionally, but I couldn't make out what they were saying. One of the GIs was carrying bricks from the pile by the roadside, and the other – the one who'd winked at me – was building the wall of the sentry box.

As I watched, Perkins straightened up and said something to the man carrying the bricks.

Again, I couldn't hear the words he was saying but from his tone I could tell he thought something was wrong – perhaps he thought the GI was being a little lazy and not carrying enough because he picked up a brick and gestured with it. Then he went to add it to the pile the chap was holding over his shoulder, but he misjudged the distance and as he threw it – carelessly, I thought – it somehow missed the other bricks and hit the airman smack in his forehead.

I gasped and jumped to my feet as the airman fell down out of sight.

'Oh Lord,' I said to myself, shocked. But then, thankfully, Perkins reached down and helped him to his feet. The other GI – the one who'd winked at me – took his other arm and I could hear their voices, louder than they'd been before.

I stood, not sure if I should run over and offer to help. From the way Perkins was pressing a handkerchief to the GI's forehead, I could see he was bleeding. There was a bit more discussion, then Perkins and the winking GI helped the injured airman to the jeep. Perkins talked to the other chap for a moment, gesturing towards the sentry box, and then he got in the jeep and drove away with the injured airman, leaving the winking GI alone.

He picked up a brick and waited – I assumed – until he could no longer see the jeep in the distance. Then I watched as he put down the brick and vanished from view.

Intrigued, I took my book and put it back in my pocket then began to walk towards the gates.

As I approached, I realised he hadn't disappeared at all. Instead he was sitting down, with his back against the stone wall, reading.

'Hello,' I called as I got nearer.

He glanced up at me and smiled. 'Hello, Miss Henry.'

I was absurdly pleased that he'd remembered my name.

'Oh please, call me Gloria,' I said.

He got to his feet. He wiped his hand on his trousers then held it out to me.

'Jerome,' he said. 'Jerome Scott.'

I shook his hand.

'Nice to meet you, Jerome.'

'Likewise.'

'I saw what happened.' I gestured to the pile of bricks. 'I saw what Perkins did to your friend.'

'He's an asshole,' Jerome muttered. Then he screwed his face up. 'Sorry.'

'Is he all right? Your friend?'

'Eugene,' Jerome said. 'His name's Eugene and he's got a girl named Liza and he plays the piano and he's scared of spiders but nothing else.' He looked right at me, his expression defiant. 'Not that Perkins knows any of that.'

I bit my lip, awkward at the heat of his anger.

'Is Eugene badly hurt?'

Jerome's jaw was clenched. 'Nah,' he said. 'Not this time.'

The implication that there might be a next time made me uncomfortable.

'Did Perkins mean to hurt him?'

'Maybe. Maybe not.'

'Perhaps you should tell someone?' I said. 'Someone in charge?'

But Jerome shook his head. 'There's no point,' he said. He sounded weary. 'Anyway, I should get on.'

He bent down and picked up his book and I saw the cover for the first time.

'*The 39 Steps*!' I exclaimed in delight.

'Yes?'

I pulled my own copy out of my pocket and showed him. 'Snap!'

He smiled for the first time. 'It's a good read.'

'It's my favourite.'

'Huh,' he said. 'You like spies?'

'I do.'

'And that's why you were watching us? Spying?'

Embarrassed that he was wise to what I'd been doing I ducked my head, but he laughed and I realised he was teasing.

'I'm glad you saw,' he said. 'Else, when Perkins tells his version later, I'd start thinking I'd imagined things.'

'You think he'll lie about what happened?'

Jerome shrugged. 'He'll say Eugene walked into the brick he was holding, or that he dropped it on his own head. No one will question it. Probably won't even ask Eugene what happened.'

'That's terrible.'

'That's how it is.' He gave me a tight smile, with no humour in it. 'Welcome to the US Air Force.'

I shifted my weight on my feet, feeling uncomfortable. 'Are they all like that? Like Perkins?'

'Nah.' Jerome shook his head. 'Not all of them.'

'Stick with the good ones, then.' I thought about Taylor getting annoyed when Perkins was telling me about the laws. 'There must be some good ones.'

He laughed. 'It ain't that easy. We do as we're told.'

'No you don't.'

'What?' He blinked at me in surprise.

'You don't do as you're told.'

'Miss Henry . . .'

'Gloria.'

'Gloria, I don't mean to be rude, but you're not an airman and you're not American. You don't know what you're talking about.'

'I know I couldn't hear what Perkins said to you before he took poor Eugene off to get his head patched up, but from the way he gestured, I'm pretty sure he told you to carry on building this sentry box,' I said. 'And I'm almost one hundred per cent positive he didn't tell you to sit down in the sunshine and read *The 39 Steps*. And yet, here you are.'

Jerome looked startled. 'Here we are,' he muttered. 'Fine, I don't always do as I'm told.'

'Can you drive?' I asked.

'Yes.'

I was impressed. 'Do you know Waldo?' I asked. 'He's stationed here at the house. Big chap with shoulders like this.' I held my hands out wide. 'And a moustache.'

'I know him.' Jerome was watching me curiously. 'Captain Waldo.'

'Right,' I said. 'I happen to know he's fed up to the back teeth with his driver. He keeps getting lost because they took away all the road signs in case the Germans invaded. So Waldo's always late.'

'How do you know that?'

'I listen to other people's conversations,' I said. 'And I watch people.'

'Like a spy.'

'My mother calls me a nosy parker.'

He laughed. 'She's right.'

'Anyway, you should volunteer to drive him,' I said. 'Then Perkins wouldn't be able to tell you what to do anymore.'

'Waldo would be telling me instead.'

'I suppose so. But no one would be getting hit over the head with bricks if you were his driver.'

'It's a nice idea, but I don't even know how I'd get to introduce myself.'

'Shut the gates,' I said.

'What?'

'Shut the gates.' I pointed to the wooden gates at the entrance to the driveway. Once upon a time we'd had metal gates, but they were long gone to make munitions. 'Shut the gates and they'll stop and ask you to open them. And then, well, I'm sure you'll think of something.'

'Right,' said Jerome. 'A spy and a fixer, eh?'

'What's a fixer?'

He rolled his eyes. 'Someone who fixes stuff.'

'Oh.' I was a little embarrassed. 'That should have been obvious.'

'Some people make things happen,' he said. 'And other people just let them happen. And some people fix them. Like you.'

'Yes, well, there are lots of things I can't fix even though I wish I could.'

'Like what?'

I looked right at him, and I had the strangest urge to sit down with him, right there on the verge at the side of the gate, and tell him all about how my father died, and my mother was sad, and my best friend had gone off to be a land girl and I was lonely, and how I wasn't sure who I was or who I wanted to be. But instead, I just smiled.

'Oh all sorts of silly things,' I said lightly.

'I'd like to hear about them,' he said. 'One day.'

'One day I'll tell you.'

He held my gaze for a second and I thought how nice he was and how unfair it was that Perkins treated him the way he did.

'My grandpa said I shouldn't be too friendly with you,' I blurted out, though I wasn't sure why.

Jerome laughed. 'Then it seems neither of us does as we're told.'

Chapter 7

Philippa

'What should I wear?' I asked Vanessa on the phone. 'Will it be glitzy?'

'Oh heavens, no,' she said, laughing. 'It's just some friends having a drink. I might stretch to a bowl of crisps if you're lucky and if I can keep them hidden from Alex until everyone arrives.'

I laughed. 'Jeans and a nice top?'

'Perfect. See you at seven?'

I ended the call and went to find Marco. He was in our bedroom staring into our MFI gold-trimmed fitted wardrobes.

'I don't know what to wear,' he said.

I flopped on to the bed. 'Jeans and a nice top, Vanessa says.'

'Jeans? For our introduction to Honeyford society?'

'You make it sound like we're in *Bridgerton*,' I said with a chuckle. 'Wear your good jeans, not the ones with the holes in the thighs, and your blue checked shirt.'

'Bossy,' Marco muttered, but he took the shirt out of the wardrobe anyway.

I went for black jeans and a white shirt, then changed to a black T-shirt because I looked like a waitress in my first outfit.

Then I changed again because I looked like I was going to a funeral. And in the end, I split the difference and put on a black and white striped top.

'I'm so nervous,' I said, as we walked down into Honeyford later. 'I feel like we're being put on display.'

'That is exactly what's happening,' said Marco. 'But it's a good thing. Think of all those potential customers. Every one of them will have a birthday and a wedding anniversary and retirement parties and all sorts of events to celebrate and Honeyford House will be the perfect location for them.'

'Marco Costello, you are a shrewd and savvy businessman,' I said.

He grimaced. 'I'm nervous too.'

I put my arm through his. 'They'll love us.'

Vanessa lived in a nice house on the edge of the village. Her garden went round the house on three sides, and as we walked up the path, we could hear music and laughter spilling out.

'Philippa and Marco,' Vanessa declared as we let ourselves in – cautiously because we were still Londoners at heart and you did not go round letting yourselves into people's houses in West Norwood, no matter how nicely they'd invited you. 'Come and meet everyone!'

Everyone, as it turned out, was a couple of Vanessa's friends from the council, who were both very eager to find out what our plans were for the house and who bombarded me with questions.

Harvey the builder was there, though I almost didn't recognise him because he wasn't wearing his usual paint-splattered T-shirt and cargo shorts, and there were a couple of others too including a man who ran a local brewery and whisked Marco away to try his beer, and it was all lovely but a little overwhelming.

After we were all introduced, I went to the kitchen to find a drink and came across an older woman with long, greying hair in a plait drinking red wine and leaning against the worktops.

'Hello,' I said. 'I'm Philippa.'

She looked delighted. 'I'm Jackie,' she said. 'I work with Vanessa at the museum.'

'Nice to meet you.'

'Have you met four hundred people already this evening?'

'I have.'

'Can you remember anyone's name?'

I smiled. 'I remember yours.'

'Drink?' she said.

'Yes please. What you're having would be great.'

She poured me a large glass of red, and we sat down at the kitchen table.

'You're living in Honeyford House?'

'We are.' I eyed her over the top of my glass. 'Are you wanting to know our plans?'

'Vanessa's told me already.'

'Oh thank goodness,' I said. 'Everyone's really nice, but there's only so much I can say about decking.'

Jackie laughed. 'Do you know much about the house's history?'

'Not really,' I admitted. 'We've been focused on its future really.'

'Are you interested?'

I found I was very much interested. 'I am,' I said. 'Do you know anything?'

'Bits and pieces. I was a history teacher before I retired, and I'm a bit of a local heritage fan.'

'Brilliant,' I said. 'What can you tell me? Vanessa said the history of the house wasn't all good. Please don't say it's got a dark and sinister history and is full of ghosts.'

'Well, it's funny you should say that . . .' Jackie said. Then, seeing my look of alarm, she shook her head. 'Nothing sinister.'

'That's a relief,' I said. 'I know it was going to be a school, then the people who bought it changed their minds and sold it to us.'

'They found a better site closer to Cheltenham,' Jackie said. 'I think it was just too much work for them to do the conversion required. And Vanessa said the adaptations wouldn't have been approved anyway.'

'I guess not.' I sighed. 'It's been empty for ages. That's why it was so cheap and why it's in such a state.'

'Various families lived there in the Nineties and early Two Thousands,' Jackie agreed. 'But none of them stayed long.'

'Oh God, is this one of those stories where it's a real millstone round everyone's neck?'

'Nah,' Jackie said, topping up my wine. 'Just some bad luck, I think. One chap lost all his money in the recession. Another family moved abroad.' She leaned forward. 'But the really exciting stuff is earlier than that.'

'Tell me.'

'In the Sixties and Seventies it was owned by Lucien Lavelle.'

'The photographer?'

'Yes. He scandalised the whole village with his debauched parties. There were rock stars and models whizzing round the place. I heard George Harrison met Pattie Boyd at one of Lucien's parties.'

'Oh my,' I breathed, absolutely thrilled. 'That's wonderful.'

'Isn't it? For a while, Honeyford House was where everything happened. Very glam. Jimi Hendrix played a gig in the garden, according to local rumours, though I've never been able to verify that.'

'So what happened?'

'In the mid-Seventies, a model called Glenda – just Glenda, no surname – took an overdose at one of the parties and she died. And that put an end to that.'

'That's so sad,' I said, frowning. 'Did she die in the house?'

'In hospital a few days later.'

'That's good.' Then appalled at my heartlessness, I gasped. 'Not good. I don't mean good.'

'I know what you meant,' Jackie said, with a little smile.

'What else do you know?'

'Before Lucien, the house was owned by a family called

Henry for a few generations. I think the last Henry was killed in the Second World War and his wife and daughter moved away after that. GIs were stationed there for a while towards the end of the war.'

'In our house?'

'The big cheeses – the officers – lived in the house. Most of them were based at RAF Eaton, down the road.' She frowned. 'And some others were in barracks on what's now the business park, off the main road, past the farm.'

'We could do local history evenings when we're up and running,' I said. 'You and Vanessa can come and tell everyone stories of Lucien's lavish orgies and the handsome GIs who wooed the villagers.'

'I'd like that,' Jackie said. 'I'm pretty sure we've got some old photos of Honeyford House, if you're interested in seeing them.'

'Ooh yes please. Vanessa did mention that. Maybe we could get copies made and frame them to put up in the bar. That would look lovely.'

'Come and see us at the museum.'

'I will,' I said, chuffed. 'Is it open every day?'

Jackie made a face. 'No. I'd like to open every day but we're trying to keep costs down. Our budgets are being squeezed.'

'Is it run by the council?' I asked.

'We're funded by the council, but it's me who balances the books,' Jackie said with a shudder.

'I can take a look if you like?' I said. Then, when Jackie looked confused, I grinned. 'I'm an accountant. I've been helping Harvey with his invoices, and Mick at the shop with his taxes. Everyone's being so kind to us – it's my way of giving back.'

'Then yes please,' said Jackie. 'I'd really appreciate that.' She got up from the table. 'Now I'm afraid I have to go. I need to take my dog out for a walk before he goes to bed.'

'Lovely to meet you,' I said.

She said goodbye and wandered off and I was left alone in the kitchen, wondering where Marco was.

I poured myself some more wine, then took my glass through into the lounge, which ran from the front of the house to the back, and had large patio doors on to the garden.

Marco wasn't there, but as I stood close to the open doors I heard his voice – he was outside.

I went out on to the patio. It wasn't properly dark yet but it took a moment for my eyes to adjust to the dim spring twilight and at first I couldn't see Marco.

Then, following the sound of his voice, I spotted him. He was lying on a picnic blanket on the lawn with Alex.

'That's the plough,' Alex was saying, pointing upwards. 'It'll be easier to see when it's darker. I think it looks more like a saucepan than a plough – see the handle?'

'I see it,' Marco said.

'But I suppose in the olden days they had ploughs but no saucepans.'

'No saucepans?' Marco said. 'But how did they cook their spaghetti?'

'Maybe ploughs were invented before spaghetti?' Alex said.

I stood where I was for a minute, enjoying their conversation but feeling a coldness creep round my heart that I was fairly sure wasn't just caused by the April evening air.

Of course I knew that Marco liked kids. His family was full of them. He was a fun uncle. The one all the children jumped on and wanted to impress, and confided in. And I loved them too. I adored them, in fact.

But with the loss of every pregnancy, I had felt it harder to be around them while Marco seemed to pull them closer. And now he seemed to have taken Alex under his wing, too. And how could I resent that? How could I resent this little lad with his broken family, being given some attention from a good, caring man who shared his love of football and stargazing and heaven knows what else?

I was a terrible person.

I watched them for a few more minutes, and then Vanessa came round the side of the house and spotted them on the blanket. As I watched, she went over to them and said hello, crouching down on her haunches. Alex, in a moment of mischief, pulled her down on to the blanket and she toppled forwards, laughing.

Marco was laughing too and for a moment I felt as though I was spying on a family – two parents and their child. Uncomfortable, I went back inside to the lounge and to my relief found Harvey to chat to.

He was telling me about roof tiles, when Vanessa appeared next to us, looking a little flushed.

'Alex is teaching Marco all about constellations,' she said.

I pasted on a smile. 'They seem to have really hit it off.'

'It's good for Alex to be around men who can be relied on,' Vanessa said, giving Harvey a smile.

'Yes,' I said vaguely, wishing it wasn't my husband she was talking about and then wishing I didn't feel that way.

'Good news,' Harvey said.

'Pardon?'

'About the pergola,' he explained. 'Ness says it's all fine.' He frowned. 'And that Marco is planning to make it himself.'

I rolled my eyes. 'He's ordered all the wood already. You'll be able to watch the progress when you're working on the roof. Just don't laugh at him.'

Harvey chuckled. 'I'll keep an eye on him.'

'I'd love to help with the pergola,' Vanessa said. 'I'm quite handy with a drill.'

'Really?' I made a face.

'Gosh, yes. I love a bit of DIY.'

'She's pretty good,' said Harvey. Vanessa looked pleased.

'What's this?' Marco came in through the patio doors, with Alex trailing after him.

'Vanessa's just offering to help build your pergola,' said Harvey.

Marco beamed at Vanessa, and I felt a prickle of annoyance.

'We're fine,' I said, pushing a strand of hair out of my eyes. 'Honestly.'

'Erm, no we're not,' Marco said. 'We need all the help we can get.'

'Then count me in.' Vanessa stood up straighter. 'We'll get it all done in no time at all.'

Chapter 8

Gloria

I had decided it was time to help my mother organise the summer fair. I thought if she really got stuck in, then perhaps I'd be able to join up and leave her for a while. Besides, it would give me something to do, and my father's birthday was approaching, and I wasn't sure how Mother would react this year. If I was involved in the fair too, that meant I could step in if she had another bad day and cover for her.

The return of the summer fair was the most exciting thing that had happened in Honeyford for ages, because everyone loved it and we'd all missed it in the years it hadn't been running.

Back when I was little it had been glorious. I remembered sun-soaked afternoons playing the games on all the stalls, and riding the carousel. In the evening there was the dance for the grown-ups but I would always tag along with my parents and fall asleep on two chairs pushed together.

I supposed this year it would be more make do and mend. Mother had already told me that the carousel wouldn't be coming because all the men who had once worked on it had joined up. And I knew the cake stalls were bound to be much barer. But I had an inkling that the fruit and vegetable competition would never be so hotly contested now everyone was a gardener. And then, of course, there was the dance – with the thrilling addition of the GIs!

I wondered if I was bold enough to go along to the dance without Patty there by my side. Perkins and the other GIs had mentioned it, but I'd not been lying when I said I wasn't much of a dancer. And perhaps Jerome and Eugene would be there too. I hoped so.

'Have you seen Fran?' Mother said as we were leaving the house. 'She said she had a surprise for you.'

'A surprise?' I frowned. 'What sort of surprise?'

My mother was picking up her folder of notes about the fair and checking her hair in the mirror in the hall. 'I don't know; she just said it was a surprise.'

'I'll go and find her.'

'Well, be quick,' Mother tutted. 'I'll set off and you can catch me up.'

I rolled my eyes. 'Fine.'

She straightened her jacket and headed outside, while I wandered off to find Fran.

I tracked her down in the kitchen.

'Finally!' she said. 'I've got a surprise for you.'

'What is it?'

'If I tell you, it won't be a surprise.'

'Where is it?'

'Stop asking questions,' she said. She gave me a little shove towards the door. 'Go to the vegetable garden, will you? I need some . . .' she looked round vaguely '. . . carrots.'

'You need carrots?' My gaze fell on a pile of carrots next to the sink. 'I'm supposed to be helping with the summer fair.'

'Go on,' she said, shoving me less gently this time. 'Go.'

Bewildered, I went out of the back door and up the path to the vegetable gardens on the far side of the house. And there, looking happy, healthy and strong in her Land Army uniform, was Patty.

'Ohmygoodness,' I shrieked. I ran to her and threw my arms round her. 'You're here!'

'For a little while,' she said. 'I've got a month at Heath Farm, over the hill.'

'I'm so pleased to see you.'

'Me too.' She smiled at me. 'I can't wait to tell you all about what I've been doing.'

'Tell me now.'

'Unless you want to start digging then I can't spare the time, but we could have a cup of tea later?'

'Come and meet me in the village,' I said. 'I'm helping with the summer fair.'

Patty raised an eyebrow and I groaned. 'It's good for my mother. And I'm so bored, Patty, I need to do something to fill my time.'

'I thought there were GIs here,' said one of the other land girls who was digging nearby. 'Don't they fill your time?'

I felt my cheeks flush. 'I've not seen much of them really,' I muttered.

Patty eyed me suspiciously. 'I'll come and find you when I get a break,' she said. 'Seems we've got a lot to catch up on.'

I kissed her goodbye and hurried off to find my mother. The sentry box was finished now, though no one was in it. I was a little disappointed not to see Jerome, because I'd been wondering if Eugene was all right, and if he'd managed to speak to Waldo, and if Perkins had got into any trouble for hitting poor Eugene with the brick, even if it had been accidental . . .

But he wasn't there.

I found Mother in the village hall with most of the WI, and Mr Fingal from the parish council.

'Ah,' she said in a low voice as I scurried over to the empty chair next to her and sat down. 'I was wondering where you'd got to.'

'Patty's home,' I whispered. 'She was my surprise.'

Mother smiled at me and patted my hand, and then we turned our attention back to Mrs Evans from the WI who was talking about making sweets for the children from sliced carrots.

Poor kids, I thought, my mouth watering as I remembered the butterscotch Grandpa had always brought me, and the tiny French pastries Mamie made for my birthday.

The meeting dragged on, until finally I saw Patty waving frantically at me through the window. Luckily, we were on to who was providing tea in the tea tent by then, and I didn't think I was needed, so I made my excuses and dashed outside.

'I've only got an hour,' Patty warned. 'But shall we go and get a cup of tea at the café?'

Arm in arm we strolled over to the café where we sat at a table outside, enjoying the spring sunshine, and ordered a pot of tea to share.

'Tell me everything,' I urged Patty. 'What are you going to be doing?'

'It's such hard work,' she told me as I poured the tea. 'I was so tired during training that I hardly knew my own name. But it was easier for me than some. At least I've grown up in the countryside. There were girls there from London who'd never got close to a cow.'

I made a face. 'Did you have to get close to a cow?'

'Yes,' Patty said, rolling her eyes. 'I've learned to milk them.'

'Urgh.'

'You're the worst country girl I've ever known.' She picked up the little jug and poured milk into my tea. I gave it a wary glance and Patty groaned.

'Gloria.'

'Sorry.'

Across the street, a jeep drove up and several GIs spilled out. Patty sat up a bit straighter.

'The Americans,' she said. 'Look lively.'

I scanned the men for Jerome or Eugene, but I couldn't see them.

Perkins was there, though, and he waved to me. I waved back and Patty looked impressed.

'You know him?'

'He was working on a thing at home,' I said vaguely. 'We got talking.'

The men all went into the pub, and Perkins started walking over to where we sat.

'What's he like?' Patty said. 'He's rather handsome.'

'He's too full of himself,' I muttered as he approached. 'Hello, Perkins!'

'Hey there, Miss Henry.'

'Gloria,' I said. 'This is my friend Patty. She's just home for a little while.'

Patty held her hand out for him to shake, pulling her shoulders back as she did. 'Nice to meet you,' she said, looking up at Perkins from under her eyelashes.

I kicked her under the table, but she ignored me.

'How are you finding Honeyford?' she asked, resting her chin on her hands. 'I'm sure it's very different from where you're from.'

'It certainly is,' he said, with a grin. 'But I like it a lot.'

'So you're settling in all right?' Patty said. I rolled my eyes because she was virtually purring like a cat. 'I thought you might need someone to show you the sights . . .'

I turned away from her as she fluttered her eyelashes at Perkins and watched another jeep arriving. This time two men in uniform got out. They were wearing tin hats with the letters MP on them, and armbands saying the same. They went up the stairs at the front of the pub but they didn't go inside. Instead they stood, one on either side of the door like guards.

'What's going on there?' I asked Perkins, curious. 'What are they doing?'

'They're military police.'

Patty raised an eyebrow. 'Why are they here?'

He shrugged. 'They investigate any crimes that might happen.

They keep the privates in line. We're here in Great Britain, but we have our own rules to live by.' He looked at me. 'Ain't that right, Miss Gloria?'

'Just Gloria,' I muttered.

'And are there any criminals among you?' Patty said.

Perkins leaned over the table. 'The only criminal round here is you, Miss Patty,' he said. 'Because you've just stolen my heart.'

Patty regarded him for a second, and then she laughed.

'Lord, that's corny,' she said. 'Better luck next time, eh?'

Perkins straightened up. 'I'll keep trying,' he said with a grin.

'How is Eugene?' I asked, annoyed by their flirting.

He looked at me with a frown. 'Who?'

'Eugene? He was building the sentry box. I heard he got hurt.'

He looked at me for a second, his eyes narrowed – though perhaps it was just the sun – and then he nodded. 'He's right as rain now.'

'Glad to hear it.'

'It's Friday afternoon and we've got the weekend off,' he said, turning his attention back to Patty. 'We're headed for a drink if you'd like to join us.'

'I have to get back to work,' said Patty sounding genuinely regretful. 'And Gloria is too young.'

I kicked her again. I may not have had much time for Perkins, but I didn't want him to know I was still only 17.

'Then I'll see you ladies later,' he said. He nodded at us, his gaze lingering on Patty, and went off towards the pub.

'Will you still be here for the fair?' I asked Patty, who was rubbing her ankle and giving me a steely glare.

'I think so. Ouch, Gloria, that hurt. You've got very pointy feet.'

'Shall we go?'

'Is Perkins going?'

I screwed my nose up. 'He says so. But let's go together.'

'Ohh, yes, let's.' Patty looked pleased. 'I'll get some of the land girls to come along, too.'

I felt a shiver of excitement. 'It'll be so good to have some fun,' I said.

Another group of GIs walked past, heading for the White Horse.

'Oh, we'll have fun all right,' Patty said, nudging me.

I giggled as two GIs approached from the other direction. These airmen were Black, like Jerome and Eugene, and they looked less sure of themselves. I watched them walk towards the pub cautiously. One put a foot on the first step and one of the military policemen standing beside the door shook his head, holding his hand out to stop the airman coming any further.

He glanced round at his friend, who shrugged. And then they both walked away, shoulders slumped.

In the window of the pub, I saw George, the landlord, watching them go. I wondered what he was thinking.

'They weren't allowed in,' Patty said, sounding shocked.

'The Black GIs are treated differently from the white ones,' I told her. 'Grandpa and I were talking about it, and you must have read about it. In America they have laws about where the white people can go, and where the Black people go.' I frowned. 'But we don't have those laws and they're not on the air base now, so I'm not sure why the police are involved. We treat everyone the same here.'

Patty looked unconvinced. 'I'm not sure that's true,' she said. 'Really?'

'You know I said I'd been training with some girls from the East End of London?'

'Yes?'

'One of them, a girl called Amelia, she's Black. Like those GIs.'

'And?'

'And at first they wouldn't let her into the Land Army. She really had to fight to be allowed to join up.'

'Gosh,' I said, feeling my faith in British people shift a little. 'That's awful.'

'That's what I thought. Some of the other girls thought it was right, though. They said she wouldn't be as educated as the rest of us.'

'I've heard some people saying that about the Black GIs.' I rubbed my nose. 'Is Amelia one of the land girls who didn't know which end of a cow was which?'

'Nope, she's great,' Patty said.

I shrugged. 'Well, there you go.'

'There you go,' she said.

We both looked over to where the airmen were walking out of the village.

'They stay in a different base,' I said. 'The officers are in our house, the white GIs are at the air base, and the others are in the barracks over the hill, by the main road.'

'I knew that,' Patty said. 'But I'd not realised why.'

'I suppose if it works for them . . .' I said uncertainly.

'I suppose,' said Patty sounding just as uncertain. Then the clock on the church tower bonged the hour and she jumped. 'I have to go,' she said. 'I can't be late back. Are you walking back?'

I glanced over to where George the landlord was sweeping the steps of the pub, having got the policemen to move aside.

'No,' I said. 'I just want to ask George something. I'll catch you later.'

'All right,' Patty said. She got to her feet and kissed me on the cheek. 'Be careful, Glo.'

'I will.'

Chapter 9

Philippa

'I read that it's meant to be a glorious summer,' I said to Marco a few days later. We were strolling through the village, enjoying the spring sunshine, on our way to the White Horse for a drink. 'Tropical.'

'Really?' said Marco with disbelief. 'Where did you read that?'

'On the internet.'

'Oh well in that case, it's definitely true,' he said. 'Everything you read on the internet is true.'

I gave him a shove. 'I'm just saying it could be good for your outdoor tables if it's a good summer. And it'll mean Harvey can finish the roof faster, too.'

'That is true.'

We'd reached the green at the end of the village and just as we were about to walk across the grass to the pub, Vanessa came flying out of the village hall across the way. She looked frantically worried and her eyes were red.

'Vanessa,' I called. 'Vanessa? Are you okay?'

She glanced up and paused as she saw us approaching.

'I'm having a nightmare,' she said. 'Total bloody nightmare.'

'What's the matter?' I asked. 'Is it Alex?'

'Alex,' she said, sounding close to tears. I felt a knot of worry in my stomach.

'Vanessa, is Alex all right?'

She looked horrified. 'Oh yes, he's fine. I'm so sorry to scare you.' She ran her fingers through her hair. 'It's his birthday tomorrow.'

'Teenager,' said Marco. 'It's a big deal.'

'I knooooooow,' Vanessa wailed, making me jump. 'And everything's gone wrong.'

'We were going for a drink,' said Marco. 'Come on, let's go and sit down and you can tell us all about it.'

He took Vanessa by the elbow and steered her up the steps to the pub and inside. I usually liked it when Marco took control when I was in a tizzy about something, but seeing him do it with someone else – someone who wasn't his mother, that was – made me feel odd.

'I'll get the drinks,' I said quickly, to hide my uncharitable feelings. I may have found Vanessa a little intimidating but she'd been nothing but kind to me, and I didn't want to see her upset.

When I came back from the bar, I found Vanessa and Marco sitting at a table in the corner. Vanessa looked a bit calmer, though she still took a big swig from the wine glass I handed her.

'The place Vanessa's booked for Alex's birthday party has let her down,' Marco said as I sat down next to him.

'Oh, what an arse. What had you booked?'

Vanessa made a face. 'It's just that five-a-side place, on the main road? He wanted to play football with his friends and then have burgers. Nothing fancy. But they've had a burst pipe and it's all flooded so they're closed and everything else is booked up.'

'Poor Alex,' I said.

'I've not even told him yet.' Vanessa took another gulp of her wine. 'Because I know he's secretly hoping his mum will get in touch, and I know he'll be disappointed if she doesn't phone.' She swigged again. '*When* she doesn't phone.'

'You don't think she'll call?' I said, feeling terribly sad for the lad. I knew just how horrible it felt to know you weren't your mum's priority.

Vanessa shook her head. 'I don't think so. Tilly's made her choice, and she seems to be at peace with it. But Alex still hopes she'll come back.' Her voice wobbled. 'So he's bound to be devastated when she doesn't send a card. And then to have to cancel his party too, oh I just feel awful.'

She looked straight at me. 'You said your mother couldn't look after you?'

My stomach twisted. I didn't like talking about my childhood. But I sensed that Vanessa had something to ask, so I nodded.

'Our home was chaotic and my mother had a lot of issues,' I said, choosing my words carefully. I didn't want to mention the bare mattress I'd slept on sometimes, or the way I'd had to take money from her purse and go to the shop by myself to buy food before I'd even started school. 'She had bad times and better times and when things were bad, I couldn't stay with her.'

Vanessa was watching me intently. 'Where did you go?'

'To a cousin when I was little, but then he moved away. And then foster homes when I was older.'

'Was it awful?'

'No.' I shook my head vigorously. 'Not awful. It was an escape.'

Vanessa's shoulders relaxed a little.

I reached out and squeezed her hand. 'Alex is a lovely lad. He's happy. That's because of you. But he'll always feel sad about his mum.'

'Do you love your mum?'

Next to me, Marco moved his chair a little closer and I was glad of his presence.

'She died,' he said. 'Philippa's mum passed away.'

'Shit, sorry.'

'Don't be,' I said. 'I did love her. I didn't have it easy growing up, but she wasn't having it easy either. I don't blame her for anything.'

Vanessa nodded, her eyes full of tears.

'I was wondering if I should buy a present and a card for Alex, and pretend they came from Tilly. Would that be awful?'

'Don't do that,' I said. 'I know why you'd want to, but he needs to know he can trust you. Don't lie to him.'

'You're right,' Vanessa said with a groan. 'Of course you are. I just want everything to be perfect for him. Poor lad. It's his first birthday since he's been with me permanently and I wanted it to be memorable.'

'There's really nowhere else?'

'There's a wedding on at the village hall,' Vanessa said. 'The pub team are playing a cricket match against the Three Feathers, so the field's out of action all day, and my garden is not big enough.'

Marco sat up straighter. 'No,' he said. 'But ours is.'

'Marco . . .' I began. 'I'm not sure . . .'

But he didn't hear me. Or he wasn't listening.

'Have the party at Honeyford House,' he said. 'They can play football in the garden, and I'll do burgers and chips for them afterwards. Philippa can decorate the restaurant, can't you, Phil?'

'Well, I suppose . . .'

'I've got some balloons and bunting and whatnot,' Vanessa said, looking much cheerier. Then she slapped her forehead. 'But the football place was supplying the cake.'

'Not a problem,' Marco said. 'I can make a cake. Football themed?'

'If you're really sure,' Vanessa said. 'I don't want to put you out.'

'Oh rubbish,' said Marco waving his hands just like his father did when he got excited. 'It'll be great. And maybe the parents will remember us and become loyal customers.'

'Always the businessman,' I said, laughing even though I wasn't overly happy about this arrangement. Ten 13-year-olds in our garden was a big ask. Would they behave themselves? Were we going to be in charge?

As if she'd read my mind, Vanessa said: 'We'll need someone to keep an eye on them.'

Marco waved his hands again. 'We can do that . . .'

This time I prodded him to stop him talking. 'You'll be in the kitchen, Marco,' I said. 'And I have certain skills but I really can't organise a five-a-side football match.'

Marco looked disappointed. 'I suppose.'

'I'll give Harvey a call,' Vanessa said. 'He coaches one of the local teams. I'm sure he won't mind helping out. He knows most of the lads anyway.'

'Then it's sorted,' Marco said. He drained his drink. 'Come on, Phil.'

'Where are we going?'

'To buy the ingredients for a birthday cake.'

So that was why I ended up spending my Saturday handing out many, many burgers and hot dogs to muddy, sweaty boys, topping up endless cups of orange squash, awarding a small plastic trophy to the "man of the match" and intervening in more than one fight.

In short, I was exhausted.

Marco, though, was clearly loving every minute. The burgers had all gone, the cake was cut and wrapped in napkins so the kids could take a slice home, and there was a "grown-ups v kids" game happening on the lawn, though as it was only Harvey and Marco against a lot of smaller, more energetic lads, I didn't fancy their chances.

I sat down on one of the new chairs on the terrace and watched. My feet were sore from standing and my shoulders ached from holding trays of food, and if I was being completely honest, my heart hurt – again – as I watched my husband with the kids – again.

The football match came to a noisy finish with the boys running round in triumph. Vanessa, who'd been watching from the sidelines went over to commiserate with Marco and Harvey. She looked really happy – her eyes were shining and she hadn't stopped smiling – and very pretty. But for once I didn't feel envy as I looked at her; I just felt glad that we'd been able to help.

Well done, Phil, I thought to myself. *Maybe you're not such a terrible person after all.*

Some of the boys came up to the terrace to pour themselves more drinks.

'Alex's dad is well cool,' said one of them.

I sat up, trying not to look like I was listening. Did they mean Marco? Or Harvey?

'His hair's awesome.'

Ah, Marco then. Poor Harvey was bald as a coot.

'Alex, your dad's epic,' the first one said as the birthday boy bounded up the steps. I waited for him to correct them and tell them Marco wasn't his dad. But instead Alex just grinned.

'I know,' he said.

Chapter 10

Gloria

I wanted to speak to George about his piano player. Mother had told me the chap who usually played at the pub – a man called Hastings who I'd never been very fond of – had gone to live with his sister in Birmingham. And that had given me an idea.

But when Patty had raced off back to work, George had gone back into the pub and I wasn't really sure about whether I should go inside or not – especially as the whole place was beginning to sound a bit raucous thanks to the Americans inside. Maybe another time, I thought. I'd just go home and find out all about the plans for the summer fair, instead.

As I walked, another US car came by slowly. I glanced up and saw – to my absolute delight – Jerome at the wheel. He saw me and nodded subtly, then he lifted one finger from the steering wheel, in a gesture that I took to mean he was asking me to wait.

I felt a tiny thrill as I stopped to look in the window of the butcher's shop, pretending to be ever so interested in some chops, but all the while keeping an eye on what Jerome was doing.

He stopped the car just a little way along and Waldo and another man got out. They both walked off towards the village hall and I

wondered if they were coming to see Mr Fingal. The parish coun-
cillors all liked to think they were Very Important when it came
to the arrival of the GIs though I thought the Americans regarded
them with an air of kindly amusement. Keeping them sweet, I
thought now, like we were with our tolerance of their race laws.

'Gloria?'

I turned away from the chops and saw Jerome coming towards
me.

'Hello,' I said.

He smiled at me broadly. 'I'm driving Captain Waldo,' he said.

'I saw!'

'Because of you.'

'No,' I said modestly. 'I just gave you the idea.'

'I got lucky,' Jerome said. 'Got time to chat?'

He gestured to one of the benches in the village square.
Honeyford was pretty much one street that broadened at one end
into a square. The church was on one side of the square, the pub
and some houses on the other, and shops – and the café where
I'd had tea with Patty was opposite. In the middle was a patch
of grass, where some of the summer fair was held. The rest of
the stalls would be on the cricket pitch, behind the churchyard.

'I'm not in any hurry,' I said. So Jerome and I walked across
the grass and sat down on the bench. 'Tell me what happened.'

'The car had to stop, of course, because I shut the gates like
you said. And when Masters – that's the guy who was driving
Waldo before – went to start the engine again, he couldn't get
it to turn over. It happens sometimes on these cars. We've been
driving them for ages, round the air base when we were doing
the runway, so I know how to handle them. Anyway, he was
getting red in the face and Waldo was annoyed, and I leaned in
the window and told him what to do.'

'And it worked?'

'It did.' He grinned. 'And I mentioned had he come up the
hill from the base at Eaton because I knew it was hard on

the brakes going down the other side and perhaps next time he'd be better going along the river, which is slightly longer but an easier drive . . .'

I frowned. 'Is it?'

'Not really,' said Jerome, 'but I wanted to show that I knew the area. And then I was so polite, and I said to Waldo that I was very sorry to interfere, sir, but I hoped I'd been of help. And he asked my name and the next day I got told to drive him.'

'That was easy,' I said.

'Right place, right time.'

He looked so pleased with himself that I couldn't stop myself grinning back at him.

'Thank you,' he said.

I waved away his thanks, but I was chuffed.

'How is Eugene?'

'He's fine,' Jerome said. 'It wasn't a bad wound really. It was more the attitude, you know? Perkins is . . .' He sighed. 'He's from the south.'

'The south of America?' I asked, interested. 'Is that bad?'

Jerome gave a little laugh. 'No, not bad. They just have different rules about Black people and white people is all.' He took his hat off and rubbed his palm over his cropped hair. 'Though at least they know what the rules are. It changes all the time at home.'

'Where are you from?'

'New York.'

I was almost speechless with delight. 'New York City?'

'That's it.'

'Oh my goodness,' I breathed. 'Is it wonderful?'

Jerome glanced around where we sat. 'It's very different from here – that's for sure.'

He looked a little thoughtful for a moment and I realised just how far from home he was. I couldn't imagine how it felt to be transplanted from New York City to a tiny, quiet place like Honeyford. I'd been to London, of course, and I thought

81

New York would be similar – full of hustle and bustle and bright lights – but on a much bigger scale.

'Are you missing home?'

Jerome fixed his gaze on his feet. 'I miss my family,' he said. 'I miss my mom and dad.' He laughed. 'I sound like such a baby.'

'Not one bit,' I said firmly. 'My dad died. I miss him too.'

'Oh shoot, I'm sorry.' Jerome looked horrified, and I touched his arm briefly in reassurance.

'Don't be,' I said. 'You couldn't have known.'

There was a moment of silence between us and I wanted to kick myself for making it awkward.

'Are you going to the dance?' I asked hurriedly. 'My friend Patty came home – she's a land girl – and we're going to go. It could be fun.'

Jerome looked unsure. 'Would we be welcome?'

'Of course you would,' I said. 'Gosh, everyone's desperate to get to meet the GIs. And Perkins and his cronies were talking about going the other day.'

I had intended to convince him but at the mention of Perkins he shook his head. 'It's best we stay away.'

'Oh,' I realised suddenly that he'd meant he wouldn't be welcome because he was Black, not because he was a GI and I felt silly. 'Really?'

'I think so.'

'Earlier on, I saw some . . .' I paused, not knowing how to word it. 'Some GIs were turned away from the pub.'

Jerome followed my gaze to where a couple of white GIs were sitting on the steps of the pub, drinking beer and laughing. I couldn't see the policemen now and their jeep had gone too.

'There were military police there,' I said.

Jerome made a face. 'Sounds about right.' I looked at him. His jaw was set. 'I should go,' he said.

'How are you finding *The 39 Steps*?' I said quickly, not wanting him to leave.

He got to his feet, but he turned to me and smiled. 'Hannay sure gets himself in all sorts of trouble.'

'He does.'

'Do you like detective stories?' I asked. 'Dorothy L Sayers? Agatha Christie?'

'I like scary stories,' Jerome said. 'I like Edgar Allan Poe.'

I widened my eyes. 'What about *Dr Jekyll and Mr Hyde*? Have you read that?'

'No.'

'Oh you'd like it,' I said. 'I have a copy you can borrow.'

He looked at me, his head tilted to one side and a small smile on his face. 'You do, huh?'

'I do.'

He smiled properly this time. 'Thank you.'

Over beside the village hall I saw Waldo emerge with Mr Fingal.

'I really should go now,' Jerome said. 'I'll catch you later.'

He put his hat back on and hurried off, without looking back.

'Making friends?' a voice said, making me jump because I'd been too busy watching Jerome go to notice anyone approaching.

I turned to see George from the pub standing next to me.

'Yes, actually.' I gave him my best smile. 'Jerome there was just telling me that his friend Eugene plays piano.'

George, who'd been landlord of the White Horse since before I was born and who had been a friend of my dad, gave me a resigned look. 'Gloria, are you meddling again?'

I widened my eyes in innocence. 'Just making small talk.'

'You heard that Hastings has gone to live in Birmingham?'

'Mother mentioned something,' I said casually.

George chuckled. 'All right then,' he said. 'All right.'

But I'd stopped listening because I could see Jerome approaching in Waldo's car. As he drove past us our eyes met and he gave me a wink again – just like he'd done that first day. I felt my cheeks redden and, suddenly full of happiness, I grinned at George. 'I'm making friends,' I said.

Chapter 11

Philippa

I had a habit of catastrophising. At least that's what my therapist had told me. I'd had quite a lot of therapy over the years. She said I spent a lot of time worrying about worst-case scenarios that I'd made up in my own head. She was right, actually, and that was exactly what I was doing now – worrying about Marco playing Dad to Alex.

The therapist – Therese – had told me I should concentrate on the facts of a worrying situation.

'What do we know is true?' she would say, tapping her chin with her forefinger and staring at me.

So now, a week or so after Alex's triumphant thirteenth birthday party, I was sitting on the terrace with a cup of tea, thinking about what I knew for sure.

I knew Marco loved me. That was a big one. And I knew I loved him too. I knew Vanessa was a good person – the way she was with Alex showed me that, not to mention how kind she'd been to us. I knew teenagers, even brand-new ones, worried about what their friends thought and that sometimes it might be easier to let them think one man was your dad instead of telling them the truth.

I knew that Marco had been spot-on when he'd said hosting

Alex's party would get us noticed among people in Honeyford. Already we'd had several enquiries about when we'd be opening and what functions we could cater for.

And I knew the terrace needed a good power wash because it was absolutely filthy.

Getting to my feet and putting my empty mug on the table, I wandered over to the edge of the patio and looked back at the house. The ceiling repairs had been delayed while Harvey waited for more wood or tiles or something, but he was back today. And Marco had worked out exactly how to build the pergola – though I was still quietly doubtful that it would actually stay upright.

Things were looking good really. That was another fact. I'd even been helping more people in the village with their accounts, and Marco had done an afternoon tea at short notice at a nearby care home, where Mick from the shop's elderly mother lived, and I was finding it rather nice to be useful.

Next on the list was tackling the garden. It wasn't so bad near the house, but towards the bottom it descended into tangles and brambles. I wasn't looking forward to it at all. But today was a lovely day so it would be the perfect time to get going. Maybe I'd start hacking away at some of the grass.

I decided I'd walk round the boundary of the whole garden and have a look at it from all angles. But before I could set off, the doorbell rang.

'PHIL!' Marco bellowed from somewhere off to the side of me – I thought he might be in the ramshackle shed, looking at bits of wood. 'DOOR!'

I slid off the wall and went to open the door. There was Vanessa, holding a large brown parcel. And behind her, with his ball under his arm, was Alex.

'I've brought you a present,' she said, sounding chuffed to bits. 'I can't wait to show you.'

'Well, in that case, come on in,' I said. 'Hi, Alex.'

'Football was cancelled,' he said with a hangdog expression.

'Oh God, not because Harvey's working here?'

'Harvey's not my coach,' Alex said wearily as though he'd told me this before, which to be fair, he probably had. 'He coaches the under tens.'

'Well, that's a relief. Come through to the garden.'

'Are Marco and Harvey doing the pergola?' Vanessa asked. 'I thought I might be able to help?'

'Marco is,' I said. 'But Harvey's on the ceiling still.'

Vanessa's shoulders slumped just a little. 'Well, if Marco needs another pair of hands . . .'

'I'm sure he'd be glad of it,' I said.

'I can help,' said Alex. 'Can I saw some wood? Or cut it with an axe?'

'No,' Vanessa and I both said together.

'I'm sure Marco can find you a job,' I added. 'You can go and find him. I think he's in the shed looking for wood.'

We sat down on the terrace and Vanessa presented me with the parcel. 'To say thank you for Alex's party.'

'That was all Marco.'

'You did it together.' She clapped her hands. 'Open it.'

I ripped off the paper and to my delight, inside was a black and white photograph of David Bowie. He was lying along the top of a carved stone wall, one knee bent to show off his huge flares. His face was turned slightly to the camera, his eyes closed and a contented smile on his lips.

'Oh. My. God,' I said. 'Is that here?' I pointed to the carved stone wall that ran along the edge of the terrace. 'Did David Bowie lie on our wall?'

Vanessa grinned. 'Well, maybe, is the answer. It looks like Honeyford House, but we can't verify it. I'd say yes though. He's bound to have been at one of Lucien's gatherings.'

'I love it,' I said, giving her a hug. 'Thank you.'

Marco appeared on the terrace with Alex beside him and I showed him the picture.

'Amazing,' he said in awe. 'Harvey! Did you see this?'

Harvey came over and almost passed out in disbelief when he saw the picture.

'I'm a huge Bowie fan,' he told us. 'I can't believe he's walked where I'm standing now. Can you get me a copy of that, Ness?'

'Of course.' She smiled at him. 'I've got a spare one actually.'

'That's lucky,' I took the picture back from Harvey and admired it again.

'Isn't it,' Marco said. I glanced at him and he winked at me. I had no idea why.

'Right, Marco,' Vanessa said. 'Tell me what you need me to do.'

'Excellent. I'm all ready,' he said proudly. 'I've cut all the wood. Now we just have to put it together.'

'Like Lego,' said Alex.

'Exactly like Lego.' He grinned. 'I've got a diagram.'

'Show me,' said Vanessa.

Harvey looked concerned. 'I'm going back to the restaurant,' he said. 'Before I get distracted.'

He headed off, with a final glance at Bowie's picture, while Marco spread out the paper on the table and the three of them pored over it. I looked at their heads all close together – Vanessa's messy bun, Marco's curls, and Alex's blonde mop and felt a bit left out.

'I'm going to walk round the garden,' I said mostly to myself. 'Draw a bit of a plan too.'

No one heard me, so after a brief pause, I left them to it.

From where I stood with Honeyford House behind me, most of the garden was to my right. It swept round, bordered with trees, and down the hill towards the village.

I decided to start my circuit on the left where the garden ran along another road. I went down the steps at the corner of the terrace and across the overgrown lawn then set off, following the curve of the garden. Things weren't too bad up here. Yes the grass was long and uncared for but I could get myself on the sit-on mower and charge about and get rid of the worst of it in no time. Up ahead, in the wall that separated the garden from the road, I saw a gate. I'd not even realised there was access there. We'd really concentrated on the house when we'd bought it, not the garden. But it could be useful, I thought. Especially if we did do weddings at some point.

I paused and looked back at the house. I could see Alex doing keepy-uppies on the terrace and Marco and Vanessa holding up bits of wood. Even from this distance, I could see Vanessa had half an eye on Alex, and I felt a teeny tiny stab of envy both because Alex had someone who cared what he was doing, and because Vanessa had a child to love.

Rolling my eyes at my own overemotional response, I turned to walk away and – ooof – found myself sprawled on the ground, my shin throbbing.

'Bloody Nora,' I muttered. I pulled my legs round and rolled up the leg of my jeans to examine my shin, which was disappointingly showing only a small red mark. What had I walked into?

I pushed my jean leg back down and felt around in the long grass until I found a wooden railway sleeper – very hard and slightly raised off ground level.

'Ohh,' I breathed in delight, getting to my feet in a slightly ungainly fashion. Now I knew they were there, I could see they were vegetable beds. Totally overgrown now, of course, but they were large and looked great. I pulled my phone out and took a few pictures. Marco was very keen on knowing where all the food he cooked with had come from and I knew he'd be thrilled with the idea of growing some of our own vegetables.

Pleased with my progress already, I set off again. Right at the bottom of the garden was a wood. Well, more of a glade really, because it was just a few trees. I rather liked it down there, though. The ground was soft and the air smelled nice. Scattered among the trees were bluebells, which were a burst of colour in the earthy ground. It was quiet and still and sheltered from the road and the house. I wondered if we could put a hammock between two of the trees. It would be a nice place to sit and read on a summer's day.

I stood a little way from the trees and looked across the garden. It was very overgrown down this end. Not just grass but brambles and all sorts. It was actually hard to walk – I had to take huge high steps like I was walking on the moon – and squash the undergrowth down with my feet as I went. I was glad I was wearing trousers because if I'd had shorts on, my legs would have been torn to pieces by the spiky plants.

I didn't go into the glade but as I walked past the trees I noticed one of them – the last one in the row – had a little dip in its roots, like a ready-made armchair for someone to sit on. Though, I thought, looking at it and assessing its size – perhaps not quite suitable for my perimenopausal behind.

Alex might like it, though. I'd have liked a little nook to hide away in when I was a teenager. Perhaps I could show him. I'd like that. The realisation surprised me. I looked up to the house, and as I did, I saw Vanessa – who was up a ladder – holding a piece of wood in place, reach too far. The ladder tipped and she fell, almost in slow motion.

I heard Marco shout, and Alex wail, and I set off up to the house, running as fast as I could through the long grass.

By the time I reached the terrace and pelted up the steps, Vanessa was lying on the ground – she was conscious I saw in relief though she looked pale. Marco was next to her, his phone in his hand and Alex was watching from a distance, his face ashen.

'Oh my goodness,' I said, slightly out of breath from running up the garden. 'Vanessa, are you all right?'

'I think I've broken my bloody ankle,' she said, through gritted teeth. 'I heard it snap.'

'So did I,' said Marco. He looked more than a little wobbly himself. 'I heard it.'

'Go and see Alex,' I said in a quiet voice. 'He's scared.'

Marco, thankfully, glanced round at the lad, who looked very young suddenly, and sprang into action. 'Let's go and get Granny a blanket, shall we?' he said. 'She's going to be right as rain, you'll see.'

I crouched down and took Vanessa's hand.

'Did Marco call an ambulance?'

'No, I wouldn't let him.'

'You need to go to hospital,' I said. 'I did my first aid badge at Brownies but I'm not sure we covered broken bones.'

Vanessa managed a tiny smile. 'I didn't want to frighten Alex,' she said. 'Tilly has been to hospital a couple of times when her partner got angry. He might get upset if he sees paramedics.'

'Marco's looking after him,' I said, feeling sorry for poor Alex, who'd had so much to deal with. 'But I can take you in the car, if you'd rather that?' I looked at her. 'If you can get up?'

Vanessa nodded as best she could. 'I can,' she said.

It obviously took every bit of strength she had, and at one point I was worried she was going to pass out from the pain, but she managed to get to her feet – well, one foot as she was leaning on me. Her face was grey now and I was nervous that she might have a funny turn, but she managed. I thought that her desire not to frighten Alex must be very strong and I admired her for it.

Marco appeared in the doorway and I shook my head. 'I'm taking Vanessa to hospital,' I said.

'Alex,' Vanessa called. I could feel her trembling with the shock and the pain, but her voice was strong. I thought about those women who had lifted cars off their children and marvelled once more at her determination. 'I've hurt my ankle, so Philippa is just going to take me to hospital.'

Alex's little worried face appeared at Marco's side. 'Who will look after me?'

Vanessa breathed in sharply then she said: 'What about Arjan?' She looked at me. 'Best friend,' she said.

'Arjan's at a wedding this weekend,' Alex said.

'Shit,' Vanessa muttered. 'Shit.'

'Is there anyone else?' I asked quietly.

She shook her head. 'I have to be careful about who he stays with.'

Marco twigged what was happening. He put his hand on Alex's head. 'How about you stay here with me for a while? Just until we know what's happening with your granny?'

Alex looked uncertain.

Marco checked his watch. 'Spurs are playing in half an hour,' he said. 'We could watch the match and order a pizza?'

Alex, Marco and I all looked at Vanessa to see what she thought. Her face was even greyer now, and I thought it was with a slightly desperate air that she said: 'That sounds good.'

'Can we get a meat feast?' asked Alex.

'Of course.'

Vanessa tried to smile but it was a little lopsided and weak. 'Stay with Marco, love. I'll be fine with Philippa.' She blew Alex a slightly shaky kiss, and reassured he went inside with Marco.

'Come on then, Hopalong,' I said. 'Let's get you to hospital, shall we?'

Chapter 12

Philippa

Vanessa needed to have an operation because her ankle was broken badly and needed pinning. I was allowed to see her before she went down to theatre.

'I feel like a right idiot,' she said as soon as I pulled the curtain back and poked my head round. 'This is all my fault.'

'It's just one of those things,' I told her. 'It's no one's fault.' Then I grinned. 'Well, perhaps Marco could take some of the blame for making you go up a ladder.'

'I insisted,' she said, groaning. 'He said it was – what was the word he used? Shoogly.'

I smiled at her use of Marco's Scottish phrase. 'I've left a message for Alex's social worker like you asked,' I told her. 'And I'll call him again when you get taken for your op to update him. And I went to Sainsbury's next door and got you a nightie – I thought that would be best with your ankle – and some toiletries and whatnot.' I brandished my carrier bag. 'And there's some chocolate in there and a couple of magazines, too.'

I put the bag on the chair next to her bed.

'Thank you.' She reached out and took my hand. 'I've always

said having Alex keeps me young, but at the moment I feel very old and very foolish and . . .' she made a face '. . . a little bit scared.'

My heart twisted in sympathy for her. 'It'll be fine,' I said. 'You'll be fine. You're not old just a bit broken. But they'll fix that. And Alex will be grand.'

Vanessa looked worried. 'Could you keep him?' she said. 'You and Marco? Just for now?'

'Oh, Vanessa, I'm not sure. Would we be allowed? What would the social worker say?'

Vanessa's eyes filled with tears. 'He'll be fine with it,' she said. 'If I am.'

'Really?'

'Otherwise, they'll arrange an emergency foster placement.' She squeezed my hand. 'He won't want that. He'll be so frightened.'

'He hardly knows us . . .' I began. I was growing more comfortable with Alex being around but there were limits.

'He knows you better than he'd know a foster carer, and he loves you,' she said. 'He said he's asked Marco to watch his football match next week.'

'Did he?' Marco hadn't mentioned that to me.

'Apparently.' Vanessa looked at me. 'If you can pass my phone, I'll email Alex's social worker now and let him know you're going to keep him for now.'

'Okay,' I said, my heart twisting at the thought of Alex having no one else to care for him. I passed her the phone. 'Go on. CC me in.'

I reeled off my email address and when a nurse appeared to get her ready for surgery, I told her what Vanessa was doing. She smiled. 'Bet that's a load off, isn't it, Vanessa? Knowing your lad is being looked after.'

'It is.' Vanessa handed me her phone again and I put it in the locker at the side of her bed.

'Should I wait?' I asked the nurse. 'I can wait. It's not a problem.'

'No, don't be silly,' said Vanessa at once.

'No, you get off,' the nurse agreed. 'It'll be a few hours before she's back on the ward. Leave your number at the desk and we'll call you with an update.'

'Okay,' I said. I leaned over and gave Vanessa a kiss on the cheek. She gripped my hand tightly and it occurred to me suddenly that Alex wasn't the only one who didn't have anyone to look after him. 'Good luck,' I said. 'Don't worry, we'll get you back up that ladder in no time.'

I left her with the nurse, gave my number to the woman at the desk and asked her to call with an update, and went to find the car.

I was, I found, slightly reluctant to go home, which was ridiculous. I found I was torn between wanting to help Alex because I absolutely understood how he would be feeling, and being nervous about having a child in the house. A living, breathing, pizza-eating reminder of what might have been.

The fact was, I told myself sternly, that Alex was a 13-year-old boy who had no one else. No one. And that was the only fact that mattered here.

After a circuit of the car park because I'd been so worried about Vanessa when we arrived, I'd not paid attention to where I'd left the car, I tracked it down. Then I sat there for a minute to ring Marco and fill him in on everything.

'She's gone to surgery,' I told him. 'She asked if we could keep Alex overnight. She emailed the social worker.'

'Of course we can,' Marco said immediately, as I'd known he would. 'What about his things?'

'Oh I didn't think of that,' I said. 'I'll go back to Sainsbury's and pick him up some pyjamas.'

'Get some ice cream too,' he said. 'And some popcorn? We can do movie night – might be a nice distraction for him because I'm sure he'll be worried about his granny, poor sod.' He paused and I could almost hear the cogs in his head whirring. 'We'll put him in the spare room. Is there bedding in there?'

This time I had to think because the spare room in our bit

94

of Honeyford House had become a bit of a dumping ground. I tried to picture the bed. 'Yes, I think I remember putting a duvet cover on there.'

'I'll check,' Marco said. He sounded quite excited. 'Are you okay with this, Phil?'

'Yes,' I lied. 'Totally fine. Of course I am.'

'It's okay if you're not,' he said quietly. 'I know it's weird, having a kid staying.' I felt tears spring into my eyes at his concern. But I wanted Alex to stay. I did.

'I'm fine,' I said again, slightly shakily. 'I'll run to Sainsbury's then.'

'Okay,' said Marco. 'I love you.'

'I love you, too.'

I arrived home, armed with treats and a pair of pyjamas that I hoped would fit and not be too babyish. When Marco's nieces and nephews had been small and I'd gone shopping for presents for them, I would pretend I was buying for our own children, but this time – the first time I'd bought something for a child since we'd accepted that we'd never have our own – it felt like a knife in my heart.

I'd overcompensated for feeling so bad by buying too much ice cream and other sweets for Alex, which had made his eyes gleam when I got back and unpacked my bags.

And then I'd managed to avoid "movie night" by spending ages sorting out the spare room for him, and clearing a space so he could make it from the door to the bed without breaking his ankle, and hunting for a night-light that I knew we'd had in a box somewhere, that I could plug into the socket in the hall so Alex could find his way to the loo if he needed to.

Once that was all done, and I'd had an update from Vanessa's nurse telling me she was back on the ward and all was well, I poked my head round the door to the living room. Marco and Alex were watching a Spider-Man film, which I knew Marco had seen about three times before, but which Alex seemed to be explaining in great detail.

'She's called MJ,' he was saying. 'Peter loves her, but he's not told her yet.'

I hovered by the door. 'Your granny's had her op and she's doing well,' I said to Alex. He nodded without speaking but I could see the relief on his face.

'Are you coming to sit down?' Marco said. 'In or out, that's what my dad always says.'

I paused, knowing I should really go and join them but not quite committing, so when my phone buzzed in my pocket, I was glad to see Vanessa's name on the screen.

'How are you?' I asked.

'Woozy. But glad it's done.'

'Do you want to speak to Alex?'

'Yes please.'

I waved the phone in front of his nose. 'It's your granny.'

'You went down like a sack of spuds,' he told her cheerfully, much to my alarm. 'It was like you fell in slow motion. But you're okay now, right? Philippa said so.'

I felt a little warm glow of having been able to reassure him.

'He's fine,' Marco told me in a low voice, as Alex chatted. 'He's quite happy to stay here and I think he'll be even more comfortable now he's spoken to Vanessa.'

'Granny wants to speak to you,' Alex said, prodding me with the phone. I took it back and he nudged his way round me and plonked himself back on the sofa next to Marco. 'Press play,' he demanded.

'See?' said Marco.

I chuckled. 'He's absolutely fine,' I told Vanessa. 'Have they said when you might get out?'

'Not yet.'

'It's no problem for us to keep Alex here tomorrow,' I said. 'It's Sunday anyway. Marco will keep him busy.'

There was silence on the other end of the phone and for a second I thought we'd been cut off.

'I really appreciate this, Philippa,' Vanessa said eventually sounding a little tearful.

Even though she couldn't see me, I shook my head. 'Don't worry one bit,' I said, knowing I wasn't being entirely truthful. 'It's no big deal.'

I tried to stay breezy the next morning too. Alex emerged from his room, looking a little wary and my heart went out to him. I remembered what it was like to sleep in a strange bed. Though in my case, of course, I'd sometimes liked being away from home; it had been an escape even though I worried about my mum when I was away from her.

I thought back to those nights in emergency foster care when my mum was having a bad patch. It always involved being dropped off by a kindly but harassed social worker, sometimes late at night, and having to go to bed in a strange room, often shared with strange children. Usually I stayed a couple of nights – a week at the most – then went home. Once I was picked up again a few hours later. And when I was 14, I was in foster care for a couple of months after my mother had a particularly bad time of it and went into hospital for a long stay. It wasn't fun, but it was a relief not to have to look after Mum when she was struggling.

Now I smiled at Alex, whose hair was even more mop-like than usual, as he wandered into the kitchen. 'Want some breakfast?' I asked.

'Yes please.' He sat down at the table and reached for his phone, which had been charging overnight. 'Can I call Granny?'

'Maybe message her first to see if she's up for a chat?' I suggested, holding up the loaf of bread. 'Toast?'

'Yes please,' he said, focusing on his phone.

I dropped two slices into the toaster and watched him type his message, his thumbs moving quickly over the screen.

'I'm not sure what will happen later,' I said, remembering how I had liked to know what was happening. 'But as soon as I do, we'll tell you.'

Alex nodded. 'Okay.'

'Do you have any plans for this morning? Football match or anything?'

He shook his head. 'Nothing.' He looked up at me. 'Can I hang out with Marco?'

Half relieved, half disappointed that I didn't have to play mum, I nodded. 'He'll be glad of your help. Just don't go up any ladders, will you?'

I was rewarded with a smile that made me feel pleased. Like I'd won a prize.

'I'm going to start cleaning some of the garden,' I told the top of his head as he looked at his phone. I took a deep breath. 'So if you fancy helping with that, just come and find me.'

'Can I use a scythe?' he said.

'No.'

'Those big scissor things?'

'No.'

He looked at me and made a face. 'Probably just hang with Marco then.'

I chuckled, despite myself. 'Whatever you want,' I said.

Chapter 13

Gloria

Mother was enjoying being involved in the summer fair and I thought it was quite funny because I suddenly saw where I got my desire to fix things from. She had two folders full of notes and receipts and though initially not many people had wanted to sign up to run stalls – I couldn't blame them, what with everyone just trying to keep going through the hardship and fear the war had brought – things had changed since she came on board.

Somehow my mother had managed to visit just about everyone she knew for miles around and cajoled, persuaded or perhaps even just bribed them into running a stall. Suddenly we had people selling little wooden toys made from old beer barrels, honey from the hives in their gardens, "new" bedsheets made from strips of worn ones stitched together, and all manner of home-grown fruit and vegetables.

In short, it was looking as though the fair would be a triumph, thanks to Mother.

She'd made such a difference to the organisation that Mr Fingal from the parish council seemed to have developed something of a crush on her. I kept seeing him gazing at her in meetings with an air of wonder.

And he wasn't the only one.

It was early evening and I was drinking tea on the terrace, enjoying the sunshine and waiting impatiently for Mother to finish her telephone conversation and come and join me.

I was appreciating spending time with her. Seeing her as she must have been before grief for my father consumed her.

It was a strange thing to say, but I didn't really know Mother very well. She and my father had always been so in love – strangers in the street would comment on their adoration for one another – that I'd been firmly in second place. I knew without a shadow of a doubt that both of them would put the other ahead of me. I hadn't minded – I'd thought it was just the way things were, until I grew old enough to realise it wasn't really always like that.

My parents had never been cruel, of course. On the contrary. They provided for me – indulged me, even – and loved me. Just not as much as they loved each other. I'd always thought that if I ever had children of my own, then I would make sure they knew they were the most important thing in my life. Always.

When Daddy died, it was like part of Mother died too. But now she was coming back to life and I had to admit, I liked it.

She was very clever, I had discovered. I'd known that, too, of course. But I'd never really appreciated her sharp brain. It was hard to appreciate someone's intellect when it was dulled with misery.

I heard her on the telephone now, speaking French as she said goodbye – she must have been talking to her own mother.

'Keep speaking French like that and Grandpa will recruit you to be a spy,' I said as she came outside and sat down with me. 'He'll parachute you into enemy territory.'

Mother laughed. 'Well, he'll be disappointed to find out that my French is very rusty, and my conversations are mostly about clothes.'

I made a face. 'My French is rusty too,' I admitted. 'I barely speak it anymore now I've left school.'

Mother poured herself some tea from the pot. 'Why don't we speak only French one day a week? Just for fun?'

'*D'accord*,' I said. 'We can do French Fridays.'

'Actually, Mamie was calling to say Grandpa is on his way and he's bringing you a present from her, which might help with that.'

'Grandpa's coming again?' I was delighted. 'Does he have another meeting with the Americans? When will he be here?'

'Any minute, apparently.'

We both looked up as we heard the sound of a car engine but it was Jerome driving Captain Waldo round to the front of the house. I sat up a little straighter and so, I noticed, did Mother.

'I might go and see if Grandpa's coming,' I said, even though we could see perfectly well from where we sat.

'Good idea,' said Mother. 'I'll come too.'

We walked round the side of the house. I smoothed down my hair and out of the corner of my eye I could see my mother straightening her skirt.

Jerome was just opening the car door to let Waldo out as we walked towards them. He gave me a tiny smile and I felt a funny butterfly sensation in my stomach that I quite liked.

'Oh look, here's Grandpa,' said Mother, sounding slightly disappointed.

I glanced at her curiously, as Grandpa's car stopped behind Waldo's and he got out.

'A welcoming committee,' he said, spreading his arms wide. Mother and I both hugged him.

'Captain Waldo, I presume?' he said, turning his attention to the Americans. 'Nice to meet you at last.

'Mr Wilmington, sir,' said Waldo.

Grandpa gave him an approving nod. 'Spoke to your man Kidd last week. He told me good things about you.'

'Well, that's very flattering, sir,' said Waldo.

101

'Are you busy now?'

'Not for an hour or so.'

'Come and have a cup of tea with us,' Grandpa said, slapping Waldo on the back. 'You don't mind, Rose?'

'Not at all,' said Mother. 'You're very welcome, Captain Waldo.'

'Thank you, ma'am.'

'Oh heavens, call me Rose,' she said. She shook his hand and I couldn't help noticing she looked up at him from underneath her eyelashes, just as Patty had done with Perkins. 'Let's go round the side of the house rather than traipsing through.'

'You, boy,' said Grandpa, clicking his fingers at Jerome. 'Fetch my bag from the boot, will you.'

We all stopped walking. Jerome froze on the spot, looking at Waldo obviously wondering what to do. I felt a prickle of discomfort down the back of my neck. Jerome didn't work for Grandpa. Grandpa shouldn't have been telling him what to do. And I knew without a shadow of a doubt that had Jerome been a white private, he wouldn't have asked him.

Waldo took a step towards Grandpa, and smiled. But it was a frosty kind of smile. 'Let me get that for you, sir,' he said.

Then he opened the boot of the car and took out Grandpa's bag, hoisting it on to his shoulder.

Next to me, my mother gave a little gasp of admiration, audible only to me.

It was rare that I saw my grandfather on the back foot, but he seemed to realise he'd made a mistake. He looked flustered for a second, then recovered his composure.

'Thank you, Captain. I'll take that.'

Waldo handed it over without a word.

'Tea?' said my mother brightly.

'Tea,' Grandpa agreed.

'You're dismissed, Private Scott,' Waldo said to Jerome. They saluted each other and then Waldo, my mother and Grandpa all began to walk round the side of the house. I hung back, wanting to speak to Jerome. I felt I should apologise for my grandfather, somehow.

'Nice chap, your driver,' said Grandpa as they went. 'Where's he from?'

'New York City, I believe,' I heard Waldo say.

'But where are his people from? I was in the West Indies for a while, you know? Back in the 1920s . . .'

His voice faded away and I looked at Jerome. He looked back at me, but just as I was about to speak, my grandfather reappeared.

'Come along, Gloria,' he said. 'I've got a present for you from your grandmother. It's a translation of *The 39 Steps*.'

'*Les Trente-Neuf Marches*,' I said, still looking at Jerome.

'Exactly,' Grandpa said. 'Come on, your mother's pouring the tea.'

Jerome held my gaze for a second longer, then he turned and walked away across the gravel, and I – feeling a little bit like I'd disappointed him – turned back to my grandfather and smiled.

'That's a marvellous present,' I said cheerfully. 'Show me.'

Chapter 14

Philippa

'We should talk about an opening date for the restaurant,' said Marco.

'Now?' I looked round at him, where he was sitting at the kitchen table in our part of Honeyford House, with a folder spread out in front of him.

'I need to think about staff, and when to order food and whatnot.'

'Well, yes, I understand that, but we're a bit snowed under this week, Marco.' I flipped the pancake I was cooking perfectly. 'Ha! Did you see that?'

Marco watched me, his expression amused. 'I did.'

'I think some of your cooking skills have finally rubbed off on me.'

'It's taken a while.'

I slid the pancake on to a plate and poured in some more batter, pleased with myself.

'I thought you didn't want Alex to stay?' Marco said, speaking quietly.

'I never said that.' I shook my head, without looking at him. 'Did I?'

'Well, you as good as did.'

'I just thought it might be weird, having a kid in the house. After everything that's happened.'

'Right,' said Marco. 'And is it weird?'

I looked down at the pancake. 'It's slightly weird that I'm cooking pancakes at seven thirty on a Monday morning.'

Marco got up and wrapped his arms round me from behind. I leaned against him. 'It's a bit weird,' I conceded. 'But good weird.'

'I know.' He paused. 'So why are you still being off about it?'

'Am I being off?'

'You wouldn't watch the film with us on Saturday night.'

'I don't like superheroes.'

'You went to the garden centre on your own yesterday afternoon.'

'Alex wouldn't have wanted to come there.'

'You could have picked up his school stuff on the way back, instead of me having to go later.'

'I didn't think of that,' I lied.

Marco shrugged. 'You wouldn't eat dinner with us last night.'

'I wasn't hungry.'

'But now you're making him pancakes?'

'He needs a good breakfast before school.'

'Phil, what's going on?'

I stayed still, looking down at the pan. 'Nothing's going on.'

Marco leaned over and took the spatula from my hand, flipping the pancake just at the right moment before it caught.

'That's annoying,' I said.

He moved away and leaned against the counter, facing me. 'It was burning.'

'No it wasn't.'

'Phil,' he said. 'Don't overthink this. Alex is staying for a little while. And then he'll go home. It's no biggie.'

'I'm not overthinking anything,' I said, clenching my jaw. 'I'm just making pancakes.'

'Burning pancakes.'

'Marco,' I snapped.

My phone rang, just at the right moment to stop Marco ending up with pancake batter over his head.

'Take over.' I thrust the spatula at him and picked up my phone. 'Hi, Vanessa, how are you feeling?'

I could tell Marco wanted to know how Vanessa was too, so I deliberately walked out of the room and into the hall, where Alex was coming down the stairs in his school uniform.

'Granny,' I mouthed at him. He blew a kiss towards my phone, his nose twitching as he smelled breakfast.

'Pancakes?'

I nodded and he vanished into the kitchen.

'Is that Alex?' Vanessa asked. 'Is he okay?'

'Right as rain,' I reassured her. 'Ready for school.'

'Wonders will never cease.'

'How are you doing?'

'Not bad, considering,' she said. 'Waiting for the doctors to do their rounds.'

'Any news on when you can come home?'

'I'm hoping tomorrow.'

I sat down on the bottom step, feeling relieved. 'That's great news. But will you manage at home?'

'They're going to give me a boot so I can walk a bit, and I'm lucky to live in a bungalow.'

'You won't be able to drive, though.'

'No,' Vanessa said. 'That's a point. I'll have to rally support to ferry Alex to and from football.'

'We can help, too. He's been no trouble.'

'That's kind, thank you.'

We chatted a bit longer, and she spoke to Alex, then he said goodbye, grabbed his bag and ran out of the front door to meet his friend on the bus to school. And I went back into the kitchen and glowered at Marco.

'The pancakes weren't burnt.'

'Let it go, Phil.'

I snorted. 'Am I overthinking that, too?'

He groaned. 'I'll regret saying that, won't I?'

I made a face at him. 'Vanessa might be home tomorrow.'

'Does she need a lift from the hospital?'

'Maybe,' I said. 'She didn't say.'

'I can go and get her.'

I snorted again.

'What?' said Marco.

'You're always going out of your way to help Vanessa,' I said, knowing I was being unfair.

'Well maybe,' Marco said, 'it's because Vanessa is nice to me.'

We glared at one another across the table for a moment and then he pushed one of the folders he'd been looking at towards me and gave me a tiny smile.

'We need to decide when to open.'

I sighed. Marco was like that – all irritated and grumpy one minute, then back to normal the next. I supposed it was better than stewing for days. My friend Clare's husband could be that way – sulky like a schoolboy until she eventually guessed what he was cross about. When I first got together with Marco, it took me a while to get used to his little bubbles of annoyance, but then I grew to like them. He was so open and honest, and very rarely did his irritation spill over into anger. I always knew how he felt and that felt good.

Now, slightly reluctantly, I took the folder and opened it at the calendar. Marco was old-school and liked to write things down instead of adding them to his phone like a normal person. The days for the next few weeks were all full of scribbles.

I squinted at them for a second, then decided I needed sustenance.

'More tea while we discuss it?'

'Yes please,' Marco said.

I got up and went to put the kettle on, and as I walked past him, Marco grabbed my hand and pulled me on to his lap.

'This is a strange situation we're in,' he said. 'I thought we were doing okay navigating the baby stuff.'

'We are,' I said, resting my chin on his curly head. 'We are.'

'And the massive life-change stuff.'

'We're doing okay with that too. I don't miss London at all. And look how hard you've worked on the restaurant.' I paused, thinking of the right words, because the truth was I didn't really understand how I was feeling. 'Alex was just an unexpected obstacle,' I said. 'And he made me wobble, just for a minute. But I like having him here, and it was the right thing to do. And tomorrow he'll go home again.'

'Sure?'

'Sure.'

I kissed him. 'Are you all right?' I said. 'It's weird for you too.'

'I will be when I get a cup of tea,' he said.

Chapter 15

Gloria

I was grumpy. I was bored of the relentless meetings about the fair, I was still annoyed with Grandpa for clicking his fingers at Jerome, and I was missing my grandmother. Patty was always busy, Mother kept sending me on errands for the parish council, and the weather was hot. I was permanently sniffing thanks to the flowers making my nose run, and all in all, I was not having a good day.

There was just a fortnight to go until the big summer fair weekend and Mr Fingal was getting his knickers in a twist about refreshments, so he'd summoned us all to the village hall for an emergency meeting with George from the pub.

Mother and I were supposed to be going to the meeting together but I couldn't find her.

'Where's Mother?' I asked Fran, who was sniffing a bottle of milk in the kitchen.

'I've not seen her,' she said. 'Is this off do you think?'

'I'm not smelling it.' I grimaced. 'Has she gone without me?'

'She wouldn't go without you,' Fran said. She went to the sink and poured the milk away. 'She might be outside. You know she likes the sunshine.'

'I'll go and have a look.'

I wandered outside, squinting in the bring light, and heard Mother's laugh coming from the front of the house. I walked round the corner and there she was, leaning against a car and laughing. She looked beautiful and very young as she stood there, with her hair pulled off her face and her skirt blowing in the breeze, the sunlight making her face glow. She was talking to Waldo, who was clearly telling her some hilarious story. He was walking like a chicken and Mother was laughing so hard, she almost doubled over and then Waldo was laughing too and for a second I didn't want to interrupt them because they looked like they were having such a nice time together. Then the church bell rang out from the village and Waldo looked at his watch.

'I have to go,' he said, sounding genuinely regretful. He gazed at Mother and she looked up at him. 'Maybe I'll see you later?'

'I'd like that,' Mother said.

She watched him go back inside the house, and I watched her watch him, feeling an odd mix of emotions. My father wasn't coming back, of course, but it was strange seeing Mother looking at another man.

Then she turned to me and gave me a wide smile.

'Darling, there you are,' she cried. 'I was just coming to find you.'

And she looked so happy and content that all my doubts fell away.

'I found you first,' I said.

Mother looped her arm through mine and we began to walk down to the village.

'Waldo's nice, isn't he?' I said.

She looked at me. 'He's very nice.'

'Handsome, too.'

'Gloria . . .' she said.

I looked at her, my eyes wide with innocence. 'What?'

'He's very nice and very handsome.'

'I don't think he liked Grandpa very much,' I said.

Mother tutted. 'Grandpa can sometimes be very set in his ways.' She patted my hand. 'Now, tell me how are you getting on with the book Mamie sent you?'

I told her a bit about the translation and what I thought of it, and we began chatting about my grandmother as we strolled on through the sunshine, arriving at the village in no time at all.

'She never calls me Gloria, always Glory,' I said, as I'd said a hundred times.

Mother laughed. 'She claims she can't say Gloria, but your father and I agreed it was because we'd named you after his mother and she was put out.'

'My middle name is Delphine after her.'

'Ah but that wasn't good enough for my mother.'

'My sympathies,' I joked. 'I know how difficult it is to have a mother who is hard to please.'

Laughing together, we walked into the hall where everyone was standing in a huddle, talking. No one looked very happy.

'What's happened?' Mother said. 'Is something wrong?'

'We're just talking about these blooming policemen,' said Millicent Hayes, who played the organ in church every Sunday and who was never afraid to share her opinion.

'What policemen?' asked Mother.

'The ones outside the pub every evening.'

'Have you been naughty, George?' Mother teased. But he didn't laugh.

'No, I bloody well have not,' he said. 'But they're not happy about my new pianist.'

'Who are they?' Mother frowned.

'The military police,' Millicent said.

Mother looked blank. 'Why would the police care about your pianist, George?'

'Is it Eugene?' I said.

George nodded. 'He's a lovely lad. And him playing has brought in more GIs from the other base. And those policemen don't like it.'

'I heard they're here to stop GIs committing crimes,' I said.

'Well, no one is committing a crime in my pub, so I don't need them there.'

'It's this colour bar, isn't it?' Mr Fingal said. He gestured to the chairs that had been put out in the hall and we all sat down, though far less formally than we had done in the past. No regimented rows of seats today – everyone moved round so we were in a group. 'They don't like the white soldiers and airmen mixing with the Black GIs.'

Jennifer Lacey, whose daughter Bess had been really horrible to me when we were small, cleared her throat. 'Well, I think they rather have a point, don't you?'

'How so?' said George.

'It's bad enough having the Americans over here, without having to welcome all sorts,' she said.

Silence fell in the hall. I wanted to argue but Mrs Lacey didn't take kindly to insubordination.

'Who's that lad I've seen you with, Gloria?' Mr Fingal said. I sat very still, wondering what I should say. Mr Fingal smiled at me, and I realised he was telling me he didn't agree with Mrs Lacey. 'He seems a nice chap?'

'Jerome,' I said. 'His name is Jerome Scott.'

'And is he nice?'

I felt a little bit squirmy, so I just nodded.

'They're good lads,' George said firmly. 'Jerome, Eugene, Stanley, the lot of them. And I can't be turning away customers.'

Mrs Lacey tutted loudly and my mother glared at her.

'Well,' said Millicent Hayes, folding her arms. 'Good lads or not, I'm not sure I'm comfortable with these . . .' She paused for a moment, eyes to the ceiling as if she was looking for the right word in the beams. 'These Americans, telling us what to do.'

'Quite,' said Mr Fingal.

'They don't like foreigners,' said my mother to me quietly, in French, which made me stifle a snort of laughter.

'I say live and let live,' said Mrs Lacey. 'Let these policemen do what they need to do. We won't bother them, and they won't bother us.'

'Right,' said George sounding uncertain.

'Anyway,' said Mr Fingal. 'Shall we get on? George has to open up in fifteen minutes.'

I fixed an interested look on my face, then I sat back in my chair and looked out of the window, while everyone discussed whether George should put tables and chairs on the green, or just serve at the pub.

I wondered what Patty was up to. She'd been so busy that I'd not seen her for ages, and I was hoping we could catch up later. Maybe we could even get the bus to Cirencester and go to see a film. That would be nice.

'Gloria?' Mr Fingal said. Everyone was looking at me expectantly and I had no idea why.

'Could you do that for us?'

'Erm . . .' I chewed my lip not wanting to admit that I'd not been listening. Fortunately, Mother came to my rescue.

'You'll go and fetch the programmes from Cirencester, won't you?' she said. 'You said you were thinking of going to the pictures, so you could walk past and see what's on.'

'I don't know what Patty's doing,' I said vaguely, but it was too late.

'Great stuff,' said Mr Fingal. 'I'll call the printer and let him know you'll be there . . .' he checked his watch '. . . in an hour. If you go now, you'll easily catch the quarter past bus.'

'Fine,' I said grudgingly. 'I'll go.'

I got the information I needed from Mr Fingal and hurried to the bus stop. It was an easy journey to Cirencester and actually I'd not been there for a while, so it was quite nice to be in town and have a look at all the shops.

I collected the programmes without any trouble, then I walked round the corner and checked the pictures. There was a Vera Lynn film on which I thought would do us. Patty and I liked musicals.

It was a gorgeous day even though it was only May. I hoped it meant the weather would be good for the summer fair. I took off my cardigan at the bus stop and shoved it into the bag with the programmes, crossing my fingers that the bus wouldn't be too stuffy when it arrived.

Alas, when it trundled up, I saw it was busy with red-faced sweaty shoppers, a group of schoolgirls, and two Black GIs – soldiers – sitting at the back, chatting quietly.

I found a seat and got comfortable for the short journey back to Honeyford.

A few stops out of Cirencester, the bus emptied a little, which was a relief. And then at the next stop – near one of the air bases – four white GIs got on. Three of them were strangers to me, but I recognised one as Corporal Taylor – the friend Perkins had been with on the day I'd met him.

The men were laughing uproariously at something, and the group of schoolgirls all nudged one another, smoothing down their hair and glancing at them sideways.

But as Taylor and the others walked down the aisle of the bus, one of them noticed the two soldiers who were sitting down already. He sighed in an overdramatic fashion, as though their very presence was an irritation he didn't want to deal with.

'You're going to have to get off,' he said to them. He gestured outside with his closely cropped blond head. 'Go on.'

The two soldiers looked at one another, but they didn't speak and they didn't move.

'Are you stupid?' said the blond man. 'We can't be on the bus with you. You need to move.'

The bus had fallen silent as soon as he spoke because his voice was louder than it needed to be and more aggressive.

Still without speaking, the two soldiers got up and went to move down the aisle towards the door of the bus, but the school-girls barred their way. I felt the hairs on the back of my neck stand up.

At the front of the bus, the driver was watching in his mirror, not yet pulling away into the road.

'No,' said one of the girls. She was tall with her hair in a long plait down her back, but she couldn't have been more than 14. 'You sit down.'

The soldiers glanced from the girls to the other men – they were caught in the middle and I could see they weren't sure who was more frightening.

'Miss, we should leave . . .' one of them said to the girl with the plait. 'Let us by.'

'NO,' she said again, more loudly. 'You were here first. If these . . .' She looked at the other GIs disdainfully and when she spoke again her voice was dripping with sarcasm. 'If these *gentlemen* don't want to be on the bus with you, then they should leave.'

The blond man's face reddened and he glared at the girls.

'This is nothing to do with you.' He jabbed his finger towards them. 'Let them go.'

'No.' This time all the girls spoke together. Then the one with the plait gave the two soldiers a tiny shove back towards their now empty seat. 'Sit. Down,' she growled. The two men sat, which made me smile but only for a second, because now there was nothing between the aggressive blond GI and the girls. He took a step towards them.

'Maybe I should throw you off, eh?' he said. 'There ain't nothing to stop me doing that.'

He loomed over them and the girls shrank back.

'I'll stop you,' I said. The words were out of my mouth before I'd even had time to think. I stood up so I was in front of the girls. 'You need to leave.'

The man was very red now, and the sinews in his neck were bulging.

'And you're going to make me, are you?'

Taylor put his hand on the GI's shoulder.

'She might not make you, Corporal Gordon, but I will.'

Corporal Gordon whipped round and he and Taylor eyed each other, their noses almost touching. I was relieved that I wasn't in his sights anymore.

The men stared at one another until the bus driver spoke up.

'I'm not going anywhere until you get off, sir. So unless you want to annoy all my other passengers, and the passengers on the bus behind, I suggest you leave.' He held his hand out. 'Here's your fare.'

Corporal Gordon looked to the other GIs behind Taylor for support but they both shook their heads.

'You have to go,' one of them said. 'Get off the bus.'

'Get. Off,' said Taylor.

For a second, I thought Gordon would argue but he didn't. He glowered at me and the schoolgirls, then shoved past us. He didn't take the refund from the bus driver and Taylor and the other GIs didn't follow.

I sat back down, feeling adrenaline pumping through my veins, and the schoolgirls did the same.

'Right,' said the driver, closing the doors. 'On we go.'

Chapter 16

Philippa

We'd chosen a date six weeks away to open the restaurant. A "soft opening" Marco called it. He was more nervous than I'd ever seen him before.

'You know what you're doing,' I said. 'You ran the pub for a decade.'

'I know.' He rubbed his head. 'But I had Jonny running it with me. And we'd both worked there for years before we took it over. It wasn't starting from scratch.'

'I think you'll be great,' said Alex from the back of the car. We were taking him home because Vanessa was out of hospital. All our nerves were a bit jangly.

'Thanks, Al,' said Marco.

'Everyone loved the burgers you made at my party,' Alex said. 'And Arjan's still going on about the chips. He says they're the best chips he's ever tasted.'

I looked at Marco, who kept his eyes on the road but smiled. 'Arjan's tougher than any restaurant critic,' I said. I put my hand on his knee. 'And Jonny may have gone back to Australia but you've got me running the business with you now. You're not on your own.'

'You've got me too,' said Alex. 'Team Alco.'

'What on earth is Team Alco?' I said, turning round to look at Alex.

'Alex and Marco,' he said, like it was the most obvious thing in the world. 'Alco.'

'Perhaps not the most appropriate nickname,' I said, annoyed that I hadn't been included and worried that Marco was getting in too deep with Alex. 'How about Marcex?'

'I like Alco,' said Alex firmly.

Marco pulled up outside Vanessa's house. 'Come on then, pal,' he said. 'Home time.'

Vanessa was in a bit of a tizzy. Frustrated by not being able to do all the things she normally did.

'Harvey said he can take Alex to football,' she said. 'And he's fine getting to school and back on the bus, but I'm so tired, I worry I'm not going to be able to cope.'

'How about we have Alex a couple of evenings after school?' Marco said. I shot him a warning glance. He'd surely done enough to help already? Vanessa's freezer was full of meals he'd made for her and Alex. But either he didn't see the look I gave him, or he ignored me. 'He could come and have his tea with us, and maybe help me out with getting the terrace ready now the evenings are lighter.'

Vanessa looked delighted. 'That's a wonderful idea. He'd really like that.'

I sat down on the armchair opposite her and tried to smile.

'He's such a lovely lad,' I said honestly. He really was a nice boy, but my feelings were all tangled. I was worried that Marco was getting too close to him and that we were somehow using this troubled teenager as a replacement for our unborn babies. And that made me feel strange and guilty and sad all at once.

So later when we'd left Alex at home and the house seemed quiet and huge without him there, I decided I should probably say something to Marco. He was, I always thought, the only person in the world who understood exactly how I felt about all our pregnancy losses and the fertility struggle, because he'd gone through it too. My losses were his losses. And even though I'd seen other marriages fall apart under stress, ours had got stronger. Somehow.

Marco was on the terrace, of course. The pergola was almost finished, and I had to admit he'd done a good job. We would have a lovely space for outdoor dining – once I'd cleared the garden, which I really had to get on with now we had an opening date sorted. Marco had worked out the menu and he was ready to hire some extra staff. No doubt he'd be employing Alex as his sous chef and maître d' all rolled into one.

I stood for a little while at the window in the restaurant, watching Marco work. Sometimes – no, often – I reminded myself that I was very lucky to have him.

I'd met him at a friend's thirtieth birthday celebration. We'd gone for a long Sunday lunch at Marco's pub and because he knew the birthday girl too, he'd joined us when service was over. And because there was a spare seat beside me, he sat there. And actually, he'd been by my side ever since.

We'd got married in Italy, in the little town where Marco's family was from, which was full of Scottish Italians. I'd wanted to marry abroad because I had no family other than my mum, who couldn't have coped with a wedding. I didn't want to put her in the position of having to say no, so marrying abroad meant she was off the hook because she was too poorly by then to travel. I'd had a Facebook message from Rick and Ellie when we got engaged saying "congratulations!" but nothing more.

So we got married in Barga, and Marco wore a kilt and we ate pasta and drank excellent wine, and I was so glad I was becoming part of his family, that it didn't seem to matter anymore that I had none of my own.

When we'd gone to bed that night, more than a little bit drunk and with cheeks that ached from smiling, Marco had kissed me and said he suspected I fell in love with his family and that was why I'd married him. And I'd laughed and said that wasn't true. But it was a little bit. I adored his parents, and his grandparents and his brother and his sisters, and their husbands and their kids. I loved the noise and the chaos and the fun and even the arguments. And I really loved the stories about their childhoods spent half in Scotland and half in Italy. I loved it all and I couldn't wait to have our own children to add to the brood.

I had imagined little dark-eyed versions of Marco, learning to speak Italian like their dad, and – well – being good at maths like their mum. But it didn't happen that way. And now we were the wrong side of 40, and I thought – I had really, honestly, genuinely thought – that I was fine. That I'd dealt with not having a child of my own.

We had a new life now, here in Honeyford. With new goals and a new focus.

But Marco being so invested in Alex was making me feel like this was all a big mistake – a façade pasted over our sadness. I knew I had to tell him what I was thinking.

I watched him for a little while longer, and then when he'd climbed down the ladder and was standing back to admire his handiwork, I went outside.

'It looks lovely,' I said. 'You've done such a good job.'

'I really want this to work.' He put his arm round me and I leaned into him.

'You probably don't need Alex to help you now,' I said, casual as anything.

Marco looked at me. 'Well, I don't really need him at all, but I like having him around.' He rubbed my shoulder with his thumb. 'He's a good lad.'

'I know.' I paused. 'Just . . .'

'Just what?' Marco took his arm away from my shoulder. 'What's the problem, Philippa?'

I took a deep breath. 'Don't get too close to him, that's all.'

Marco didn't get angry very often, but when he did the warning signs were obvious because his face went pale and he clenched his jaw. He was doing that now.

'What do you mean?'

I put what I hoped was a reassuring hand on his arm. 'I mean, he's not our son, Marco.'

He looked at me for a minute and I thought he was going to explode. I'd only seen him really angry a couple of times in all the years we'd been together. Once at a traffic warden who'd ticketed our car because we'd stayed in the hospital car park five minutes too long after another scan where I'd been told my unborn baby had died. And once at his brother Enzo, about something tiny that had escalated until all their childhood resentments came out and were shouted about, and then forgotten almost as quickly.

But now I expected him to lose his temper. I could see a pulse in his temple, flickering.

'Marco,' I began.

He opened his mouth and I braced myself. But instead of the tirade I was expecting, Marco started to cry.

Immediately I flung myself at him and took his hand to guide him to one of the chairs on the terrace. It still had plastic wrapping on because we'd not opened them all yet but I didn't care. We both sat down and I held him close, almost crying myself because I hated to know that he was still so sad, even though I felt the same.

'I don't think he's our child,' he said, when he'd gathered himself. He wiped his eyes, unashamedly. Marco was never one to bottle up his emotions and I was glad about that because we'd had such a lot of emotions over the years that we would have burst if we'd even tried. 'I don't think that at all, Phil. I just like being around him.' He took a deep breath. 'I like kids, and he's a nice one.'

I smiled a tiny smile. 'He is a nice one,' I agreed. 'I was worried you were . . . I don't know. Projecting.'

'Projecting?'

'I'm not completely sure what that means,' I admitted. 'But I was worried you were putting all your love for our unborn babies into this one lad. Like a replacement.'

Marco took my hand. 'No,' he said. 'I have more than enough love to go round.' I was relieved, but he frowned. 'I know you're finding it difficult, though.'

I squirmed a bit, because he knew me so well. 'I do like having Alex around.' I smiled. 'It's very quiet without him. But he just landed on us . . .'

'It's what happened to you, when you were a wee girl,' Marco pointed out. 'Rick and Ellie did the same for you. And those foster families you spent time with.'

'I know.' I screwed my face up. 'And it was always temporary, wasn't it? Rick and Ellie moved away, and the foster families were only ever for a short while. It wasn't forever.' I took a breath. 'Like our babies.'

Understanding dawned on Marco's face. 'Oh, sweetheart,' he said. 'You don't want to enjoy having him here because you know he's not going to stay?'

I blinked away tears. 'When I was a kid, I'd go to the park sometimes on my way home from school and watch the families. I used to love it when the mums got cross with the kids for doing something a bit dangerous, you know? Like swinging too high, or hanging off the climbing frame upside down. Because I knew that meant their mums loved them and cared about them.'

'Your mum loved you,' Marco said.

'She tried to love me.' I took a breath. 'But I wanted to have a family, and every time I did, like with Rick and Ellie, and the foster homes, and the pregnancies, it got taken away.' I looked at him. 'I don't want to get too close to Alex because it feels the same.'

I didn't mention how watching him, Vanessa and Alex looking at the stars had reminded me of watching families in the park.

We sat there for a while on our plastic-covered chairs, looking out over the tangled garden, and then Marco sat up.

'How about we plant something?' he said.

'Well, I thought we could do some big pots up here. You can actually buy them from the garden centre already filled with plants . . .'

'No.' Marco shook his head. 'I meant like a tree or a bush or something. Something that will last forever. In memory of our babies.'

I had no words. All in all, I'd lost five babies. Some very early on, some later in my pregnancies. We'd talked about a memorial of a sort but so far all we had done was give a donation to the charity that had helped us. I pinched my lips together.

'Or not,' Marco said hurriedly. 'If you don't want to . . .'

'No, I do.' I nodded. 'I do. I think it's a lovely idea.'

I looked down the sweeping garden to where the small wood was. Under the trees a scattering of bluebells had appeared though I'd been disappointed there weren't more.

'Can you plant bluebells?' I asked. 'Or do they just appear?'

Marco made a face. 'No idea.' He pulled his phone out and typed a few words, then scrolled through the results.

'You can plant bluebells,' he said. 'You plant the bulbs in late spring.'

'That's now.' I was delighted. 'Let's plant hundreds of bulbs under the trees and make our own bluebell wood.'

'They won't grow until next year,' Marco warned.

'That's fine. We'll know they're there.'

'Oh, look at this!' Marco was still reading. 'It says bluebells are a symbol of everlasting love.'

'Perfect.'

Marco got up and held out his hand to me. 'Come on, then.'

'Where are we going?'

'To the garden centre.'

* * *

123

The garden centre didn't have any bluebell bulbs. But there was a helpful chap working there, who told us we could order them online from a historic nature website. He gave us all the information we needed about planting them and sold us a lovely basket he called a trug – which Marco found hilarious for reasons I didn't quite understand – and a planter thingummy so I didn't have to bend down the whole time.

'Right,' I said when we pulled up at home. 'Let's have a really good crack at the garden, shall we? I'll do the bottom by the woods if you want to drive your lawnmower round and cut the grass.'

'Sounds like a deal,' Marco said.

I turned the key in the ignition to turn off the engine and he put his hand on my knee.

'Are you all right?'

Cautiously, I examined my feelings. 'I think so,' I said. 'Are you?'

'I think so, too.' He squeezed my thigh. 'The bluebell wood is a lovely idea. We could give it a name.'

'The wood?' I made a face. 'Like what?'

'Memory wood?' he said. Then he shook his head. 'God, no, that's awful.'

I laughed. 'It doesn't need a name.'

'I suppose not. I just want it to be perfect.'

'It will be.' I took my seatbelt off. 'It's really quiet down there and there's a spot where I wondered if we could put a hammock between two of the trees. And right at the end . . .' I tilted my head to the side and tried to see. 'Look.' I poked my finger at the windscreen in the direction of the trees. 'See that very last oak tree? It's got a lovely hollow in its roots, like a gorgeous armchair.'

'It's the perfect place,' said Marco.

'It will be, if we actually get a move on and do some work.'

'All right, Monty Don,' he said with a grin. 'Let me go and get changed and we'll crack on.'

* * *

It was backbreaking work. For me at least. I was regretting letting Marco bomb about on the ride-on lawnmower we'd hired. Though he did have to keep stopping to sweep up the cuttings and then take them over to the ever-increasing compost heap.

We'd decided to leave the veg patches for now. We couldn't do those and the garden and the terrace before we opened, what with Marco being busier and busier in the restaurant, and I knew I had lots of advertising to do and forms to fill in for the licence, and Food Standards Agency and all sorts. When I thought about how much we had to do before we opened it made me feel queasy.

I stood up and wiped my forehead on my sleeve. I wasn't doing badly, actually. I'd started near the first tree in the glade, and hacked away at the brambles and prickles that had grown up, separating the wood from the lawn.

It was scratchy, horrible work, but I was making good progress and it was very satisfying. I was fortunate in that I enjoyed my work, even though most normal people turned their noses up and said accountancy was boring. But I got a lot of pleasure from doing accounts and making everything neat and balanced – you didn't have to be a therapist to understand that my chaotic childhood made me appreciate the beauty of order and organisation – and I was getting the same pleasure now. Satisfaction in a job well done. My arms ached and my legs hurt, and I was covered in scratches and my hair was a tangle but I felt better than I'd felt for months. Years, even.

I piled another armful of brambles into the wheelbarrow and with some effort because it was slightly uphill, pushed it over to the compost heap.

'You look very sweaty,' Marco said, emptying yet another bag of grass cuttings on top of the detritus I'd just dumped.

'You definitely got the easy job, sitting on the bloody mower,' I said, giving him a kiss. 'I'm knackered.'

'I'm just about done.' He turned and surveyed the lawn. It

wasn't the neat stripes I'd been picturing, but it was short and way more groomed than it had been and Marco looked extremely proud of it, so I patted him on the back.

'Well done,' I said. 'It's going to be so lovely in the summer. We should get some solar lights too, otherwise as soon as it gets dark all our hard work won't be seen from the terrace.'

'Good idea.' Marco nodded. 'Want a hand with the brambles?'

'I'm almost done, too,' I said. 'But yes, please.'

We strolled across the garden down to the trees, me pushing the wheelbarrow. 'I'll cut and hack, and you gather,' I said. 'But you'll need gloves because it's so prickly.'

We started cutting back the final patch of overgrown plants and very quickly the wheelbarrow was full up again.

Marco took it off to dump it and I headed for the last little bit. It was close to the tree with the hollow in its roots and it was really just overgrown grass, thank goodness. And a few tiny oak trees that had clearly decided to sprout from fallen acorns.

I took the secateurs and started cutting the grass away and then, in amongst the long weeds and sprouting plants, I saw something made from stone.

Curious, I knelt down and pulled it out of the grass cuttings, brushing it off as I lifted it.

It was a little garden ornament, about knee high. A cherub, I supposed you would call it. It had curly hair carved from the stone and its head rested on its knee. On its back were two feathered wings and its eyes were closed.

'What on earth is that?' Marco said, coming up behind me and making me jump.

'I found it in the grass.' I stood up so I could show him properly.

He shuddered. 'It's bloody horrible.'

'Aww I think it's quite sweet,' I said, wiping the cherub's head clear of dried mud. 'Look at its little face.'

'Is it supposed to be a dead angel?'

'No, it's not a dead angel.' I gave him a shove. 'It's a cherub and it's asleep.' I held the statue out at arm's length and examined it. 'I think.'

'It's creepy,' Marco said. 'Where was it?'

'Down there.' I pointed with my foot.

He crouched down and pulled away some more grass and fallen leaves and muck. 'Here?' he said.

'I guess so.' There was a little broken base, which was obviously where the cherub had once sat. 'Give it over and I'll see if it's fixable.'

Marco pulled the base out of the ground, shook it to get rid of the worst of the mud, and handed it over to me.

'Look, it'll sit right on it, I think.' I tried to hold the statue in one hand and the base in the other but it was too cumbersome. So instead I sat down on the ground, next to Marco, put the base down and balanced the cherub on top.

'Bit of superglue and it'll be right as rain,' I said.

'Terrific.'

'I think I'll put him right in the middle of the terrace,' I teased. 'We'll make a feature of it. Ooh, we could call the restaurant *Cherubs*. What do you think?'

Marco nodded, mock seriously. 'Absolutely. Perhaps we could go for a kind of faux Grecian theme throughout, actually.'

'Yes!' I laughed, leaning back on my hands. 'Pillars? Mosaics?'

'I think mosaics are Roman,' Marco said, tutting. 'You should know that, being married to an actual Italian. What? What's the matter.'

When I'd leaned back, I'd put my hand on more stone. I turned round so I was kneeling up and felt under the grass, pulling it away so I could see what was beneath.

'What is it?' Marco said, peering over.

I'd cleared away the grass to reveal smooth round stones – from the river I thought. They were arranged in a small rectangular shape with the hole where the statue had stood at one of the narrow ends.

'Is it buried treasure?' Marco asked.

I felt sick suddenly.

'No,' I said. 'I think it's a grave.'

Chapter 17

Gloria

'These aren't your usual type of stories, Gloria,' Mrs Poole the librarian commented as she stamped the books I'd chosen.

'I thought I'd try something new,' I said.

'Edgar Allan Poe?' She lifted the book up and looked at it. 'This is a marvellous read. Quite spooky, mind you. Oh, and *The Turn of the Screw*? Henry James is one of my favourites.' She gave a little delighted shiver. 'It's ever so creepy.'

'I'm looking forward to trying them,' I said.

'American horror,' said Mrs Poole with satisfaction. 'You should try Washington Irving, if you like these. *The Legend of Sleepy Hollow* is wonderful. It's about a headless horseman.'

'Sounds great,' I said honestly, though I wasn't sure if I would like these books. I was generally more interested in living, breathing villains than spooks and spectres. But, I told myself I wanted to branch out, expand my interests. And yes, perhaps I hoped to have something to talk about with Jerome the next time I saw him, but where was the harm in that? I was simply being welcoming. Learning more about our American visitors.

Mrs Poole stamped my final book and handed them over.

I said goodbye and headed outside. It was another warm day – summer was coming early this year by the look of it – and I paused for a moment on the library path, turning my face to the sun like a flower.

'Hey,' said a voice and I opened my eyes to see Jerome. My heart jumped, just a little bit and I smiled at him.

'Hey,' I said, though it sounded odd in my English accent.

'Borrowing or returning?' he asked.

'Borrowing.' I was suddenly embarrassed that all the books I was clutching were ones I'd chosen with him in mind.

'Show me.' Before I could argue – and actually, how could I argue anyway without seeming like a fool – Jerome took my books and looked through them, smiling slightly.

'These are all American authors,' he said.

I looked down at my feet. 'Yes.'

'Edgar Allan Poe?'

'Yes.' I dragged my embarrassed gaze upwards and saw he was smiling, but not in a way that made me think he was laughing at me. Instead, he gave me back the books and opened the bag he was carrying.

'I'm returning some,' he said. 'Look.'

He pulled out *The Mysterious Affair at Styles* by Agatha Christie and *The Nine Tailors* by Dorothy L Sayers. I laughed out loud.

'English crime,' I said. 'What did you think of them?'

'Loved 'em,' he said, grinning.

We stood there on the path, smiling at each other for a second and I thought how handsome he was. He had a dimple in his cheek that gave his smile a mischievous look, and he was so smart in his uniform.

'How would you like . . .' Jerome began, just as I said: 'I was wondering . . .'

We both laughed again, a little awkwardly this time.

'You first,' I said.

'I have to return these books,' he said. 'But then I have like a half-hour before I need to be back at the base. I wondered if you would like to take a walk?'

I was chuffed. 'I was going to ask you the same thing,' I said. 'I'd love to know what you thought of Hercule Poirot.'

'So let's go,' he said. 'How about we head down to the river?'

'Perfect.'

He dashed inside with his books, and was back in a jiffy. Then we strolled along in the sunshine.

'Did you enjoy the books?' I asked.

'I'm thinking of growing a moustache like Hercule Poirot,' Jerome said. 'And perhaps affecting a Belgian accent.' He frowned. 'But I don't know what a Belgian accent sounds like.'

'A bit like French,' I said. 'Like this.' I stopped walking and he turned to look at me as I stroked my imaginary moustache. '*Bonjour, tout le monde*. My name is Hercule Poirot,' I growled in my best attempt at a Belgian accent.

Jerome laughed in delight and I was pleased to have amused him.

'You speak French?' he said.

'This way.' I tugged his sleeve to divert him from the pavement, down the little path that led to the river. 'I do. My grandmother is French. My mother and I are both very rusty though, so we've been speaking French to one another all day on a Friday.'

'Has it helped?'

I gave a Gallic shrug. '*Peut-être.*'

Jerome laughed again. 'I have no idea what that means but I like it.' He looked round at me. 'You're funny.'

'Thank you,' I said. 'I think.'

'And smart, speaking two languages that way.'

As we walked we'd grown closer, and our arms were brushing each other. I didn't move away.

'I didn't learn French from a book, though,' I said. 'It's just from Mamie speaking to me.' I grinned. 'She pretends she can't understand me when I speak English, but she can. She barely has an accent when she speaks English.'

131

'She sounds like a character.'

'She is.' I nodded.

Jerome frowned. 'Is she all right? Your grandmother?'

'I think so?'

'She's not in France?'

'No, she's in London with my grandfather. My mother keeps asking her to come and stay here in case there are more bombs, but she won't.' I looked over my shoulder, checking we weren't being overheard. 'She hates the countryside.'

We were away from the shops and road now, following the little stony path to the river. Jerome nodded. 'I get that,' he said. 'I thought I'd hate it too.'

'But you don't?'

He looked at me. 'It has its good points.'

My stomach squirmed and swirled with excitement and nerves and something else I'd never really felt before.

'Goodness, it's warm,' I said, to cover up how flustered I was. 'We should swim.'

Immediately I realised that of course we had no bathing costumes, and that made me flustered too.

'We could just put our feet in the water,' Jerome said, helpfully. 'Cool our toes.'

'We could.'

We walked on towards the water.

'My grandmother is the boss of our family,' Jerome said. 'She's hilarious and terrifying. My dad can't even speak to her most of the time, because he's scared she'll yell at him, and she's his mom.'

I looked at the warmth in his eyes. 'You're not scared of her though?'

'Nope. I think she's perfect,' he said. 'Fearless. You know her parents were freed slaves?'

'Gosh,' I said. I knew about slavery, of course, but it always seemed something far away to me. Lost in the mists of time and

132

which had happened way across the ocean in the colonies. Not something so close. So real. 'What's her name?' I asked.

'Elaine,' Jerome said with a smile. 'Elaine Scott.'

'That's a strong name.'

'Strong woman.' He nodded. 'How about your grandma. What's she called?'

'Delphine. It's my middle name.'

'It is? Gloria Delphine? That's a name that should be on everyone's lips.'

I chuckled. 'Well, that's not very good for a spy,' I said. 'The last thing I want is to be talked about. I'll have to come up with an alias.'

Jerome looked at me, an amused expression on his handsome face. 'Somehow,' he said, 'I think people will talk about you whatever your name is.'

I ducked my head, embarrassed by his compliment but liking it too.

'Come on,' I said, tugging his hand. 'We're almost at the river.'

I ran ahead and he followed. I found a spot right at the edge where we could sit. Jerome took off his boots and thick socks and dangled his toes into the water.

'Oh man, that feels good,' he said. 'You try.'

I was only wearing little gym shoes, but I took them off anyway, and put my feet into the cold water next to his and wiggled my toes. You could hardly tell our skin was different colours when you looked through the ripples in the water. Our feet just looked like feet.

'Tell me about New York,' I said. 'What does it sound like?'

'What does it sound like?' Jerome looked round at me curiously. 'No one's ever asked me that before.'

'When I think about Paris, before the war, obviously, I think of chatter,' I said. 'The sound of a café, with people talking nineteen to the dozen, and the little chink of spoons on saucers.'

'All right,' he said, leaning back on his elbows. 'I see what you mean. What does London sound like?'

I thought for a moment, leaning back too, so our arms were touching. 'London sounds like trains,' I said. 'Train doors slamming shut, and the hissing of steam, and the guards shouting.'

'New York sounds like shouting too,' Jerome said. 'The newsies on the corners selling the papers, and folks calling to one another across the street, and kids playing. Raised voices, but not in anger. Just in life.'

'Just in life,' I repeated. 'I like that.'

'Honeyford sounds like animals,' he went on. 'It's so quiet here except for the cows. Sometimes you can't hear anything at all.'

'You can always hear something,' I said. 'It's never completely silent. Listen . . .'

We both stayed very still, ears straining. The river was rushing over the stones on its bed, and I could hear that. I could hear the breeze in the trees, and the birds singing.

I looked round at Jerome. He was still leaning back, with his eyes closed and his face up to the sky.

'What can you hear?' I said, quietly.

'The river,' he said, not opening his eyes. 'And the birds.'

'That's a song thrush,' I told him.

'And the wind in the leaves overhead . . .'

As he spoke the air was suddenly split by the sound of an aeroplane engine, coming in low – heading to Eaton, no doubt.

'It's so quiet,' I shouted over the sound of the plane.

'So very, very still,' Jerome shouted back, and we both fell about in laughter.

'I wanted to fly,' he said as the engine faded.

'I suppose that's why you joined the air force.'

'There's a unit back home that trains in a place called Tuskegee,' Jerome said. 'There are some Black pilots there. But there aren't many and I didn't get picked to train there.'

'It must be dangerous,' I said.

'Yes, but that's why we're here, right? It's all dangerous. Except we're not allowed to take part in active combat. We just get to build runways, and dig ditches, and drive folk around and tip our hats to them.' He sighed. 'It's not how I thought it was going to be, that's all.'

'I know.' I sighed. 'I'll tell you something that will make you laugh.'

'Go on.'

'I was on the bus the other day, and there were two soldiers on the bus too. Black soldiers.'

'Right.'

'And these other GIs got on. Airmen. Corporal Taylor was one of them – you know him?'

Jerome nodded.

'And another one of them was called Corporal Gordon. He was a big chap, burly, you know?'

'Burly,' said Jerome. 'I like that word. I get you. Go on.'

'And he told the soldiers they had to get off the bus. But they didn't. And do you know why?'

'Why?'

'Because a group of schoolgirls stood up to him and he had to get off instead.'

'Schoolgirls?'

'And the bus driver, too.'

'And you?'

'A bit. But it was the girls who really did it. And Corporal Taylor and the other GIs, to be fair. They stood up to their friend and that's never easy to do, in my experience.'

Jerome grinned. 'I'm finding that not everyone in Honeyford is on board with segregation.'

'I don't think English people enjoy being told what to do.'

'Apparently not.'

Our faces were quite close together now. I looked right into his dark eyes and found I couldn't stop smiling.

'Gloria?' Jerome said, still holding my gaze.

'Yes?' I'd never been kissed before but I was almost certain it was about to happen. What should I do? Should I close my eyes? Pout my lips?

I felt Jerome's breath on my face and tilted my head a little.

'I have to go,' he said.

Oh.

He sat up straight and took his feet out of the water, shaking them dry like a dog. He started pulling on his socks and shoes, so I did the same, feeling horribly disappointed.

'So, I guess I'll see you soon?' he said, getting to his feet.

'I suppose so.' I picked up my library books and stood up too. 'Bye then.'

I turned to go but he caught my hand and pulled me towards him, and kissed me so thoroughly I had no time to prepare, but somehow it didn't matter. And then he let me go again and sauntered off, looking like the cat who'd got the cream. I suspected I probably looked the same.

'Jerome!' I called after him and he paused and turned back to look at me. 'Bye!'

He gave me that cheeky wink again. 'Bye then, Gloria Delphine.'

Chapter 18

Gloria

George was so annoyed about the reaction to Eugene playing piano for him that he had put a sign up outside the pub. It said *Englishmen and Black GIs only.*

'I can't believe he's done that,' I said to Patty in hushed tones as we gazed at the sign.

She shook her head. 'He's a brave man.'

'Do you think the Americans won't like it?'

'I don't think Jennifer Lacey will like it,' Patty said. 'She's got a right bee in her bonnet about the GIs and I heard her telling Millicent that she thought segregation made sense.'

I made a face.

'I know,' said Patty. 'Crikey, it's hot.'

'It's going to be a glorious day,' I agreed looking up at the sun, which was burning already, even though it was still early. 'I can't believe it's only May. I hope it stays this good for the fair.'

Patty glared at me. 'Well it's all right for you, little miss do-nothing. This weather is awful for us stuck in the fields all day.'

'Is it, heck,' I said with a laugh. 'You love being outdoors and you love the sunshine.'

Patty grinned. 'Yes, you're right, I do. Speaking of which, I should get on.' She kissed me on the cheek. 'What are you up to today?'

'Oh you know me,' I said. 'Little miss do-nothing.'

'Are you going to see Jerome?'

'Perhaps.' I tried to sound casual but I couldn't stop smiling and Patty gave me a good-natured shove.

'Lucky you,' she said. She tied her headscarf over her hair. 'Listen, if you're free tomorrow evening, there's a group of soldiers from Jamaica who have arrived for training near Fairford. Some of us are going over to the base for a mixer.'

'What's a mixer?' Patty was only a few months older than me, but sometimes she seemed so much more sophisticated.

'Like a dance, where we can all mix.'

'Could be fun,' I said, already thinking about what dresses I had in my wardrobe that might do. But then I groaned. 'No, I told my mother I'd go to the pictures with her.'

'My mum says Rose is like a new person.'

'She's so much better,' I said, nodding. 'Honestly, Patty, it's like the sun has come out after a long winter.'

'I'm glad.'

'It's a funny thing, because I never really felt like I knew my mother. I was always at school, and she was always so focused on Daddy. But suddenly we're becoming friends.'

Patty made a face. 'Lord,' she said. 'Perhaps I should start inviting my mother to dances.'

I giggled at the thought of Fran kicking her heels up.

'So, no Jamaican mixer?' Patty said.

'No Jamaican mixer.'

'Then I shall have to keep all the Jamaican soldiers for myself.' She kissed me on the cheek. 'Goodbye!'

'I don't need a Jamaican soldier,' I called after her. 'I have an American!'

'Do you?'

I turned to see my mother standing a little way away from me on the green in the sunshine. She looked younger and prettier than she had done for ages. Years, probably.

I felt myself flush and she laughed.

'Have you met someone, Gloria? A gorgeous GI?'

I darted over to where she stood, all the paperwork for the summer fair in her arms.

'Shh,' I said. 'Don't shout about it.'

She stroked my cheek. 'You should shout about it,' she said. 'Tell everyone.'

'I'm not sure yet,' I said. 'I like him a lot, but I'm not sure he feels the same way.'

I'd not seen Jerome since we'd kissed beside the river and I kept replaying the moments over and over again in my head. Was this just a bit of fun, or was it more? Because the way I felt when I thought about him felt so deep and real, I couldn't bear the idea that he might not share my affection.

'He might just see me as a bit of a diversion,' I admitted. 'I don't know.'

'Look at you,' Mother said. 'My little girl, in love for the first time.'

'I'm not in love,' I said weakly. 'Well, maybe I am.'

My mother did a little bounce on her toes like a schoolgirl. 'Tell me all about him,' she said. 'We've got time before we get sucked into this meeting. Where did you meet him?'

I tucked my arm into hers and slowly we strolled through the village towards the hall.

'I met him when he was building the sentry box at home,' I told her. 'He winked at me.'

'How cheeky,' she said in delight. 'I like the sound of him already. What's his name?'

'Jerome Scott.'

'Nice.' She nodded. 'Better than the endless Roberts and Johns we have here in England.'

'Mother!' I said, but she shrugged.

'It's true.'

'I suppose so.'

'Is he handsome?'

'So handsome.'

'Tell me what he looks like.'

I paused. 'He's got dark hair and dark eyes,' I began. 'Actually, Mother, you know him. He's Captain Waldo's driver.'

Her eyes sparkled at the mention of Waldo.

'Mother,' I said. 'Do you like Captain Waldo?'

'Of course I do. He's a very nice man.'

'But do you *like* him?'

She squished her face up like a giddy schoolgirl. 'I think I might,' she admitted. 'Do you mind?'

'Why would I mind?'

'Because of Daddy.'

I stopped walking and turned to her. 'Daddy died three years ago. You deserve to be happy.'

'But . . .'

'But nothing. Daddy was a good man. And so is Waldo.'

'You're very wise for such a young woman,' Mother said.

'I read a lot of books,' I joked. We started walking again, almost to the village hall now.

'Back to Jerome,' Mother said. She smiled at me. 'He seems like a nice lad.'

'He is.'

'It might be trickier than it otherwise could be,' she said diplomatically. 'With these rules they have.'

'I know.' I sighed. 'I'm worried about Grandpa. I didn't like the way he spoke to Jerome. And he told me not to get too friendly.'

My mother laughed loudly. 'Did he now?'

We'd reached the village hall and she sat down on the bench outside and patted the seat next to her, indicating I should sit too.

'Let me tell you something about my father,' she said. 'He adores my mother.'

'Everyone adores Mamie,' I pointed out and Mother laughed again.

'That's true,' she said. 'But my father thinks she is the most wonderful woman in the world. And he thinks that I am even better. And you, *ma cherie*, you are the most wonderful of us all.'

'He does think the world of us,' I said, smiling at the thought of my doting grandpa.

'And because he thinks that, he also thinks that no man will ever be worthy of us.'

'Really?'

'Really.'

'But he loved Daddy.'

'He did.' She paused. 'Eventually.'

'He didn't always like him?'

'Good heavens, no,' Mother said. 'He thought he was a wastrel. Because your father liked art, your grandpa was convinced he was a good-for-nothing artist who'd see me starving in a garret.'

'He thought that? Even when he met Daddy's parents and saw Honeyford House?'

'Well, then he decided poor Geoffrey was a good-for-nothing aristocrat who'd lounge around all day, and fritter away his income.'

'Poor Daddy.'

'Oh, that wasn't the worst of it.'

'It wasn't?'

'No. Grandpa discovered your father had been married before.'

I almost fell off my seat in shock. 'WHAT?'

'Oh yes, it's a terribly sad story. He married his childhood sweetheart Felicity straight after the Great War.'

'How did I never know this before? Where is Felicity now?'

'She died, poor woman. Spanish flu. Very sudden. They'd only been married a month when she passed away. Your father was devastated for a good many years.'

'Until he met you?'

'He always said I'd reminded him how to laugh,' my mother said, going a little misty-eyed. 'I was so glad. He deserved to be happy. But goodness me, my father wasn't pleased that I was going to be a second wife.'

'Grandpa can be very stubborn,' I pointed out. 'I'm surprised Daddy didn't give up on you.'

'Never!' said Mother. 'We were in love, and we were determined to be together.'

'That's sweet . . . and sad.' I took Mother's hand. 'And if Daddy could love again after Felicity, then surely you see that you could love again after Daddy?'

'Perhaps.' She dabbed her eyes. 'My father is from a different generation, Gloria, and he spent a long time working in the West Indies and India when he was younger. It's different over there. He's used to calling the shots.'

She tucked a strand of my hair behind my ear.

'Your father and I fought to be together. And if you really want to be with Jerome then you should fight, too. Grandpa's not stupid. He'll learn.'

'What are you both doing sitting out here in the sunshine?' said Mr Fingal, as he came up the path. 'Come on, ladies. There's work to do.'

The moment between my mother and me was broken, but I was pleased I'd told her. And goodness, I'd learned a few things too. I couldn't wait to tell Patty. And Jerome. If I managed to see him later. I'd discovered he had no agency over his activity. If he was needed for a job, then he had to do it, no matter how little free time he'd had. I wasn't sure when I'd get to see him.

But despite my worries, when I finally emerged blinking into the bright sunshine after the gloom of the village hall, much later, he was there. Leaning against a tree on the green, smiling his lovely smile.

My stomach flipped and I ran to him, not caring that I wasn't being casual or breezy.

'I was hoping you'd come today,' I said.

'Of course,' he said. 'I missed you.'

'I missed you too.'

'Did you see the sign on the pub door?'

'I did.' I nodded. 'George is in there.' I nodded towards the village hall, where discussions about whether to allow jitterbugging at the dance were still going on. 'But he wouldn't discuss it.'

'George sounds like a good guy. Eugene thinks the world of him.'

'George does not like being told what to do,' I said, with a chuckle. 'How much time do you have?'

'Not long.' Jerome made a face as he checked his watch. 'Like ten minutes.'

'Oh what a shame,' I said.

'But, I can get away again tomorrow evening, if you want to do something? It's going to be a lovely evening. I thought perhaps we could climb that hill behind your house and look at the stars.'

'That sounds wonderful,' I said, delighted. 'I'll bring a picnic.'

'Even better.' He took my hand briefly and squeezed my fingers. I felt his touch like an electric shock pulsing through me. 'I'll meet you out the back gate of Honeyford by the vegetable patches at six o'clock tomorrow.'

'Great.'

'And I wanted to give you this,' he said. He looked a little shy suddenly, as he dug into the pocket of his trousers.

'What is it?'

He opened my hand and dropped a little brooch into my palm. It was an American flag, outlined in gold, with red, white and blue enamelling.

'It's a sweetheart pin,' he said. 'It's to show that your guy is a GI.'

I was so pleased I could hardly speak. 'It's precious,' I managed eventually. I pinned it to my dress. 'Are you?'

'Am I what?'

'My guy?'

Jerome grinned at me. 'I'd like to be.'

'I'd like that too,' I said. I smiled at him, feeling a flood of contentment. 'My guy is a GI.'

'I really have to go,' he said.

Across the green, there was an angry shout. We both turned to see two white officers reading the sign George had put up at the pub.

'I'm out of here,' Jerome said. 'I'll see you tomorrow.'

He hurried off and I touched my fingers to the little pin brooch. 'My guy is a GI,' I said happily.

Chapter 19

Philippa

'It's not a grave,' Marco said.

We stood together looking over the rectangle of stones.

'No, it's not a grave,' I said.

'Definitely not.'

I shook my head. 'I know that it looks like a grave, because it's the right shape.' I bent down and propped the broken statue up in the hole. 'And this cherub would serve as a kind of headstone. But it's not a grave.'

'No, absolutely,' Marco agreed. 'It's actually too small to be a grave.'

'Way too small.'

We both looked down at the stones.

'It does look like a grave though, doesn't it.'

Marco put his arm around me.

'It does. A grave for a tiny person. Like a cherub.' He gestured to the statue, clearly trying to lighten the mood, but I gasped, putting my hand over my mouth.

'Or a baby.'

'No,' said Marco firmly. 'Absolutely not.'

'It could be.' I felt tearful all of a sudden. 'It could be a grave for a baby.'

'It couldn't be, my love.' Marco wrapped his arms round me. 'Because we would know.'

'How would we know?' I sniffed. 'How?'

'Well, I'm not sure of the laws, but I don't think you can just bury anyone wherever you feel like it,' he said. He looked thoughtful, like he was trying to remember. 'Or perhaps you can. But I'm sure you have to tell someone. The council perhaps?'

'What about it if it was a miscarriage,' I said in a small voice. 'Like mine.'

Marco kissed my head. 'Then there wouldn't be a grave.'

'There could be.'

He looked wretched. 'I suppose.'

I shook my head. 'In the olden days stillborn babies were buried outside the walls of the churchyard because they hadn't been baptised,' I said. 'Perhaps a grieving mother wanted their baby remembered in a better way.'

'Perhaps.' Marco sounded uncertain. 'Or perhaps someone might have made this for a different reason.'

'Like what?'

He screwed his face up. 'I don't know.' He shivered and I slipped my hand into his. I felt oddly at peace with the idea that this could be a grave. If there was one thing I understood, it was grieving mothers.

'It's a lovely spot, you know. Close to the oak tree with the hollow. Far enough from the house that it's peaceful and secluded.'

'It is a nice spot.'

'A resting place.'

'No, not necessarily.'

'I wonder if we can find out?' I said, almost to myself. 'If it really is a grave.'

'How would we?' Marco frowned. 'Why would we?'

'Just so we know for sure.'

146

'I don't think so, Phil . . .'

'You said yourself, you probably have to tell someone.'

'Well, yes, if you do it officially.'

'So, I could check.'

'Do you really want to know?'

I thought about it. 'I think so.'

'Okay then,' Marco said. 'But I might just concentrate on the menus for now.'

I squeezed his hand. 'I understand.'

'What should we do with it?'

We both looked down at the stones. 'I don't know,' I said. 'We can't move it. Not until we know for sure if it's a grave.'

'It feels funny leaving it here, though.'

'It's been here the whole time we have,' I pointed out. 'Covered in grass and weeds.'

'Hidden,' said Marco firmly, sounding very much like he wished it had stayed that way.

'You can't see it from the house. Even if we mend the cherub, you won't be able to see it. None of the customers will be able to spot it.'

'You're going to mend the cherub, aren't you?' Marco sounded resigned, which made me smile a tiny smile.

'I'm going to try.' I picked it up again and then bent to scoop up the base, too.

'I'm . . .' Marco began. He swallowed. He looked a little pale and sad. 'I'm finding this a little bit difficult.'

'I know.'

'I don't mind if you make some enquiries, but I can't help.'

'I know,' I said again.

'Are we good?'

I nodded. 'Yes.'

He gave me a kiss. 'I'm just going to have a shower, and then I'm going to start writing some menus,' he said. 'Just . . . be careful, Phil.' He put his hands to his heart. 'It's all still a bit fragile.'

147

My own heart ached for him. 'I will,' I said.

He walked off up towards the house, his shoulders slumped. I watched him go for a moment and then I put the statue back in the hole, pulled out my phone and took some photographs. I didn't know how to find out if this was a grave, but I knew a woman who might.

'It definitely looks like a grave,' Vanessa said, later. She was scrolling through the photos on my phone. 'But it's small.'

I held my hands apart to show her how big it was. 'Not much more than a metre.'

'Hmm.' She handed me back my phone. We were sitting in her lounge. She was on the sofa, with her broken ankle up on a footstool and I'd been pleased to see she was looking much better – in good spirits, considering.

'We thought that perhaps it was for a baby,' I said. 'Because of the size, and the cherub statue.'

'I can see that.' Vanessa said.

'Could it be a grave? Legally I mean?'

She nodded and my stomach twisted. 'Absolutely,' she said. 'You can bury a body on private land without planning permission. It does lower the value of your house, mind you.'

'Understandably.' I made a face. 'So, you just dig a hole and pop in the body? You don't need to do anything official?'

Vanessa shook her head. 'No, there is some red tape. You're supposed to mark it on the deeds. And keep a record of the burial on the deeds.'

'So we could check?'

'Yes. Though I'm pretty sure this sort of thing would have come up in the searches done when you bought it.'

'You'd hope so, wouldn't you?' I said, rolling my eyes. 'But I'll check again anyway.'

'If it is a baby, though . . .' Vanessa began. She looked thoughtful. 'If it is a baby, then perhaps it would be a secret.

148

Especially if it's old. An unmarried mother, perhaps. Someone who didn't want anyone to know she'd been pregnant? Though in that case, why build a memorial?'

I felt sick. 'Well,' I began, my voice shaking a little. 'Perhaps the mother wanted a place to remember her baby, but didn't want others to know. Or maybe she just wanted it to be private.'

Vanessa looked at me, her eyes soft. I gave her a little nod.

'I've had miscarriages,' I said quickly, dropping my gaze, hoping she'd understand that I didn't want to share the details. She reached out very briefly and touched my arm. 'I'm sorry to hear that.'

There was a pause and then I said: 'So you think it could be old?'

'I'm only speculating,' Vanessa said. 'If I was at work, I could help you more. Shall I call Jackie and see if she's got any bright ideas?'

'Jackie from the museum?'

'That's the one.'

I smiled at her, thankful she'd not made a big fuss about what I'd told her. 'Yes please.'

Vanessa picked up her phone and while she chatted to her colleague, I scrolled through my emails and reread everything from our solicitor about the deeds of the house. There were reports about the flood risk from the river, and the fact the field behind our trees was inexplicably owned by the Church of England, and some stuff about access to the road, and just about everything you could possibly imagine had been checked, and there was definitely no mention of any burials in our garden. I found the map of the land that was attached to the deeds and zoomed in on the little glade of trees but there was nothing marked.

'There's no mention of a grave in any of the documents I've got,' I told Vanessa as she ended the call. 'Nothing flagged up by our solicitor.'

'Jackie wants to know how old it is,' Vanessa said. 'Because your house was built in 1803, apparently. So there have been a

149

lot of people who have lived there since then who could have had a baby, secretly or otherwise.'

'Oh,' I was deflated. 'I have no idea how old it is.'

'She says if you can work it out, or at least narrow it down a bit, she can work out who was living there then.'

'Okay,' I said. 'I'll try.'

'What about the statue?' Vanessa asked. 'Maybe that could give us a clue. How worn is it?'

'Not very.' I found the photos on my phone again and stared at them. 'Not weather-beaten like old headstones are. Though it's been sheltered I suppose.'

I zoomed in on the picture. 'Perhaps I could find out who made it? There might be a name on it somewhere?'

'Perhaps.'

'I'll have a look when I get home.' I sighed. 'We're assuming it is a grave, but it might be something completely different.'

Vanessa rearranged the cushion behind her back. 'It might be linked to Lucien Lavelle and his parties in the Sixties. Or something from the war?'

'It could be anything, I suppose.' I felt a bit glum. It seemed like it would be impossible to find out for sure what the stones meant. 'But I am absolutely sure it's a grave. I've just got a feeling.'

'What sort of feeling?'

'We were clearing the garden,' I said. 'When we found it. We'd decided we were going to plant some bluebells down there.' I rubbed my thighs with my palms. 'As a sort of memorial to our babies. Marco found out bluebells are a symbol of everlasting love.'

'That's nice,' Vanessa said.

'So perhaps that's why I'm so convinced? In fact, I'm worried that because I had that idea in my mind, I'm sort of projecting my own feelings on to someone who may not even exist.'

'Because you chose that spot to remember your babies, you think someone else could have done the same?'

'Yes.' I screwed my face up. 'Marco can't handle it. He doesn't want to know. But I feel a sort of affinity with this mother. If she even exists. I understand her. And I want to know who she was.'

'I can understand that,' Vanessa said. 'And I'm happy to help if I can. Because frankly, I'm bored out of my mind and it'll be a good distraction.'

I smiled. 'Thank you,' I said.

There was a knock at the front door and then a voice called: 'Helloooo?'

'Marco?' I said.

My husband came into the room and looked just as surprised to see me as I was to see him.

'I didn't know you were here,' he said, looking faintly ruffled.

'I thought Vanessa might have some ideas about the grave.'

Marco grimaced. 'It's not a grave.'

I glanced at Vanessa as if to say "see?" and she nodded.

'I just came to see Vanessa,' Marco said. 'How are you doing?'

'Better, thanks,' said Vanessa.

There was a slightly awkward pause.

'I'm going to go,' I said. 'I just came to show Vanessa the erm, the garden thing.'

'Right,' said Marco.

'See you at home?'

'See you there.'

I gave Vanessa a kiss, and headed for the front door wondering why on earth my husband was paying house calls on another woman in the middle of the day.

Chapter 20

Gloria

I had been sent on yet another errand by the summer fair committee. This time I'd been sent to collect umbrellas from just about every house in the village because my mother had the idea that if it rained on the day we could somehow string them up across the green to provide shelter.

The heat showed no sign of breaking, so I thought rain was unlikely, but Mother liked to be prepared. So I'd spent the day gathering brollies and delivering them to the village hall. And now I was hot and tired and a bit grumpy to be honest, so I'd found a spot in the shade at the edge of the green and I lay down on the grass.

I'd started out reading my book, but quite quickly I dropped it on to my chest and dozed, the sounds of the village washing over me as my mind drifted.

And then an ear-piercing wail split the peaceful afternoon.

Startled awake I sat up suddenly to see the telegram boy – David – cycling past me. My heart clenched with sadness and I scrambled to my feet.

'David?' I said as he went by. He stopped riding and put his toes on the ground to steady himself.

'Millicent Hayes,' he said. 'Her Sidney.'

'Sidney,' I breathed. 'Poor sod.'

David gave a little nod and carried on cycling, and I looked across the way to where there was a bit of a kerfuffle happening outside the village hall. I could see Mr Fingal gesturing and a small group of people gathering, and as I walked towards them I could hear panicky voices.

'Call an ambulance,' someone was saying. 'Or run for the doctor.'

Millicent was sitting on the bench outside the hall, where I'd sat with my mother not so long ago. Her face was grey, and she was gasping for breath.

'She's having a heart attack,' Mr Fingal said. His voice was shaky. 'Gloria! Run for Dr Christie. Millicent's had a shock.'

I turned to run, but behind me were Eugene and another airman whose name, I knew, was Stanley Silver but whom I'd never spoken to.

'What happened?' asked Eugene. 'Was it her who was screaming?'

'Her husband's been killed.'

Stanley grimaced.

'I'm going for the doctor,' I said. 'Mr Fingal says she's having a heart attack.'

Stanley put his hand out to stop me leaving. 'She's not having a heart attack,' he said. 'Let me help.'

He walked over to where Millicent sat, and crouched down in front of her. He took her hands in his and Millicent didn't object. She was still taking shuddering, raspy, shallow breaths and her gaze was vague. I thought she might be about to pass out and the thought scared me. Was Mr Fingal right? Was she having a heart attack?

'Millicent is it?' he said. He looked round at me, and I nodded.

'Millicent,' he said, looking straight at her. 'Millicent, you've had a fright. A bad one. And it's made your heartbeat a little off.'

Millicent put her hand to her chest.

'That's it,' said Stanley soothingly. 'We need to get things back

153

in a rhythm, okay? So you just keep looking into my eyes, and breathe when I breathe. Can you do that, Millicent? Okay?'

Millicent nodded and to my relief she started to breathe more regularly, and her skin lost the ashen sheen it had taken on.

Eventually after what felt like ages but was probably only about ten minutes, Stanley turned to the group of people who were still gathered.

'Millicent needs to go home and lie down, but she shouldn't be alone. Who's going to go with her?'

Out of the corner of my eye I saw Jennifer Lacey start to speak but then Celia Griffiths, one of my mother's friends, stepped forward. 'I'll take her,' she said. 'I lost my son Tim. I know how she's feeling.'

'What's your name?' Stanley asked.

Celia told him and he turned back to Millicent.

'Millicent. Celia's going to take you home. Are you ready to go?'

Millicent nodded and Stanley helped her to her feet.

'I'll come see you tomorrow if that's all right with you?' he said.

Millicent nodded again. Celia put her arm round her and slowly the women walked towards Millicent's little cottage.

As they went up the path, it felt like the whole group watching breathed a sigh of relief.

'You were amazing, Stanley,' I said. 'Where did you learn to do that?'

Stanley ducked his head, shy suddenly. 'Medical school,' he muttered.

'You're a doctor?' I was surprised – and a little embarrassed by my surprise.

'Not yet.'

Mr Fingal put his hand out and shook Stanley's firmly. 'Thank you, son,' he said. 'Good job.'

'Yes, bloody well done,' said someone else, and then more voices spoke up, praising what he'd done. Poor Stanley looked absolutely crippled with embarrassment.

'I think Private Silver and Private Lee need to go now,' I said, wanting to spare Stanley. He caught my eye and mouthed "thank you" and then he and Eugene melted away across the green.

'You should go home and tell your mother,' Mr Fingal said to me. 'She'll want to know.'

'You're right,' I said with reluctance. Mother liked Millicent and, just like Celia, she knew what it was like to lose someone. But she was doing so well. I didn't want to send her spiralling back down into grief just when she was beginning to drag herself out.

'I'll go now.'

Once more I found my mother talking to Captain Waldo. They were sitting together on the terrace this time, drinking lemonade. My mother was wearing a pretty dress with strawberries printed on the fabric that I remembered from before the war. I'd not seen her wear it for a long time.

'Mother,' I said, drawing near. 'Mother, I have some bad news.'

The colour drained from her face. 'What is it, Gloria? Who is it? Tell me quickly.'

'Sidney Hayes.'

Mother put her hands on the table in front of her, palms flat, steadying herself. 'Poor Millicent,' she said.

'It was awful. She was wailing and then she couldn't breathe.'

Mother swayed slightly, even though she was sitting down, and Waldo put his hand on her arm, anchoring her. She leaned towards him, and I was glad he was there.

'Private Silver helped her,' I told him. 'He's going to be a doctor.'

Waldo frowned. 'Silver?' he said thoughtfully. 'Silver?'

'He's not based at Eaton, sir,' I said. 'He's at the other barracks.'

Understanding dawned on Waldo's face. 'He's going to be a doctor?'

'A good one, I think. He was so kind and calm with Millicent. I don't know what would have happened if he'd not been there. We were all just standing round like lemons.'

'Excellent,' said Waldo. 'Good man.' He turned to Mother. 'Rose? Are you doing okay, there?'

My mother looked pale and shocked. 'Is Millicent alone?'

I shook my head. 'Celia took her home.'

'Good,' Mother said. 'Celia knows how it feels to get the telegram. She'll help.' She rubbed her forehead, looking sad. 'There are rather a lot of us in the village who know how it feels now.'

'You can all help each other,' Waldo suggested.

'Oh I'm not sure that's a good idea,' I said, wary of putting too much pressure on Mother. 'It's a very personal thing . . .'

'That's a wonderful idea,' said Mother, interrupting me. 'Do you know, I read that during the Great War some women set up Happiness Clubs for bereaved families. Like a support group where women could meet and help one another. Perhaps we should do that in Honeyford?'

'The Honeyford Happiness Club,' said Waldo. 'It has a nice ring to it.'

'Mother . . .' I said again. 'Do you think this is a good plan? Helping other women could bring back memories of when Daddy died.'

My mother looked straight at me. 'Oh, I expect it will,' she said. 'But that's fine.' Waldo still had his hand on her arm and now she patted his fingers with her other hand and took her arm away so she could reach out to me. 'Darling, I'll always be sad that I lost your father. Just as I know you'll always miss him, too. But losing him is part of my life now, just as being married to him was. And I have to get on with that life.'

I stared at her, completely taken aback. 'Yes,' I said eventually. 'That makes sense.'

'I've come through the darkest of times, and perhaps now I can help others do the same. And they can help me too. On the bad days. Because there will always be bad days.' She got up from the table. 'I'm going to telephone Margery at the post office and see what she thinks. Her husband died at the Somme, you know?'

156

'I didn't know that,' I said. 'She must hate having to send out those telegrams.'

'Undoubtedly.' Mother gave me a quick kiss, then rested her hand on Waldo's shoulder for the briefest of seconds, and hurried off into the house, leaving Waldo and I staring after her in wonder.

'Your mother,' Waldo said eventually, 'is really something.'

I laughed. 'She's definitely something,' I said.

Chapter 21

Philippa

Marco was going full steam ahead with the plans for opening the restaurant and I had to admit I was impressed.

The new tables and chairs had finally been unwrapped, and were stacked outside on the finished pergola, which looked great.

He'd been to the local college and recruited a part-time sous chef to help him in the kitchen, and Jackie's daughter Lauren was coming round to have a chat about doing some shifts as a waitress.

I was filling in forms and sorting out bank accounts and payroll software and was thoroughly enjoying it. I was also busy spreading the word on social media and in the local paper, and putting up adverts in Honeyford. I had to admit, the mums from Alex's party seemed to have spread the word already, not to mention Mick from the shop, and Harvey, and Vanessa.

I was glad we both had something to focus on. Finding the cherub in the woods had really unsettled both of us, and my determination to find out what it was, combined with Marco's determination to ignore it altogether, had unsettled us even more.

I felt as though we were on slightly shaky ground, but I didn't know how to change it.

And of course, there was Alex. He had been round a lot in the past few days, coming back for his dinner after school. He'd proved a willing and enthusiastic assistant when Marco was finishing the pergola, and now he was supposedly helping out in the kitchen when Marco practised dishes. Though from where I stood it seemed that most of the time when he was round, he and Marco were playing football on the newly trimmed lawn, or playing on the Xbox that Marco had bought from eBay. He'd never been very interested in computer games before.

Marco had started clearing out the spare room properly. He said it was good to have a space for Alex to stay if he wanted to. I'd not argued but I did wonder why he thought Alex would need to stay over. It wasn't like Vanessa was planning to break her ankle again.

Vanessa, in fact, was doing really well.

So well that she turned up on our doorstep with Jackie and Lauren.

Lauren had come for a chat with Marco about waitressing, and Jackie had wanted to have a look at the "grave", so I'd been expecting them. But there was Vanessa too, on crutches but looking back to her old self. She was wearing her maxi dress and her hair was pulled up in her trademark tousled bun, with a few tendrils escaping on to her tanned shoulders. Her makeup was perfectly applied. In short, she looked great. She looked, I thought, like she was off out somewhere, rather than popping round to a friend's house on a weekday morning.

'Vanessa,' I said. 'You're looking much better.'

She kissed me on the cheek.

'I was dying of boredom at home so when Jackie said she was coming round I thought I'd tag along. I hope that's okay?'

'Of course.'

'How are the workers?' she asked as we went inside.

'The pergola's finished, as I'm sure Alex mentioned,' I said. 'And thank goodness, the ceiling's almost done too. We're just waiting for the plaster to dry before Harvey does the last bits.'

159

'Great,' said Vanessa half-heartedly. I supposed the pergola might still be a sore point for her.

Marco came out of the restaurant to greet Lauren.

'You brought a support team?' he said, smiling at her.

She groaned. 'Mum and Vanessa insisted on coming to see some grave or something.'

Marco's expression darkened. And instead of saying hello to Jackie and Vanessa properly, he bundled Lauren off to the kitchen and to show her the restaurant and the terrace.

Slightly embarrassed, I offered Jackie and Vanessa a cup of tea.

'He's very excited,' I said, making excuses for Marco, as we went into our part of the house. 'And very nervous.'

'I'm not surprised,' Jackie said. 'It's going to be great, though. I've heard lots of people talking about it.'

'That's really good.' I filled the kettle and switched it on. 'We're going to start taking bookings this weekend, if I can get the software up and running properly.'

When I'd made the tea, Vanessa leaned back against the sofa cushions and said: 'Tell Jackie all about the grave.'

'Yes please,' said Jackie. 'Ness has filled me in on bits and pieces but I want to know everything.'

Feeling faintly disloyal because Marco so clearly didn't want to know more, but still desperate to solve the mystery, I filled her in on what we'd found and showed her the photos. The broken statue was under the sideboard in the living room, in a carrier bag. I'd not wanted it out where Marco could see it. I got that out and she looked at that too, but I'd thoroughly examined every inch of it to see if I could find a name or any other information about where it had come from and there was nothing.

'It's all very strange,' Jackie said. 'Could we go and have a look at the stones in the garden?'

'I'll come too,' said Vanessa.

'Can you manage on your crutches?' I didn't want her hurting herself even more than she already had.

'It's at the end of the woods isn't it?'

I nodded.

'Maybe we can walk down the drive and go that way. It'll be easier.'

Leaving our empty mugs in the kitchen, we went outside. I was pleased to see that Marco and Lauren were still in the kitchen – I could hear them chatting – and I didn't have to explain where we were going.

Making slow progress, but faster than I'd expected, we skirted the side of the house, and headed along the drive.

'How's the building work coming along?' Jackie asked as we went. 'My husband is a friend of Harvey's.'

'Is he?' said Vanessa, looking slightly red in the face from the exertion of walking. 'I didn't know that. Why have you never told me that?'

Jackie gave her an odd look. 'You never asked,' she said.

'Almost done,' I said. 'Thank goodness.'

We reached the curve in the driveway where it bent round to meet the road, and walked straight on instead, on to the grass. Jackie and I hovered on either side of Vanessa to make sure she didn't fall, but she made it safely, if slightly out of breath, to the little copse of trees.

'The stones are just down here,' I said, leading them to the right spot.

Jackie stood and looked down at the stones, with the hole at the top where the statue had been.

'Goodness,' she said. 'It really does look like a grave.'

'I know.' Standing there brought back all the feelings from when I'd found it. A longing to know for sure what it was and who'd made it. And again that sort of tug of understanding for whoever had built this memorial. Because I was convinced all over again that a memorial was exactly what it was.

'I wonder if the archaeology society might be able to help,' Vanessa said. She was talking in a quiet respectful voice, like you

161

would if you were standing next to an actual grave, and I appreciated it. 'They might know if there's a way to tell . . .' She broke off. 'Well, a way to find out what's underneath without digging.'

I shuddered. 'I'm not sure I want to know,' I said. 'I'd rather find out more about who made it.'

Jackie crouched down and picked up one of the stones. 'These must be from the river,' she said. 'By the ford.'

'That's what I thought.'

She dangled her fingers into the hole left by the statue. 'And this is where the cherub was?'

'That's right. Like a headstone.'

'It's a mystery, that's for sure,' said Vanessa. 'I don't really know what to suggest.'

'It makes me feel a bit sad,' Jackie said.

'Me too,' I said. 'I really wish we hadn't found it.' I sat down next to her, and tugged on a weed growing in the hole to get rid of it. As I pulled it out, I caught a flash of something sparkly underneath.

'Look,' I said. 'What's that?'

Not caring if I got my hands dirty, I brushed away the soil to reveal a tiny gold brooch. I pulled it free of the mud, and shook it off.

'Oh my,' I breathed.

It was only small. A little lapel pin in the shape of a flag, dulled by the earth that had covered it. I got to my feet, slightly awkwardly, then I put the pin into my palm and held it out for Jackie and Vanessa to see.

'It's an American flag,' I said. 'I think? It's hard to see the colours.'

'Jackie, look,' said Vanessa. 'Look what it is.'

Gently Jackie took it from me. 'I know exactly what this is,' she said, her tone excited. 'I've seen lots of these.'

'What is it?'

'It's a sweetheart pin.'

I liked the name. 'A sweetheart pin?'

162

'American soldiers would buy them to give to their sweethearts during the war. Sometimes parents would wear them too as a mark of pride that their son was serving. It was a patriotic thing.' She smiled. 'We've got a whole box of them at the museum because so many girls from round here had romances with the GIs who were stationed nearby.'

'Gosh,' I said. 'I wonder then if whoever left the stones here had a romance with a GI? Didn't you say there were Americans stationed here during the war?'

'Yes, officers lived here,' Jackie said. 'The house would have been owned by the Henry family then.'

'Someone was killed weren't they?'

'Mr Henry,' Vanessa said. 'I read about him when I found the Bowie picture. His family had owned Honeyford for decades, but after he died his wife and daughter moved away and sold the house.'

'Did they move away before the GIs arrived? Because if not, perhaps one of them owned the sweetheart pin.'

'I don't know but I'm sure I can find out,' Jackie said.

'Perhaps this memorial is for the man who died? Mr Henry?' I said. 'Or for a GI who was killed? Or maybe the mother or daughter had a romance with a GI and got pregnant?' I paused. 'Or maybe it's nothing to do with the GIs at all.'

'It's a good starting point, though,' Jackie said.

A shout from up at the house made us both look up. Marco and Lauren were on the terrace, waving.

'Looks like they've finished,' Jackie said. She stood up and brushed the dust from her jeans. 'Let's head back up. I'm in work later, so I'll look up who was living here – if anyone – when the GIs arrived and send you the information.'

'Thank you,' I said. 'I really appreciate the help. I'm even more intrigued now.'

Vanessa took my arm and gave it a squeeze. 'Me too,' she said.

* * *

163

Later, I was sitting at the kitchen table doing some work when Alex appeared at my elbow.

'What are you doing?' he asked.

I looked at him. 'What are you doing?'

'I'm helping Marco.'

'You don't look like you're helping Marco.'

He grinned. 'He's counting tins of tomatoes. It's very boring.'

'Fair enough.' I saved my spreadsheet. 'I didn't know you were here.'

'Granny's got a hospital appointment.'

'She didn't mention it when I saw her earlier. Is she okay?'

'Just a check-up.'

'Good.'

There was a pause.

'Where's the grave?' he said.

I looked at him in surprise. 'How do you know about that?'

'I heard Granny talking to Jackie about it.'

'It's not a grave.'

'It looks like a grave.'

'How do you know?'

'That's what Granny said.'

He sat down at the table next to me.

'History is my favourite subject.'

'I thought football was your favourite.'

He looked at me as if I was mad. 'Football isn't a subject.'

'Sorry.'

'I like thinking about the people who used to live and what they did and that.'

'Really?' I was surprised.

'Yes.' He nodded quite vigorously. 'I like thinking about all my family going back and back and back. Because I've got two parents, but I don't see them really. Not right now.' His face twisted, just briefly and my heart went out to him. 'And I've got four grandparents . . .' He gave me a devilish glance. 'You know like on *Love Island* they say "on paper"?'

'You watch *Love Island*?' I raised an eyebrow and he grinned again.

'I watch bits on YouTube,' he admitted. 'When Granny's not around.'

I laughed and he carried on, pretending to be irritated at the interruption.

'On paper, I've got four grandparents, but actually I only really have Granny. But then going back, there's eight, and sixteen, and thirty-two . . .' He spread his fingers out on the table, like he was playing the piano and pushed down. 'Like roots on a tree.'

'A family tree,' I said.

'Yes.' He looked a bit embarrassed. 'And trees are strong because of their roots so thinking about all those people who came before me makes me feel strong. Are you okay? You look like you might cry.'

I was feeling a bit teary, but now I laughed instead.

'I don't have much family either,' I said. I took a deep breath. 'My mum wasn't always able to look after me properly. Bit like your mum.'

'Who did you live with?'

'My mum most of the time. But it wasn't always great. Then sometimes with family, but they moved to Canada. And then in foster homes for a while.'

'Was it horrible?'

'Actually no,' I said, remembering Vanessa asking me the same question. 'It sounds like it should be horrible – and I know some kids have had an awful time in care – but it wasn't like that for me. It was . . .' I thought. 'It was safe.'

Alex, bless him, nodded, looking much wiser than his years. 'Before I came to live in Honeyford, I felt worried all the time, and scared some of the time. Living here stopped me feeling like that.'

165

'That's it,' I said. 'That's exactly how I felt.'

We looked at one another in understanding.

'When Granny fell I was really frightened that she wouldn't be all right,' he said. 'And Marco made me feel safe.'

I pinched my lips together. 'Good,' I muttered. 'That's good.'

There was a little pause.

'So,' he said, clearly having moved on from our moment of sharing. 'Is it a grave?'

'I still don't know.'

'Is it really old?'

'I think it's from the war.' I reached out and picked up the sweetheart pin that was propped up on my laptop. 'Your granny and Jackie and I found this.'

'It's an American flag,' he said, looking interested. 'There were lots of Americans here in the war.'

'There were.'

His eyes gleamed. 'Is one of them buried in your garden?'

'I hope not,' I said. 'Urgh.'

My phone pinged and I picked it up. 'Speak of the devil, this is Jackie now,' I told Alex, scanning the message. 'Apparently there was a woman called Rose Henry who lived here during the war. Her husband's name was Geoffrey and their daughter was Gloria.'

'Is one of them buried in the grave?'

I shook my head. 'Geoffrey was killed early on in the war, before the Americans came.'

'What happened to Rose and Gloria?'

'They moved away, Jackie said. I don't know where to, but I expect we can find out.'

Alex did a little jig on his chair. 'We could ask someone. Ages ago at my junior school I had to do a project on the war and what people did. That's how I know about the Americans.'

'We could. Though I don't expect there are many people who remember the war now.'

He frowned. 'No, they'd be too old. Unless they were very

young during the war, and then they probably wouldn't remember anyway.'

'Exactly. But we could find birth and death and marriage certificates, I think. That might help.'

Alex put his fingers on the table again. 'We can make their family tree.'

'Maybe.'

'Unless Rose and Gloria went to live in America. Loads of women did that. They married the Americans and they all went off together to New York on the same boat.' He frowned again. 'Maybe not all on the same boat. But loads of them went.'

'It could be harder to find them if they did that,' I said, impressed at his knowledge. 'But I know where we could start.'

'Where?'

'Google.'

Chapter 22

Gloria

It took my mother precisely two days to set up the Honeyford Happiness Group. I was astonished and impressed but very reluctant to come along to the inaugural meeting, even though she begged me to join them.

'I don't want to talk about death,' I said, though what I really meant was that I wanted to go down to the village and see if Jerome was around because I'd only seen him at a distance since our evening picnic on the hill, which had been every bit as wonderful as I'd hoped it would be. I was desperate for some time with him. If I was in Margery's front room, I would be even more unlikely to see him.

'Gloria, stop being so grumpy,' Mother said. 'She's being so grumpy, Dad.'

Grandpa was here again. He was back and forth from London more often now the Americans were really settled in, though he'd never tell me what he was doing, which rankled. Today he'd arrived before breakfast so he'd joined us at the table but he was only drinking tea.

'Why are you being grumpy, Gloria?' he said, with a twinkle in his eye that told me he was joking.

'I'm not being grumpy. I just don't want to go and talk about sad stuff with a group of . . .' I stopped because I'd been about to say "old women" and nothing got my mother in a huff like her being reminded that she'd not see 40 again. 'About sad stuff,' I muttered.

'That's not the idea of it,' Mother said. 'We're not going to be sitting around crying.'

Grandpa looked interested. 'So what are you going to be doing?'

'Useful things,' Mother said. 'You know the WI are picking plants to be made into medicine – they need volunteers for that. And we can do some sewing and mending. Collecting donations for families who are struggling. Margery says we could even do some gardening as her vegetable patches need attention. And then, if while we're doing that, someone wants to share some memories or chat about how they're feeling, we can do that too.'

I actually thought that sounded like a marvellous idea. I said so, and Mother beamed with pride.

'I always think that when you're feeling gloomy, you should do something to help someone else. It always helps.'

I didn't want to point out that in those long dark days after Daddy died, she'd barely left the house, let alone thought about helping others. Because she was doing it now and she was positively glowing with excitement.

'I think it's all great,' I said. 'But I still don't want to come.'

My mother gave me a long stare. 'Well, that's a shame,' she said. 'Because Hilary Vincent is coming and you remember her daughter? Beverley?'

'Yes,' I lied, because I didn't want her to launch into an explanation of who Hilary's daughter was.

'She's home at the moment. She's a Wren. I thought you might like to speak to her. See if it's something you fancy.' She paused, taking a sip of her tea. 'If you want to join up that is.'

I looked at her in delight. 'Really?'

'Well, you're nearly eighteen.'

'Would you be all right here on your own?'

'I'm not on my own. Fran's here half the time, and so is your grandfather . . .' Grandpa raised his teacup to her and she smiled at him. 'And I'm going to be busy with the Happiness Club, of course.'

'The Wrens are a good bunch of girls,' said Grandpa approvingly. 'I've been down in Portsmouth with them recently and they're very game.'

'You've been in Portsmouth,' I said, narrowing my eyes. 'Why would you have been there?'

'Never you mind,' he said. 'What do you think about the Wrens?'

'Maybe,' I said, feeling a little bubble of excitement inside. 'Or what about the WAAF?'

'Working with planes?' Grandpa said. 'Tough job.'

'Or the ATS?'

'That's not easy, either,' he said.

'I think they're all tough jobs,' said my mother, giving Grandpa one of the looks she gave me when she wanted me to think about what I was saying. 'Look how hard poor Patty's working in the Land Army.'

'She's still got time to have fun,' I said with a chuckle.

'Ah yes,' Grandpa said. 'Speaking of Patty . . .' He put his cup down on his saucer with a clatter. 'And fun . . .'

'What about her?' I said, popping the last of my toast into my mouth.

'I wanted to have a word about her. And the Jamaicans.'

'How do you know about that?' I glared at my mother who shrugged.

'Fran was talking about it,' she said. 'I didn't know it was a secret.'

'It's not a secret.' I looked at Grandpa. 'What about Patty and the Jamaicans.'

'I heard there was a dance at the base?'

'Apparently.'

'I don't want you mixing with those lads, Gloria.'

I rolled my eyes. 'So, I'm not to get too friendly with the Americans, and I'm not to mix with the Jamaicans?'

'Oh, Gloria,' Grandpa said.

'Who can I be friends with then?'

'You can be friends with whomever you choose,' Grandpa said patiently.

'As long as they're not American or Jamaican?'

'The Americans are fine, as you well know,' Grandpa said.

'Glad to hear it,' Mother muttered.

'You're being facetious,' Grandpa went on.

'I've not been to the Jamaican base,' I said. 'I've not got any plans to go to the Jamaican base. But Patty says they're all lovely lads. And they're practically British, anyway, aren't they? Jamaica is British.'

'Well, sort of,' Grandpa said. 'Yes and no.' He leaned back in his chair and looked at me. 'I worked in Jamaica you know.'

'I did know that, funnily enough,' I said. Now I really was being facetious. My mother shot me a warning look.

'There's a difference between us and them,' Grandpa went on. 'Between we British folk and the people from the colonies. A hierarchy.'

'What about the Americans?'

'Well, that's different again,' he said. 'We're allies.'

'Jamaica is an ally.'

'Gloria, do you understand what I'm saying to you?'

I was beginning to understand what he was saying and I wasn't sure I liked it one tiny bit. I looked at my mother, who was regarding Grandpa with a curious and somewhat disdainful expression on her face, and then – to keep the peace really – I nodded.

The grandfather clock in the hall donged loudly and we all jumped.

'I must be off,' Grandpa said. 'But don't forget what I said, Gloria.'

I wanted to point out that really he hadn't said anything at all. 'Don't go to the Jamaican base?' I said sweetly. 'All right then.'

Grandpa gave me a hard stare, then he picked up his hat and put it on.

'I'll let you know when I'm next in the area, Rose,' he said to my mother, kissing her on the cheek. 'I might be around for the summer fair, actually. Could try to persuade Delphine to come along.'

'Not much hope of that,' said my mother.

'It's worth a try.'

He nodded to me. 'Goodbye, Gloria,' he said. 'Behave yourself.'

'Always,' I lied.

We heard him leave through the front door and my mother made a face. 'He's awful about the Jamaicans,' she said. 'He's always said they're workshy. My mother said that's not true at all.'

'That's what Corporal Perkins said about the Black GIs,' I said. 'But the only time I saw them all together, he was the one lazing about while Eugene and Jerome built the sentry box, just the two of them.'

'Hmm,' said Mother. 'How is Jerome?'

'I've not seen him since our picnic and that was days and days ago,' I said miserably. 'He's always busy with Waldo.'

'Really?' Mother's eyes flashed with mischief. 'Why don't you go and get ready, and maybe I can have a chat with Waldo.'

'Get ready for what?'

'For Happiness Club.' She looked at me, her eyes wide. 'You are coming, I presume?'

'Gosh you're sneaky.'

She smiled. 'Nonsense. Run and get washed and dressed. Go on.'

Knowing there was very little point in arguing, I dragged myself up from the table, and headed upstairs to get ready for Happiness Club, wondering how on earth I'd managed to agree to going when I didn't actually remember saying those words.

Mind you, it would be interesting to meet Beverley and find

out about being a Wren. Maybe I could sail off on a ship and have adventures? Though I remembered being slightly queasy when Mother had taken me on a rowing boat in Pevensey Bay one summer, so perhaps I'd be better in the ATS after all.

But what was important was that Mother seemed fine with me going. I had no need to worry that she was going to fall apart, or be lonely. It was exciting. Suddenly my future, which had seemed small and uninspiring, spread out in front of me.

Dressed and hair brushed, I dashed downstairs and found Waldo in the hallway.

'Gloria,' he said. 'Rose asked me to tell you to meet her at Margery's.'

'She's gone without me?' I said, a bit put-out. 'Thank you for letting me know.'

'And I thought you might be interested to know that Private Scott is free all afternoon,' he added. 'In case you were at a loose end.'

I turned to look at him, feeling my cheeks redden, and I touched the little stars and stripes badge I had pinned to my chest. 'Perhaps you might let Private Scott know that I'll be on the green at lunchtime,' I said. 'If he'd like to find me there.'

'Will do,' Waldo said. 'Enjoy the first meeting of the Honeyford Happiness Club.'

'Do you know,' I said, my spirits boosted, 'I think I might.'

Chapter 23

Philippa

Despite my confidence in the power of Google, I couldn't find Gloria and Rose.

Well, I could find them, but I didn't really discover anything that was remotely helpful and I had to subscribe to a load of genealogy websites to do it, which irritated me. I made a note on my calendar to cancel all the free trials and carried on searching.

First of all, I found Rose and Geoffrey Henry's wedding certificate. They'd married in 1922 in the church in Honeyford, when Rose was 23 and Geoffrey was 35 – he'd been married before, I discovered, and he was a widower when he and Rose wed. And I found Gloria's birth certificate, which told me she was born in 1926.

And then, nothing.

I sat at the kitchen table, staring at my laptop screen, doing sums in my head. Jackie had told me the GIs arrived in 1943, so Rose would have been 44 by then – possibly on the verge of being too old to get swept off her feet and have a baby. But Gloria, the teenage daughter, full of hormones and excitement? Well, she'd have been 17 when the Americans arrived. She was my prime candidate for having got pregnant by a GI.

But could I find a birth certificate for any baby? Nope. Nor a wedding certificate nor a death certificate for our Gloria. Or a baby. If there was a baby, of course.

So it was a dead end. Disappointed, I messaged Jackie telling her I'd hit a stumbling block, and asking if she had any suggestions. While I waited for her to reply, I saw Marco walk past the window. Of course, that wasn't odd in itself, because he was running round all over the place at the moment, getting things ready for the opening. Though he was quite subdued and not nearly as excited as I'd expected him to be and something about the slump of his shoulders as he passed the window put me on edge.

I shut my laptop, and went outside expecting him to be rearranging the patio heaters, or looking at the way we'd put the tables on the pergola. But he wasn't. Instead, he was halfway down the garden, heading for the bluebell wood.

The bluebell bulbs we'd ordered had arrived, and they were piled up with the equipment by the back door. Marco had barely given them more than a cursory glance when they'd been delivered and he wasn't carrying anything now, so I wondered what he was up to.

'Marco?' I called, but he was too far away and he couldn't hear me, so I followed him.

I walked down the sloping grass, towards the trees and there he was, sitting in the little hollow near the stones.

'Marco?' I said. 'What are you doing here?'

He looked up at me, and his face was so sad, it almost broke my heart. 'What's wrong?'

'It looks like a grave,' he said. 'I can't think about anything else.'

'Oh, love.' I sat down next to him and took his hand. 'We don't know for sure.'

'We chose this spot to remember our babies, because it's quiet and still and the perfect place to come and sit and think,' he said. 'And I can't help wondering if someone else felt that way, too.'

'Perhaps.'

He leaned his head back against the trunk of the tree. 'I thought I was doing okay,' he said, sounding genuinely surprised. 'I thought I'd made my peace with it.'

'Me too.'

'I was so excited about the restaurant and even the ups and downs with the ceiling, and Vanessa's ankle, and the pergola and everything, even that didn't dent my enthusiasm.' He rubbed his forehead. 'But this? This has knocked me for six, Phil.'

I sighed. 'That's how I felt with Alex when we first met him. I saw you getting close to him and it just made me feel awful, even though he's a sweetheart.'

'Maybe we're not as healed as we thought.'

I put my head on his shoulder. 'Maybe we never will be.'

'I don't know what to do,' Marco said eventually. 'This was our new beginning. We were supposed to be starting the next phase of our lives together but instead I've got a constant reminder of all the sadness that went before.'

I opened my mouth to speak but he'd not finished.

'I know I said I didn't want to think about this,' he went on. 'But I can't stop thinking about it. Every time I go out on the terrace, I think about it. And that makes me think of our babies and what might have been.'

'I understand. Maybe planting the bluebells . . .'

But he shook his head. 'I can't deal with opening the restaurant with this hanging over us.'

'What are you saying?'

'I'm saying, we can't open a restaurant in a graveyard. I don't want to do it.'

I felt cold. 'But, Marco,' I said. 'This is your dream. Our dream. It's all arranged. You've given Lauren a job, and found a sous chef, and built a bloody pergola. We're opening in two weeks.'

But he looked straight ahead, his jaw set. 'I can't do it, Philippa. Not if there is a grave in the garden. I want to cancel the opening.'

176

'For a little while?' I said, my voice shaky. 'You want to post-pone?'

'I want to cancel it for good.'

'And then what?' I couldn't quite believe what he was saying.

He shrugged. 'Sell? Go back to London? I don't know. But I don't want to live in a house with grave in the garden.'

'It might not be a grave,' I said, a little desperately. 'What if I find out what happened?'

Marco looked round at me, his eyes damp with tears. 'It's impossible to find out, Philippa. Not unless we dig it up. And I'm not doing that. No way.'

'God, no,' I said, appalled. 'That's not the answer.'

We stayed quiet for a moment. I felt like we were teetering on the brink of something. Something huge and uncontrollable. And I knew – I absolutely knew – that my sweet, sensitive, kind husband needed me to understand what he was saying. And I did understand because I'd felt the same horror when we'd found the little cherub. But I also understood money and I knew without a shadow of a doubt that if we didn't open the restaurant, we'd lose everything.

'Marco,' I began, my mind full of figures and projections. 'Sweetheart. We're in an awful position here. And it's not like we can ask anyone for help.' I tried to laugh but it came out a bit squeaky. 'I don't expect many other couples have stumbled on a grave in their back garden. But I really think if we just talk it all through, we can find a way to live with this.'

'Philippa, you're not listening to me. I don't want to do it. I'm not going to do it.' He got up and brushed his trousers clean. 'I'm going to call Graham.'

I looked up at him blankly. 'Who's Graham?'

'From Hodgson and Dobbs.' Then when I still didn't know he sighed. 'The estate agent.'

'No,' I said, scrambling to my feet. 'Absolutely not.'

We stood facing one another. Marco looked sad and broken. I suspected I just looked angry.

'I know you like to pretend that you're the creative mind and you don't understand the business side of things,' I said, feeling my pulse beginning to pound in my temple. 'But you do understand. You're a clever man. You know that if we walk away now we'll be left with nothing. We've sunk all our savings into this, Marco. Every penny.'

But he just shrugged. 'I don't care.' He looked down at the stones on the ground. 'This is bigger than money.'

'We couldn't afford to buy in London again,' I warned. 'Not now.'

'We'll get something smaller. A one-bedroom flat. We'll make it work.'

'Marco,' I said, begging now. 'Marco, we can't give all this up for a one-bedroom flat.'

He looked at me. 'Why not?' he said sounding cold and calm. 'It's not like we need space for a family, is it?'

His bleak words made me gasp.

'I'm going to phone Graham,' he said.

Then he turned and walked back towards the house, leaving me in total shock.

I stayed where I was for a little while, watching him get smaller. I desperately wanted to follow him, and shake him out of this awful fog he was in. To make him understand that this couldn't be the end of his dreams. But I was still angry and I knew we'd only argue if I went back to the house now.

So instead, I walked the other way, up towards the drive and the funny brick building at the entrance, trying not to think about how Marco had suggested selling ice creams from there in the summer. It wasn't exactly the right spot for it, was it? Overlooking what may or may not be a grave. I sighed. Perhaps Marco was right. Perhaps we couldn't open a restaurant here.

But no. No. There had to be another way. I walked out on to the pavement and followed the road down to the village, thinking.

My heart was telling me that the memorial we'd found was for a baby. But I could see that was exactly what I'd think because of my history with baby loss. It was just an awful coincidence that it was in the same spot we'd chosen to remember our own babies.

If I stepped back for a second, and thought logically, then I could also see that the cherub couldn't possibly mark a grave. After all, if you were secretly burying someone in your garden then why would you mark it? And if it wasn't secret, it would have been on the deeds.

If I could convince Marco that chances were, it wasn't a grave, then perhaps that would give me time to really get to the bottom of what it was. I'd found the sweetheart pin, and I'd found Gloria Henry, who was the perfect age to have had a romance with a GI. Or perhaps it was her mother whose name I'd forgotten – Rose was it? Perhaps it was Rose Henry who'd fallen for an American. Maybe one who'd been killed – weren't lots of Americans involved in D-Day? It was totally plausible that the memorial was for him.

I stopped walking halfway to the village, my mind made up. I'd go back to the house, make Marco see sense and beg him to let me continue my investigations before he made up his mind. And if we had to postpone the opening by a few weeks, then so be it. It was better than walking away.

I turned round and began marching back up the hill, calmer now and more determined.

When I got back to the house – a little sweaty and out of breath – I walked round the side and in through the back entrance.

'Marco?' I called. 'Marco?'

He wasn't in our part of the house, so I went back into the hall and through to the hotel.

'Marco?' I pushed open the door to the restaurant and saw him standing in the middle of the room, underneath the new ceiling. And in his arms, looking just as beautiful as she always did, was Vanessa.

Chapter 24

Gloria

Patty and I were in the river. It was another gorgeous day and Patty had time off, so we'd grabbed our bathing suits and gone to our favourite spot for a dip.

Along the stream, we could hear the shouts of the children paddling near the ford, but we preferred to be near a bend in the river, where the water was deeper and we could float.

I lay on my back in the water, feeling the sun on my face.

'Tell me everything about your afternoon with Jerome,' Patty said. 'What did you talk about?'

I waved my hands through the water slowly, enjoying the feeling of the cool ripples. 'We didn't do much talking.'

Patty shrieked and splashed me. 'You scarlet woman, you!'

I laughed, paddling to move away from her.

'He's so nice,' I said with a contented sigh. 'He's funny, and clever. He was telling me about America. He says he wants to get involved in politics when the war is over.'

'Your grandpa would approve of that,' Patty said.

I wasn't sure that Grandpa would approve. Not after the way he'd spoken to Jerome, and all the things he'd said about the GIs and the Jamaicans. In fact, I wasn't entirely sure anyone would approve. Except my mother, of course, who was so hopelessly romantic that she didn't see any obstacles in our way. And Captain Waldo, who seemed to be just the same.

'Maybe,' I said. 'It feels a little bit . . .' I paused staring up into the blue sky and listening to the birds singing overheard. 'Like we're doing something wrong.'

'Wrong?' Patty stood up in the water and shook herself like a dog. 'I'm going all wrinkly, I'm going to dry off.'

I did the same. 'Perhaps wrong isn't the word. It's more like we need to keep things a secret.'

'I think that's just sensible,' Patty said, wringing her hair out. 'Everyone's a little bit hot and bothered about it all. Didn't you say there was a to-do on the bus?'

'There was a to-do,' I said with a grin. 'Tempers are rising.'

'It's the heat,' Patty said, fanning herself. 'It makes everyone edgy.'

'Perhaps. But now George has put his sign up at the pub and Jerome said some of the white GIs are awfully annoyed about it. They don't like Eugene playing piano, either.'

'It's not just George who's got a sign,' said Patty. 'Apparently there are similar signs at the Queen's Head on the Cirencester road, and on the Crown at the other end of the village.'

'Really? That's quite good. Safety in numbers, perhaps?'

'It is and it isn't good.' Patty lay down on her towel. 'Like Jerome said, people are awfully cross about it. Not just Americans. Some of the locals don't like it either.'

'Jennifer Lacey thinks George is terrible,' I told her. 'She thinks we should go along with the American race laws, because it's better that way. Quite a few people round here treat the Black GIs differently.'

'I've heard there was a fight at the Crown,' said Patty. 'Black GIs and some villagers taking on white GIs and other locals.'

'Where are you hearing all this?' I looked down at her, as she lay with her arm over her face, shielding it from the sun.

181

'Oh, you know?' she said casually. 'From Victor.'

I prodded her with my big toe. 'Who's Victor?'

'One of the Jamaicans. He's had a few run-ins with the Americans himself. He's got no time for them at all.'

'Patty!' I plonked myself down next to her. 'You've been letting me rabbit on about Jerome and you haven't so much as mentioned this Victor!'

She grinned and sat up. 'Ohmygoodness, Gloria,' she said, her words running together in her eagerness to get them out. 'He's wonderful. He's so big and strong and funny – oh Lord he had me screaming with laughter – and such a good dancer.'

'I can't believe you're only telling me this now,' I said. 'Did he kiss you?'

Patty sat up straighter, a prim expression on her face. 'A lady never tells.'

'He did! He kissed you!'

She laughed. 'He did,' she said. 'It was lovely. He wrapped me in his arms and I never wanted to let go.'

'Oh, my, Patty,' I teased. 'I've never heard you gush like this. You were never this doe-eyed over William Martindale.'

'Well, no . . .' She sighed. 'Poor William.'

'Nor Paul Tomkins.'

Patty scoffed. 'No.'

'Nor Christopher Higgins.'

'Gloria!' Patty giggled. 'Stop making me sound like I've had a string of boyfriends.'

'I'm just saying you've never been this smitten with a boy before.'

'Well, that's the thing, isn't it?' Patty said. 'Victor isn't a boy. He's a man.'

'Oooh!' I said, laughing. 'Are you seeing him again?'

'Later on today,' she said. 'He's coming to the village. Come and meet him. He's so lovely.'

'I will!' I said. But I frowned. 'He's from Jamaica?'

'Yes, I said that.'

'So he's Black like Jerome?'

'Obviously.' She tutted. 'That's why he's not a fan of segregation.'

I hugged my bare legs and rested my chin on my knees. 'Will that be a problem?' I said, thoughtfully, remembering what Grandpa had said. 'Will anyone mind?'

'No,' Patty said immediately. Then she paused. 'Will they?'

'Jamaica is a British colony, though, isn't it? It's part of the empire?' I said, just as I'd said to Grandpa.

'Yes.' Patty nodded. 'Of course. So that means Victor is British.'

'Yes,' I agreed uncertainly.

There was a small silence as we both thought about it.

'It's odd, isn't it?' Patty said eventually. 'I don't really understand what it's all about.'

'Jerome says the race laws in America are similar to what the Nazis are doing in Germany.'

Patty looked horrified. 'Surely not?'

I shrugged. 'That's what he said.'

'Maybe he's confused.'

'Maybe.'

I closed my eyes, trying to picture the map of the world on the wall of my classroom, with all the countries coloured pink to show the British Empire.

'Where exactly is Jamaica?' I said.

'In the Caribbean.'

'Which is where?'

'Did you not learn anything at school?' Patty said with a tut. 'Or was your head just filled with Agatha Christie novels.'

I rolled my eyes. 'Where is it?'

Patty picked up one of the smooth, round stones that lined the riverbank. 'This is North America,' she said, putting it down on the grass. She picked up another smaller stone. 'Then this is Mexico . . .' she put it beneath the larger rock. 'And . . .' Her knowledge failed her. 'Some other countries. And Panama! Where the canal is.'

'Right,' I said.

'And this . . .' Patty put down another big stone. 'Is South America.'

'Okay.' I nodded. 'None of this helps me to know where Jamaica is.'

She gave me a good-natured shove and jabbed her finger on the grass next to the smaller stone. 'Round here somewhere.'

'And where's New York?' I squinted at the stones wishing I'd paid more attention in geography.

'Here.' Patty touched the side of one of the top rocks. 'And we are . . .' she picked up another stone and stretched out as far as she could then dropped it on the grass '. . . all the way over here.'

'That's far,' I said.

'It is.'

I felt a sudden despair.

'Maybe we'll never see them again,' I said bleakly. 'Victor and Jerome. They're not going to be here forever, are they? They'll stay in England for a while and then they'll go off to France and do whatever awful dangerous thing they're training for and that'll be it.'

'Gloria,' Patty began.

'And if they're lucky, they'll be safe, and then they'll get to go home to Jamaica, or to New York, while we stay here. And if they're not . . .' I swallowed. 'My father didn't come home, Patty. And nor did poor William Martindale. Nor Mr Fingal's Lawrence, or Millicent's Sidney.'

I picked up the stone that Patty had used for North America and threw it into the river where it sank with a plop.

'Gloria, don't get upset over something that might never happen,' Patty said. She took my hand. 'Listen, you know as well as I do that we can't plan for our futures now. Who knows what's going to happen?' She shuddered. 'Some of the stories

184

the girls from London have told me about the bombs down there, well. It doesn't bear thinking about. And you've lost your dad. And there's so much sadness, and pain, and death, everywhere we go.'

I nodded.

'So, I think if we get a chance of happiness for today, then we should grab it with both hands and hang on to it tightly. Even if it is just for today.'

I looked at my friend, with her freckles and her hair drying in a frizzy halo around her head, and thought she was maybe the wisest person I'd ever met. 'I think you're right,' I said.

'Well, obviously.' Patty grinned. 'Come on then. I've only got a couple of hours before I need to meet Victor and it's going to take me at least half of that to do something with my hair.'

She got to her feet and then she held her hand out to me and I got up too.

Arm in arm we went back to Patty's house in the village. Fran made us both egg sandwiches – she kept chickens now – while we sat in the sun in the garden to dry our hair.

'Your mum's like a new woman,' she said, handing me a plate.

'She is,' I said. 'I don't want to jinx it, but she does seem to have turned a corner.' I picked up my sandwich.

'I'm glad,' Fran said. She put her hand on my shoulder. 'I think having you home has helped.'

I was surprised, but quite pleased. 'Do you really?'

'Of course. Her rattling around in that big house, all alone for yonks won't have done her any good. It's your dad's house, isn't it? All his ancestors staring down at her from those paintings in the halls. She never felt like she belonged. But now she's got you back with her, and you're in your own bit of Honeyford and it must feel more like home.'

I made a face. 'I've been thinking about joining up,' I said. 'Do you think I shouldn't leave her?'

'A year ago, I'd have said no,' Fran said. She looked thoughtful.

185

'But, actually I think she'll be fine. She's got me and her friends at the Happiness Club. She's not alone anymore.'

I was relieved. 'She's got good friends,' I said with a grin. 'And Captain Waldo being around isn't doing her any harm, either.'

'Well, indeed,' said Fran with a smile. 'They've rather hit it off, haven't they? I'm very pleased for her. She deserves to be happy.'

'She does.'

'Do you think we've got time to do something with this skirt?' Patty said, appearing by the back door. 'It's so threadbare it's positively indecent.'

Fran squinted at the skirt she was holding up. 'We could pick apart the seams and put in another panel,' she said. 'But not today. I've not got time.'

Patty made a face. 'I've got nothing else to wear, Mum.'

'Rubbish,' said Fran. 'You've got plenty.'

'You can wear this if you like,' I said, pulling at my frock. It was a pretty yellow summer dress with polka dots and a white collar. I had plenty of clothes, and because I'd been away at school I'd barely worn half of my wardrobe. Make do and mend hadn't really affected me.

'What will you wear?' Patty asked, looking me up and down. 'Do you think that colour will suit me? It might make me sallow.'

'Not now you're brown as a berry from being outdoors in the sun all day every day. Try it, if you like.'

'You could wear my gingham dress. That'll look nice on you. I would wear it except it's what I wore the last time I met Victor.'

'I don't care what I wear,' I said with a laugh. 'Victor will only have eyes for you, anyway.'

We finished our sandwiches and went to get changed. Patty was all jittery and it made me laugh because she was usually so sure of herself.

'You really like him, don't you?' I said, pinning up one of her curls.

'I don't know yet,' she said primly. Then she grinned at me in the mirror. 'But I think I could.'

I put the final pin in her hair. 'There, that looks pretty,' I said. 'I can't wait to meet him.'

'I hope you like him.'

'I will.'

She put her hand on mine on her shoulder. 'When can I meet Jerome?'

'At the summer dance, I hope.'

Patty clapped her hands. 'Look at us, with our sweethearts. It's like a fairy tale.'

'Does that make me the wicked stepmother?' Fran said, sticking her head round the door. 'I thought you said you were meeting him at six o'clock, Pat? It's five past already.'

'Oh Lord!' Patty jumped up. 'Come on, Gloria. Let's go.'

Giggling like schoolgirls, we ran along the street to the pub where Patty had arranged to meet Victor. We sat on a table outside and she went in to get some drinks.

'It's busy,' she said, coming out again with two orange juices. 'There are some GIs in there.'

'White GIs?' I asked. The sign was still up, and there were no military police outside.

'Nope.' Patty looked pleased. 'There's that Stanley Silver and a few others. Playing darts with Walter Garside and that lot and looking like old mates.'

'That's nice.'

'Yes.' Patty looked up at the clock on the church. 'I wonder where Victor's got to?'

'He's probably waiting for the bus,' I pointed out. 'None have come past since we've been here.'

'That's true.' She looked relieved.

We drank our drinks and chatted. Across the other side of the green I saw Perkins and another GI walk past. They were talking animatedly and I felt a sort of crackle of nervous energy from them. When they got closer to the pub, they both paused and looked over. I kept my eyes on Patty and pretended I'd not noticed them, and after a little while, much to my relief, they walked away.

The bus came and went, and Victor didn't appear. Patty was jiggling her leg up and down and drumming her fingers on the table.

'Patty, stop it,' I said.

'Sorry.'

'Maybe something's come up,' I said. 'An emergency at the base or something.'

'Perhaps.'

'He wouldn't just not turn up without a good reason. You said yourself he's a nice chap.'

'Well, I thought he was a nice chap.' She pursed her lips. 'Perhaps I've got him all wrong.'

Another bus drove past, and we both watched it go by, without speaking.

'We should just go,' Patty said after a minute. 'I don't want to make a fool of myself.'

My heart ached for her. 'We could give it another five minutes,' I suggested. 'Or we could get another drink? Make a night of it? Go home and raid my mother's gin?'

Patty gave a little laugh without any humour in it.

'I suppose.' She sighed. 'I really thought he might be Mr Right, you know?'

'I know.'

'Do you think your mother would mind if we raided her gin?'

'I can't imagine she'll even notice.'

'Come on then.' She picked up her bag and stood up and as she did, there was a shout from the other side of the green.

'Someone! I need help!'

'What's going on?' I said, narrowing my eyes through the twilight.

But Patty was already off, sprinting down the steps and across the grass. 'It's Victor!' she shouted over her shoulder. 'Victor!'

I paused for a second, and then I turned the other way, pushing open the door to the pub.

'Someone needs help!' I shouted. 'George! Come on! Private Silver! We need you!'

Then I spun round and followed Patty. She was on her knees, next to a man in uniform who was lying still on the grass. Another man was next to him, his RAF blue jacket covered in blood.

'Oh, bloody hell,' I breathed. 'Patty?'

'Victor?' she was sobbing, cradling the man on the ground. 'Victor, please.'

'What happened?' I asked.

The other airman looked shaken. 'I found him by the bus stop,' he said. 'He's in a bad way.'

'Has he been hit by a car?' I asked.

He shook his head. 'I think someone's attacked him.'

Patty was holding Victor's head in her lap. His eye was swollen shut and his face was bloodied but I could hear him breathing, which was a relief because frankly when I'd first seen him flat out on the ground, I'd worried he was dead.

Behind me, I heard George shouting for Private Silver to come quick, and people were coming out of their houses to see what was going on. I tugged Patty's arm.

'Let them help him,' I said. 'Let Private Silver see him.'

She stood up and I put my arms round her as she cried. 'Who's done this?' she said. 'Why on earth would anyone do such an awful thing?'

Chapter 25

Philippa

They didn't spring apart like cheating lovers did in films. They didn't move at all at first, which felt like a bit of a kick in the teeth, frankly. Marco was hugging Vanessa, patting her smooth, tanned back. She had her forehead pressed to his chest.

'Marco,' I said. I felt dizzy. 'Marco!'

This time they did move, slowly. Vanessa looked upset. Marco looked guilty.

'Philippa,' he said. 'Vanessa was just . . .'

It had been a difficult day. An emotional, horrible, difficult day. I stared at my husband who still – STILL – had his arm round another woman. And I lost my temper.

'What?' I demanded. 'What was Vanessa just doing?'

'I was upset,' Vanessa said. 'Marco was comforting me, that's all.' She moved away from him, but for some reason that made me even more annoyed.

'Why are you here?' I said to Vanessa. 'Why are you always here?'

She opened her mouth and then shut it again as I carried on. 'You turn up unannounced all the time,' I said. 'In your tiny shorts, with your hair all . . .' I gestured wildly round my head, knowing I was being utterly unfair and not caring one bit. 'And now you're embracing my husband in my house?'

'Philippa, that's enough,' Marco said. He looked absolutely furious. 'You have gone too far.'

'Oh I'm just getting started,' I said. I glared at Vanessa. 'What is this? Is it that you've got a second chance to be a mum now you've got Alex, and you need a dad to add to your family?'

Vanessa lifted her chin and looked straight at me, and I saw sympathy in her eyes, which surprised me enough that I stopped talking for a second.

'I'm going to go.' She took a step towards me, and lifted her hand as if she was going to touch me, then clearly thought better of it. 'I'm going to go, but I will see you later and I will tell you everything.'

I ignored her. She stood there for a second, looking at me, and then she turned and walked out of the restaurant, leaving Marco and me alone.

'What's going on, Marco?' I said. 'First you want to sell the house, now I find you all over another woman?'

'You're being ridiculous, Philippa.'

'Me? I'm being ridiculous?'

'Vanessa was upset about her ankle, and not being able to do so much with Alex, and I gave her a hug, that's all.'

'But why is she here?' I growled. 'Why is she always here?'

'Because she likes us?' Marco shrugged. 'Because she's a nice person? I don't know.'

'And you were at her house the other day,' I pointed out. 'Dropping in to see her.'

'So were you,' he said, not unreasonably.

I clenched my fists. 'I went to talk to her about the grave.'

'I went to talk to her about Alex.'

'Oh did you?' I was so far down into my anger that anything Marco said now was going to trigger me more. 'You and Vanessa and Alex. One lovely happy family, eh?'

Marco looked at me in disgust. 'Don't,' he said.

'This was supposed to be our new start.' I spread my arms out wide. 'This was supposed to be the beginning of a new chapter. And now you've ruined it.'

'It's all my fault, is it?'

'Well it's not mine.'

We stared at one another, my breathing ragged.

'Did you call the estate agent?'

'No.' Marco pulled his shoulders back. 'I didn't call him because I'm going to wait until I'm back.'

'Back from where?'

'Ayr.'

'Ayr? Why are you going to Ayr?'

'Because I need a break. And my parents need a hand in the shop because Antonia's off sick.'

'You need a break?' I said, shaking my head in disbelief. 'From what, exactly?'

'From this.' He gestured to the restaurant and to the pile of Harvey's tools that were still in the corner. 'From that.' He pointed out to the garden in the vague direction of the bluebell wood.

'From me?' I said.

He looked at me, but he didn't answer.

'Marco?'

'There's a train from Cheltenham at three,' he said. 'I'll go and pack a bag, then I'll get a taxi.'

'Isn't this a bit of an over-reaction?'

'I told you I can't be here. You're not listening.'

I rubbed my head. 'I don't understand,' I said, sounding desperate. 'I don't understand what's happening. We've been through so much together, and now you're walking away?'

'I just need a break,' Marco said again.

'Is this because of Vanessa?'

He looked at me and shook his head. 'Now who's over-reacting?'

And then, without saying another word, he walked past me and out of the restaurant.

I didn't want to say goodbye, so like a kid, I went upstairs to one of the bedrooms in the house that wasn't being used yet. They were all empty with just faded marks on the carpets and walls to show where the furniture once stood. I lay down on the dusty floor and stewed for a while, going over everything in my head while my annoyance faded. The grave and Marco's reaction to it. Our baby losses. The bluebells that still hadn't been planted. Alex. Vanessa. The way I'd spoken to her. Marco had been right. I'd crossed a line there and I knew I needed to apologise. Just not yet. I couldn't do it yet.

I stared up at the patchy ceiling and wondered what on earth I was going to do.

Downstairs I heard an engine, and I went to the window to see a car pulling up outside and Marco coming out. I watched as he put his bag into the boot of the car and then looked up at the house for a second. Looking for me, I thought.

Suddenly, I was off and running down the stairs so fast I almost missed my footing. I flew out of the front door, and caught Marco just before he got into the car.

'Are you coming back?' I asked, out of breath. 'You are coming back, aren't you?'

'I'm coming back,' he said. 'Of course I am.'

Then he got into the car, shut the door and off he went, and I burst into tears, partly sad that he'd gone, partly confused by what had happened, and partly just feeling bloody horrible about everything.

Still sniffing and wiping away tears, I went back inside and through the house to the back door where the bluebell bulbs were. Marco's brother, Enzo, was a real fitness freak. The type who ran marathons for fun and went for a swim as a hangover cure. Not that he was ever hungover of course. He always said that the best way to feel better was to go outside and get sweaty. For years I'd ignored him, thinking the best way to feel better was to eat a load of chocolate and drink a bottle of wine. But now I wondered if he might have a point. So I went and changed into a pair of scruffy shorts and an old T-shirt, then I spent a good half hour looking for the key to the shed, which I eventually tracked down in the pocket of Marco's jeans in the laundry basket.

Already a bit out of breath and slightly sweaty before I'd even really started, but not yet feeling better, I got the wheelbarrow out of the shed, loaded it up with the bulbs and everything I needed, and then set off across the lawn to the wood.

Twice I hit a divot and tipped the wheelbarrow over, spilling everything on to the lawn, and had to start again. The second time nearly pushed me over the edge.

'Bollocks to it,' I muttered under my breath, as I threw everything back into the wheelbarrow. 'Stupid bloody bluebells.'

But I balanced the spade on top and carried on down to the wood. And there, keeping my eyes averted from the memorial, and staying well away from that part of the garden, I planted five hundred sodding bluebell bulbs. Pushing them into the earth with the very useful tool the man at the garden centre had sold us – and which I was hugely grateful for.

It took me three hours. Three whole hours. By the time I'd finished, I was sweating buckets, I was absolutely filthy, and, I had to admit, I did feel a bit better.

I put the final bulb into the ground and straightened up, feeling like I'd achieved something. Perhaps Honeyford wasn't working out as planned, but these bluebells would grow and flower, whatever happened.

At least, I hoped they would.

A shout from the house made me look up and for a second my heart lifted. Was it Marco?

But no. I squinted into the light. It was Jackie.

She came down the garden towards me as I pushed the wheelbarrow back to the shed.

'All right?' she said.

I didn't speak. I parked the wheelbarrow and went to open the shed.

'I saw Vanessa.' Jackie picked up the spade and brought it over to me.

'Is she okay?'

'She's fine. But she wanted me to come and check on you.'

'Why?'

'Because she didn't think you were fine.'

I felt tears prick my eyelids. 'I'm fine.' I pushed the wheelbarrow into the shed and slammed the door shut.

Jackie reached out and touched my arm.

'Where's Marco?'

'Gone,' I muttered. 'Gone to see his parents in Scotland.' I sighed. 'He won't stay here with the grave in the garden.'

'Still think it's a grave?' Jackie said.

I shook my head. 'No, not really. But it looks like a grave and that's bad enough.' My voice wobbled. 'Marco says he wants to sell the house when he gets back. He says he can't open a restaurant knowing people are looking out over a grave while they eat.'

'What if we make a real effort and try to work out what happened here?' Jackie asked. 'That's the other reason I came actually, to tell you I've had a few ideas about where to look.' She smiled. 'Vanessa's been thinking about it too. I wanted to invite you to the museum tomorrow to make a start.'

'I couldn't find anything when I looked,' I said. 'It's too hard.'

'Hard, but not impossible. We might have to think outside the box a bit, but we'll get there.' She paused. 'Unless you want to sell too?'

I shook my head. 'If we sell, we'll lose everything.' I swallowed. 'Maybe even each other.'

Jackie regarded me for a second.

'Vanessa doesn't fancy Marco, you know?'

'She was all over him when I walked in,' I said, feeling my irritation rising again.

'She was upset because Alex had been a bit teenagery and had told her she was being a rubbish granny. Marco was just being nice.'

I pinched my lips together, feeling more than a little ashamed of myself.

'But why did she come here when she was upset?' I said. 'She's always sniffing around.'

Jackie laughed. 'I can't believe you've not worked it out,' she said.

A little put out, I tutted. 'Not worked what out?'

'It's not Marco Vanessa's got the hots for, it's Harvey.'

Chapter 26

Gloria

Victor didn't die. Thank goodness. But he was very poorly for a few days and everyone was terribly worried. He was taken to the big hospital in Cheltenham and Patty sat by his bedside every minute she could.

At first, everyone in the village tutted a bit and said things like 'isn't it dreadful' but no one really believed he'd been attacked, because things like that just didn't happen in Honeyford.

'It's bound to have been a car,' people said. 'It's so hard to see in the blackouts.'

It hadn't been properly dark when whatever happened, happened, but that didn't seem to stop people guessing.

'No one likes to think that something like this could happen on their doorsteps,' my mother said when I told her what everyone was saying. 'They're just trying to make sense of it.'

'It makes no sense at all,' I said.

On the fifth day after his "accident" Victor woke up for long enough, and he felt well enough, to talk about what had happened.

And that's when things really fell apart.

I had gone to Cheltenham to take Patty some sandwiches and

a flask of tea. I knew she was desperately worried about poor Victor, but I was worried about her, and so was Fran.

Patty was working then going straight to the hospital on the bus to see Victor every day. She'd hardly eaten and she'd barely slept and I wanted to make sure she was all right.

So I packed a little bag with some food and some clean clothes and a book I thought she might like, and set off to the hospital.

When I arrived at the ward, I found Patty sitting next to an empty bed, tears streaming down her face and my stomach lurched with fear.

'Patty,' I said. 'Where is Victor? Is he . . .? Did he . . .?'

To my relief, she shook her head. 'He's going to be all right,' she said. 'He's awake, properly, I mean. And he's talking.'

She threw herself into my arms and sobbed. 'He's going to be all right,' she said.

I stroked her hair. 'I'm so glad.'

Patty gathered herself and dried her eyes. 'They've taken him for a blood test or something,' she said. 'All the nurses are delighted.'

'I'm sure they are.'

'He'll be back in a minute. Will you wait?'

'Of course,' I said. 'I have to meet him.'

'You really do,' she said, nodding. 'Because I've decided I'm going to marry him.'

'Really?' I smiled. 'Have you told him that?'

'Not yet.' Patty dabbed her eyes with her handkerchief. 'But I normally get what I want.'

'That's true.'

I sat down on one of the chairs next to Victor's empty bed. 'Has he said anything about what happened?' I asked Patty.

'Not yet.' She made a face. 'I don't see how it could have been a car, though.'

'Me neither. Most of the people who have cars aren't driving any more now because of petrol rationing and it's hardly a busy road.'

Our speculating was interrupted as the doors to the ward were pushed open and in came Victor in a wheelchair being pushed by an adoring-looking nurse.

'You're doing ever so well,' she was saying. Victor was sitting up, his head and one arm bandaged, and still looking dreadfully battered and bruised, but he was smiling broadly and he blew Patty a kiss as he approached.

'My love,' he said.

'Has he behaved himself?' Patty asked the nurse.

She shook her head. 'Not even a tiny bit,' she said, laughing. 'But I didn't mind. It's just nice to see him awake.'

'It really is,' Patty said.

There was a bit of a kerfuffle as the nurse and Patty helped Victor to get back into bed, and the nurse fetched some tea, and we all rearranged ourselves as Patty introduced me.

'I told Gloria she had to stay to meet you, because we're going to get married,' she said matter-of-factly to Victor.

He looked at her. 'We are?'

'I think it would be for the best,' Patty said. 'Don't you?'

Victor didn't look so much as taken aback. He simply nodded. 'Absolutely. As soon as possible, I'd say.'

'Good, then that's settled.' Patty grinned. 'Now, tell us what happened. Can you remember?'

Victor leaned back against the pillows. 'Bits and pieces,' he said. His accent was unlike anything I'd heard before, low and melodic. I liked it. 'I'd been on the bus, and I got off at the stop before the village, where you'd said to get off.'

I thought it boded well for their future marriage that he was already doing what Patty told him to do. Patty obviously thought the same because she touched his hand approvingly.

'Go on.'

'That's it really. The bus drove away and I walked a few steps, then suddenly, they jumped me.'

'People?' Patty said. 'Men?'

'Yes.'

'Not a car?'

'No, it was definitely men. Two of them I think.'

'You didn't see them?' I was disappointed that he'd not got a look at whoever did this.

'They were behind me. But I heard them talking.'

'Did you recognise their voices?' Patty said. 'Were they British? Local lads?'

But Victor shook his head. 'Americans,' he said.

'Are you sure?' Patty asked.

'I'd bet my life on it.'

It took a day or so for the news to get out, but Victor told the British police what he remembered, and soon everyone was talking about it.

'I can't stop thinking about it,' Jerome said to me. 'They say it was Americans who gave him that beating.'

'That's what Victor said.' I looked at his worried face. 'But no one thinks it was you, you goose.'

We were sitting in the shade near my favourite oak tree. Jerome had spotted me sitting reading when he was driving Waldo back to the house and had sneaked away for five minutes before he needed to get back to drive someone else somewhere else.

'That's not what I'm worried about,' he said. 'I'm not worried anyone will think I hurt Victor. I'm worried he got hurt because of me. Or Eugene. Or any of us.'

'Not because of you,' I said, remembering Patty telling me that Victor had no time for the American rules. 'Because of them. The only people responsible are the people who did this.'

'Americans,' said Jerome. 'Americans who don't want white folk mixing with Black folk.'

'But Victor's not American,' I pointed out. 'He's Jamaican. And that means he's British, really. He's in the RAF for heaven's sake. Surely an American wouldn't beat up a British airman?'

'It's hard to see uniforms in the dark,' said Jerome. 'Perhaps they just didn't know he was RAF. Or perhaps they knew and they just didn't care.'

'You really think that Victor's right and it could have been GIs?'

'I know plenty who are quick with their fists,' Jerome said darkly. 'Perkins for starters.'

In a flash, I remembered Perkins and another man walking through the village on the evening Victor had been beaten.

'Surely not,' I said. 'Perkins is an idiot but surely he couldn't be so cruel?'

Jerome shrugged. 'It's possible.'

I couldn't believe it. But I accepted that Jerome knew him better than I did.

'The police will work it out,' I assured him. 'Don't worry.'

He bit his lip. 'If it was one of us,' he said. 'It'll be passed on to the MPs.'

'Right. Well, they know what they're doing, don't they? They'll deal with it.'

'They'll deal with it,' he said. 'But perhaps not in the right way.'

'What do you mean?'

'I'm just not sure justice will be done. Not for Victor, in any case.'

I felt my stomach drop like when I missed a step on a staircase. Wartime was strange and often frightening, but I found comfort in the rules, and the knowledge that somewhere people like my grandfather knew what they were doing. That someone was in charge. But my faith in Grandpa had been shaken lately, so perhaps I'd been wrong about more than just that.

'I have to go,' Jerome said. 'Or they'll be looking for me.'

He leaned over and kissed me softly.

'It'll be all right,' I said, not sure if I was reassuring him or myself. 'All this stuff with Victor. It'll be sorted out.'

'Sure,' he said, getting to his feet. But I wasn't sure he believed me.

I sat by the tree for a while, thinking about Victor and waiting for another glimpse of Jerome as he drove by. When passed me in the car, I saw him turn his head a little bit and I let myself think he was looking for another glimpse of me, too.

It was another hot day, when the air felt heavy and it was too warm to do anything much but lie still. But I wanted to hear what everyone in the village was saying about Victor's attack, so I dragged myself to my feet and wandered down to Honeyford.

The village was quiet, and I wasn't surprised really. It was the hottest part of the day, with the sun high in the sky. George at the pub had put up another sign declaring that the white GIs were not welcome in his pub. This one was even bigger than the first one.

Mr Fingal, who was walking his dog on the green, saw me looking and came over. 'Everyone's very cross,' he said. 'About what happened to Patty's young man.'

'Victor.'

'That's him.' Mr Fingal scratched the top of his dog's head. 'The parish council has called an emergency meeting.'

'About Victor?'

'Folk don't feel safe,' he said. 'It's not right.'

'No.' I bit my lip. 'Mr Fingal, do you think the police will do anything? Will they find out who did it?'

'Seems it's been passed to the Americans to handle,' he said. 'Because Victor said it was one of them who did it.'

'Two of them,' I said. 'There were two of them, and one of him.'

'Well, I'm sure they'll get to the bottom of it, Gloria.'

'I hope so.'

An engine made me look round as a jeep came through the village, filled with GIs. I saw Perkins at the wheel and grimaced as he waved to me.

The jeep pulled up and the men all jumped out. I said my goodbyes to Mr Fingal and began hurrying away, heading towards the library, but Perkins shouted my name and I turned.

'Hey! Gloria!'

'Hello,' I said, not wanting to be drawn into conversation.

He jogged over to where I stood. 'I was hoping to catch you.'

'Really?'

'I wanted to ask you . . .' he began. He took off his cap and rubbed his head and as he did, I noticed his knuckles were swollen and bruised. And under his hat was the remains of a bump on his head. He looked very much as though he'd been in a fight.

'Have you hurt yourself?' I said.

He looked startled and followed my gaze to his hand. 'Oh this?' he said. 'Just got it caught in a door.'

'A door?' I said. 'Right.'

There was a pause.

'I wanted to ask you if you're going to the summer dance?'

'I am.'

He smiled at me. He was very good-looking and he knew it, which, I thought, made him much less attractive. 'Want to come with me?' he said. 'As my date?'

'No.'

He looked shocked. I guessed people didn't say no to Perkins very often.

'Why not?'

'I'm going with my friend Patty,' I said. I let my eyes drop down to his hand once more. 'She's in a terrible state because her chap, Victor, was beaten to within an inch of his life, for no reason. Just near here actually. It's an awful thing.'

'That's sad,' Perkins said.

'He's British, you know? Victor. To all intents and purposes.'

Perkins looked at me. 'Is he?'

'Jamaica is part of the British Empire. And Victor is training to be a pilot, in the RAF.' I smiled at him sweetly. 'I'd have thought you'd seen him around?'

'I don't know about that . . .' Perkins shifted on his boots.

'Everyone's terribly cross about it.'

'I'm sure.'

'But Victor remembers everything that happened so I'm sure we'll get to the bottom of it in no time. I say, Perkins, are you feeling under the weather? You've gone a little pale.'

'I should go,' he said.

'Don't let me keep you.'

He turned away and went back to the other men, who were waiting by the jeep. They were all looking at the sign on the pub window and I wondered if they were planning to try to force their way in. The air was crackling with tension, and I had a horrible feeling they might.

It seemed I was right, because the group began to move together towards the pub, their faces ugly with determination.

But as I watched, my heart thumping in my chest, one of them nudged Perkins and they all looked up. I looked too, to see the men of the village – the few that were left – appearing from houses and shops all around me and coming together in a line outside the pub.

They stood together, barring the GIs from going any further, and Mr Fingal said, quietly at first and then more firmly: 'You need to leave.' He cleared his throat and, because he was an Englishman after all and nothing if not polite. 'Please.'

I looked at them, this mishmash of chaps from elderly Mr Fingal, and George from the pub with his dodgy leg, and Clive, the butcher's boy who wore glasses half an inch thick, and Martin from the hardware store who was brandishing a tennis racquet, and Billy Shawcross who lived alone in the house on the end and who'd not been the same since he was in the trenches in the Great War, and the others, and I felt like crying with pride.

The GIs – there were four of them – all straightened up and stood facing the villagers. The atmosphere was thick and hot, and I felt sweat dripping down my neck.

It felt like we were in a Western film, with rival cowboys staring at each other before the big shoot-out. Except, I thought with a lurch of fear, the GIs all looked like they were in a John Wayne picture, while the villagers looked more like Laurel and Hardy.

No one moved. I wondered if the GIs had guns. All the villagers had was Clive's butcher's apron, George's broad shoulders, and Martin's tennis racquet.

I could hear myself breathing. What would happen, I thought, if no one moved at all? Would we just all stay here, frozen, until the sun went down?

Perkins took a step forward towards Mr Fingal.

Mr Fingal was a good thirty years older and smaller and slighter than Perkins, but he didn't so much as flinch. I rose up on my toes ready to run and – I wasn't sure exactly what I'd do – but I was ready to rush at Perkins if he tried anything.

'You need to leave,' Mr Fingal said again.

'Do as he says.'

I turned to see Corporal Taylor standing in the shadows at the edge of the green. I wondered how long he'd been standing there.

'This ain't nothing to do with you, Taylor,' said Perkins. 'Back off.'

But Taylor didn't listen. Instead he walked slowly and deliberately across the green and joined the line of local men.

'Leave,' said Mr Fingal, his voice stronger now.

Perkins looked at him for a long moment. I felt my hands sweating. Was he going to give poor Mr Fingal a thump? But then eventually, Perkins nodded.

'Come on, guys,' he said, not taking his eyes from Mr Fingal. 'Let's get out of here.'

It took a few minutes, but to my absolute relief, the men all walked away. Feeling a little light-headed, I watched as they all climbed back into the jeep and drove off.

The villagers and Taylor all stayed where they were until they were out of sight and then they all fell about laughing in disbelief.

'Bloody hell,' said Clive, straightening his little white butcher's hat and pushing his glasses up his nose. 'I thought we were toast.'

'Me too,' said Taylor, looking pleased with himself as Martin slapped him on the back. 'It could have backfired.'

'They know better than to mess with us,' George said in satisfaction. 'They won't try that again.'

Chapter 27

Philippa

I slept awfully that night, tossing and turning in my bed, which felt too big without Marco. I kept checking my phone in case he'd messaged – he hadn't – and going over imaginary conversations with Vanessa in my head, trying to work out the best way to apologise for the awful things I'd said.

Eventually, as the sun began to come up, I admitted defeat and went outside into the garden in my pyjamas. I sat on the terrace with a coffee and watched the sky lighten.

I had a lot of things to put right, I thought. I needed to get to the bottom of whatever the grave really was. I had to let Vanessa know how sorry I was. And I needed to save my marriage.

My phone beeped and I leapt on it, my heart thumping. To my delight and trepidation, there was a voice note from Marco. Holding my breath, I pressed the button to listen.

'My mother says I'm an idiot,' he said. 'Well, what she actually said was "*ma sei scemo*?" but she means I'm an idiot.'

I smiled. "*Ma sei scemo*" was one of my mother-in-law's favourite expressions. It meant "what's wrong with you?"

Another voice note arrived, and I tapped the screen to play it.

'But I know what's wrong with me,' Marco said. I could hear seagulls in the background and wondered if he was on the beach. 'I'm just really sad about our babies.'

'I'm sad too,' I whispered, even though he couldn't hear me.

I waited to see if he had anything else to say, but there were no more voice notes. So I pressed record on my phone.

'I've always wanted a family,' I said. 'But I'm beginning to understand that families don't have to be mum, dad and two kids. I think they can be whatever you want them to be. Our babies are part of our family but there's also room for other people too.' I took a breath. 'Like Alex.'

I pressed send before I could change my mind, and went inside to get dressed.

I wasn't very enthusiastic about going to the museum. But I knew I had to face Vanessa and I also knew that if I wanted Marco to come home I needed to get to the bottom of the grave mystery. So I trudged down to the village, ready to eat some humble pie.

Jackie was sitting behind the little reception desk when I arrived. She got up to let me in because I was early and the museum wasn't officially open yet, and she gave me a hug.

'Heard from Marco?'

I nodded. 'He left a voice note.'

'Feel better?'

'A bit.' I stifled a yawn. 'Sorry, I didn't sleep very well.'

Jackie laughed. 'I'll go and get us some coffee, shall I? The café here doesn't open until ten, but I'll pop along the road. We might need some pastries, too.'

'Sounds good.'

'Go on through and get settled at a table,' she said. 'I'll not be long. Vanessa is around somewhere but she had to make some calls first thing about a school trip so she's probably in the office.'

She headed outside and I went through the door beside reception, into the main museum, which was really just one large room.

208

On the far side, an opening led through to the café. And on the other side was a door that said, "staff only".

And sitting at one of the tables, frowning at his phone, was Alex.

'Hello,' I said. 'Shouldn't you be at school?'

'Inset,' he muttered. 'Granny's taking us to the climbing place later, but she said she had to come to work first.' He looked up at me and grinned. 'On condition I do tons of homework, she said. But I've not done any.'

'Oops.'

He shrugged. 'It's fine. I can do it on the bus tomorrow.'

'Won't your writing be messy if you have to balance your book on your knee on the bus?'

'My writing's messy anyway.' He laughed. 'It's probably better if the teachers can't read what I've written.'

'Fair enough.' I laughed too, already feeling happier.

'Why is Marco in Scotland?' Alex said, making my good humour vanish instantly.

'He's gone to stay with his parents.'

'He's upset by the grave?'

I stared at him. 'What makes you say that?'

'Because he won't talk about it, and he got cross when I mentioned it, and . . .' He looked at me. 'Because I heard Granny telling Jackie that's what it was.'

I pinched my lips together tightly for a second. 'He is upset by the grave.'

'You don't have kids,' Alex said.

'No.' I felt a flutter of nerves in my stomach, like I always did if someone asked if we were parents. But Alex just nodded.

'Okay,' he said.

There was a pause.

'Can I sit here?' I asked.

'Course.'

I sat down and took off my jacket, hanging it on the back of the chair.

'I've got an idea,' Alex said. 'About the grave.'

'Have you?'

'You should find out if it's really a grave or not.'

'That's why I'm here,' I said.

Alex looked pleased.

'I don't think it is a grave, though,' I said. 'But it would be good to know for sure. Then Marco might not feel upset about it, and we can open the restaurant.'

'What if it is a grave?' Alex said, slightly gleefully. 'What if it's an actual grave?'

I rested by chin in my hands. 'Then I have no idea what we'd do.'

Alex thought hard. I could virtually see the cogs whirring in his mind.

'You know the cemetery by the church on the green?'

'I do.'

'It's got a fence round it.'

'Yes. It would be a bit weird if it didn't.'

Alex nodded. 'So why not put a fence round your grave?'

'It's not my . . .' I began but he was still going.

'You could make it a thing,' he said. 'Put up a fence. Make it a graveyard.'

'With one grave?' It was an odd conversation to be having but I was rather enjoying it.

'Well,' Alex said. 'You could make more graves.' His eyes shone. 'For pets.'

'I don't have any pets.'

'Other people's pets.' He leaned forward across the table. 'I watched that Stephen King film, *Pet Sematary*.'

'Does your granny know that?'

He shook his head vigorously. 'Absolutely not.'

I laughed again.

'The grave might be for a dog or a cat,' he said. 'It's only little isn't it?'

'Do you know, Alex? I'd not even thought of that.'

'People do really love their pets,' he said wisely. 'Arjan did a funeral when his hamster died and we all sang "Candle in the Wind" because Arjan's mum said it was a funeral song.'

'There's a whole pet cemetery in Hyde Park,' I told him.

'Winston Churchill buried all his cats in his garden,' Alex said.

'Did he? How on earth do you know that?'

He grinned again. 'Internet.'

'Obviously.'

'So we're agreed then?'

'Are we?'

'If it's a grave, you can put a fence round it.'

'I'm afraid if you put a fence round it, it becomes a graveyard.' Vanessa emerged from the staff-only door. Immediately, I began to sweat, but I tried to smile at her.

'That's why I think Philippa should put a fence round it,' Alex said patiently, as if she'd not understood.

'But if it's a graveyard,' Vanessa said, sitting down next to her grandson and smiling at him indulgently. 'It needs planning permission. And it becomes a whole big thing.'

She looked over at me.

'Hi, Philippa.'

'Hi.' I swallowed. 'Vanessa, I just wanted to say . . .'

She held up her hands, stopping me talking, and turned to Alex.

'I think I left my phone at home,' she said. 'Could you run and get it for me?' She pulled a bunch of keys out of her pocket and gave them to Alex.

'Can't you go?' he said.

'I could,' said Vanessa. 'But it'll take me the best part of an hour to get there because of my stupid ankle.'

'Fine,' said Alex.

'It might be charging in the kitchen.'

Alex looked sulky, but he got up anyway, slouching out of the museum and along the road.

As soon as he was out the door, I tried again.

'I'm so sorry,' I said. 'Honestly, I don't know what came over me. I said some awful things and I want you to know I didn't mean them.'

Vanessa made a face.

'Listen,' I said. 'I don't want to make excuses but I also wanted to explain a bit about what's happened.'

'Go on.'

This time I gave her the details. I told her about our baby losses, and how my chaotic childhood meant all I'd wanted was a family, but that hadn't happened. And I told her I was worried that Marco's affection for Alex would get confused with something else. And it actually felt quite nice to unload.

'When I saw you together, I just lost it,' I said. 'But I really am sorry.'

Vanessa reached across the table and squeezed my hand. 'I'm sorry too,' she said. 'You've had a rotten time of it.'

'It's not been easy,' I admitted.

'I should have told you why I kept turning up on your doorstep.'

'Harvey?'

She flushed. 'God, it's ridiculous,' she said. 'We had a fling when we were teenagers and I've always held a torch for him. But then when Alex came to live with me, I met up with him again because he sometimes helps out with the football club, and all those feelings came back with a vengeance.'

'Just ask him out,' I said. 'He's not going to turn you down, is he? You're the most glamorous granny I've ever seen. I bought a maxi dress so I could look like you.'

Vanessa chuckled loudly. 'Are you serious?'

'Totally.'

She pointed to my old battered denim jacket on the back of my chair. 'See that jacket?'

'Yes?'

'I bought one just the same.'

I put my head in my hands. 'Oh my God,' I moaned. 'We're both idiots.'

'Shall we start again?' Vanessa said.

'Yes please.'

She stuck out her hand. 'I'm Vanessa,' she said. 'Pleased to meet you.'

Chapter 28

Gloria

I was staring into my wardrobe, trying to decide what to wear to the dance when my mother knocked gently on my bedroom door.

'You look pretty,' I said. She was always elegant, my mother, but tonight she was wearing a blouse covered in stars and a black skirt that I was sure I'd never seen before. 'Is that new? Did you save up your coupons?'

Mother stood up straighter. 'No,' she said. 'I made it.'

My jaw dropped. 'You did?'

'Celia helped me. We did it at Happiness Club.' She gave me a little sideways glance. 'She would have helped you too if you'd bothered to come to more of the sessions.'

Celia took in mending and was a dab hand at sewing. Since the war had started she'd been doing a roaring trade in helping people get new life out of worn sheets and pillowcases, curtains and tablecloths. She'd even taught Patty and me how to darn our stockings, which was possibly her greatest achievement because neither of us was remotely clever with a needle. And now she was sharing her skills with the village widows, thanks to my mother.

Mother gave me a twirl. 'This is my old skirt,' she said. 'I put extra fabric in it because it had gone a bit shiny round my behind.'

'Clever,' I said in admiration.

'And the blouse is made from a tablecloth,' she said. 'Can you imagine?'

'You'd never know. I like the stars.'

'I wanted to show my support for the Americans,' she said, with a little smile. She put her hand to her chest, and I noticed for the first time that she was wearing a sweetheart pin, just like mine.

'Mother,' I said in surprise. 'Where did you get that?'

She giggled like a schoolgirl. 'From Waldo,' she said.

'Your guy is a GI,' I said in wonder.

'I suppose so,' Mother said. She caught my hand in hers. 'Do you mind?'

'Not one tiny bit.' I gave her a quick hug. 'Waldo's a lovely man, and I'm glad you're happy.'

'What are you wearing?' Mother asked.

'I can't decide,' I groaned. 'I probably should have thought about it before now.'

'Well how about this?' she said. From behind the door, she produced a little white blouse and a gingham skirt with a frothy petticoat.

'Oh my goodness,' I said, absolutely delighted. 'Where did that come from?'

'I made that too.'

Speechless, I could only stare at her.

'Are you going to try it on?'

'You made this for me? Really?'

Mother laughed and I thought how nice it was to hear her happy after so many months of misery. 'I thought the skirt would be fun for when you jitterbug.'

'I don't know how to jitterbug.'

'I expect Jerome will teach you.'

I flushed. 'I hope so,' I said. 'I'm not a great dancer.'

'Pah, you've just not had the right partner,' Mother said. 'Until now.'

She handed me the skirt and I took off my dressing gown and pulled it on. The fabric stuck out in a most satisfactory way, and I twirled from left to right to make the skirt swirl around my legs.

'You'll never guess what this one's made from?' Mother said, looking beyond delighted. 'Guess, go on.'

'Another tablecloth?'

'No!' She laughed again. 'Potato sacks. They print them with the gingham pattern so they can be reused. Celia's got a pile of them that folk have passed on.'

'Well I never,' I said.

Mother handed me the blouse. 'This was a bed sheet.'

I held it up. It had little puffed sleeves and neat buttons. 'Goodness.'

'Put it on.'

I did as I was told and tucked in the blouse. Being in the countryside we knew we'd avoided the worst of the food rationing but things were still scarce and I was far thinner than I'd once been and, I looked down at my chest, my bust had all but disappeared. But the skirt and blouse flattered my frame and I felt rather sophisticated.

Mother came and stood next to me and we both admired our reflections. She'd done her hair and pinned it up under a little black hat, which made her look terribly chic.

'You look like a true Frenchwoman,' I said. 'Mamie would be pleased.'

'*Merci*, darling.' She did a little wiggle of pleasure, then she picked up a strand of my hair, which was still hanging down around my shoulders. 'What are we going to do with this mop?'

It took a while, but we eventually managed to wrestle my hair into something approximating victory rolls and pinned it up at the back too. I shook my head to make sure it wouldn't fall out when I was dancing – if I decided to dance, of course – and was relieved when it stayed firmly put. Mother helped me line my eyes with kohl and even let me use some of her mascara, which she guarded very jealously because it was so hard to come by now, and we dabbed our lips with a tiny bit of lipstick.

'It's going to be a wonderful evening,' Mother said.

'Thanks to you.'

She waved away my praise.

'It was everyone,' she said. 'Everyone in the village worked so hard on the fair and on this evening's dance. It's going to be marvellous.'

We gathered our belongings and headed outside. Mother said Waldo would take us in his car. Jerome had the night off so he was making his own way to the dance with Eugene and Stanley. Fran and Patty were meeting us there, but Victor was still too poorly to come along.

As we went outside, though, it was Grandpa who appeared, looking very smart in his suit.

'Ladies,' he said, bowing as though we were royalty. 'You look very beautiful.'

'Thank you,' we both chorused.

'Showing your support for the Americans I see?' He nodded towards my pin.

I touched my fingers to the flag. 'Doing our bit,' I said, catching my mother's eye and giving her a conspiratorial smile. Of course there was no reason for my grandfather to know what a sweetheart pin was. I quite liked knowing something he didn't.

'This is a lovely surprise, Dad,' she said.

'I was in the area and I thought I'd make the most of it,' he said. 'I can't stay, but I can drive you to the dance.'

Over Grandpa's shoulder I saw Waldo. He realised what was going on, and I saw him give my mother a little nod, telling her to go right ahead. I thought again what a lovely, sensitive man he was.

We got into Grandpa's car and reached the village hall just at the same time as Waldo did.

'Well, hello there, Mr Wilmington,' he said to Grandpa, shaking him firmly by the hand.

'And Mrs Henry.' He reached out and took my mother's hand. 'Perhaps we could have a dance later?'

My mother smiled at him, and I thought how beautiful she was.

'A dance would be lovely,' she said.

Fran and Patty arrived, and there was a hubbub as we all said hello and admired one another's frocks, while Grandpa got fed up with waiting and went inside to get a drink.

I put my arm through Patty's.

'I wish Victor was here,' she said as we went inside.

'Me too.'

Inside the hall looked fabulous. There was a band already in position on the stage, and people dancing. It wasn't overly big, but it was full to the rafters of men in uniform, and some women, and others in civvies. The music was jaunty, the drinks were flowing and everyone seemed in wonderful spirits.

'It's terrific,' Fran said to my mother. 'You've all worked so hard.'

'It's come together beautifully,' Mother agreed.

Across the room, I saw Jerome standing to one side with Eugene. He smiled at me, and it was as though everyone else disappeared and all I could see was him.

'Smitten,' I heard Patty murmur behind me, but I didn't care.

I walked over to meet Jerome and he walked towards me. As we reached each other, he smiled down at me and took my hand, and honestly all I could see in that moment was him.

'Hi,' he said.

'Hello.'

We gazed at one another.

'You look so beautiful.'

'So do you. Handsome, I mean. You're the handsomest man in the whole room.'

Jerome grinned. 'Ah stop,' he said. 'You're making me blush.'

We laughed, and the rest of the room came back into view. I

218

became aware of my mother hovering close by, clearly desperate for an introduction.

'Do you want to dance?'

I shook my head. 'Would you come and meet my mother?' I said, loudly, knowing she'd hear. 'Because she'll never leave us alone for ONE MINUTE until you do.'

Mother appeared at my elbow.

'Jerome, hello,' she said. 'I'm Rose Henry. I'm so delighted to meet you.'

Jerome took his hat off, and shook my mother's hand. 'It's a pleasure to meet you, ma'am,' he said.

Out of the corner of my eye, I saw Fran nudge Patty approvingly, and I thought that perhaps I should have warned Jerome about how overenthusiastic my friends could be. But it was too late now.

He seemed to be doing well, though. My mother was laughing at something he'd said and they were smiling at one another. I couldn't hear what they were saying because the music had struck up again, but I was pleased they were chatting. I made a relieved face at Patty and she pretended to wipe her brow and I laughed.

As Mother leaned in to hear what Jerome was saying, Waldo came over. Jerome immediately stood to attention, and I felt a rush of pride in his manners. I touched my sweetheart pin where I'd put it on my blouse, just over my heart, thinking how lucky I was, and how lucky my mother was.

'Fancy a dance, Rose?' Waldo asked.

'I'd love that,' Mother said.

She took Waldo's hand, but Grandpa appeared, with one of the American bigwigs. I didn't know his name but I'd seen him around. He was a tall, broad, imposing man with ruddy cheeks.

This time both Jerome and Waldo stood to attention, and I couldn't help notice that Jerome sort of shrank back, away from the group.

'Rose,' said Grandpa. 'This is Colonel Peter Kidd. This is my daughter, Rose Henry.'

'Pleasure to meet you,' my mother said, shaking his hand.

'I have to go,' Grandpa said. 'You know how Delphine gets if I'm away for too long.'

As far as I knew, Mamie was perfectly happy at home in London on her own, and I suspected Grandpa was using her as an excuse. But Mother and I kissed him goodbye, and off he went.

'Could I have a quick word, Mrs Henry?' the colonel said to my mother.

'I'll get us some drinks,' Jerome said in my ear. He was clearly uncomfortable being around the colonel. He disappeared into the crowd.

The colonel drew my mother towards him.

'Mrs Henry,' he said. 'I don't want to speak out of turn, but I felt I needed to say something.'

'What about?' my mother said.

'Well, I know things might be different for you folks here in England, but I don't think I can stand by and watch . . .' He paused. 'It's not right for you to be mixing with the Black boys here.'

My blood went cold, and I raised my eyebrows at Patty. She'd been talking to her mum but now she stopped and paid attention to what the colonel was saying.

'How do you mean?' my mother said. Her voice was like cut glass and was it my imagination, or did she raise it just a little to be heard more clearly, and did the people around us stop talking for a moment?

'Well,' the colonel said. He was the sort of man who had presence. The type who was used to people doing as he said. 'I meant exactly as I said. You're a fine woman and you shouldn't be mixing with the Black boys. Not chatting with them, and definitely not dancing with them.' He reached out and tweaked my mother's cheek, like you'd do to a child. 'Just watch yourself, honey,' he said.

I winced. He'd regret that, I thought.

My mother turned to me. '*Zut alors*,' she said. Then she directed a tirade in French at me, so fast that I struggled to keep up but which I was fairly sure meant that she thought the colonel was a colossal bore and needed to be taught a lesson.

'Uh-oh,' I said under my breath.

Slightly behind my mother, a Black GI was standing very still. He had lighter skin than Jerome and striking green-brown eyes. I didn't recognise him, but he'd been listening to the conversation and now he grinned broadly.

'*Oui, oui*,' he said to my mother, and in flawless French with a slightly strange accent, he told her that he agreed with every word she said.

'He's Creole,' I heard Jerome say. He'd come up behind me while I was watching Mother.

'Creole?'

'From New Orleans, Louisiana. Some folk speak French down there.'

I nodded, impressed.

'What is your mother going to do?' Jerome said. 'She's up to something.'

'I have no idea,' I told him in a low voice. 'But brace yourself.'

My mother grinned at the Louisiana GI and he vanished off into the crowd.

'Colonel Kidd,' Mother said, her tone affable, though I thought the colonel would be a fool if he mistook that for friendliness. 'I am sure with your years of experience in the armed forces, you're used to your men doing exactly as you ask.'

Colonel Kidd nodded.

'But,' my mother continued. 'I'm afraid you are mistaken if you think you can tell me – or indeed, any of my friends from Honeyford – what we should be doing.'

The crowd in the hall had fallen silent. The band had stopped playing. In the middle of the room, couples stood in each other's arms, their eyes on Mother. Everyone was watching her. I felt an enormous swell of pride.

'You see,' she went on. 'Here in Honeyford we do exactly as we wish, and we do not take kindly to instructions.'

Colonel Kidd opened his mouth and my mother held her finger up to silence him. 'I'll thank you to allow me to say my piece,' she said. 'So we will be dancing this evening with whomever we wish. Isn't that right, ladies?'

She looked round and to my surprise, I realised she was flanked on all sides by the members of the Happiness Club. Celia, Margery and Millicent, and all the others.

The women all nodded, as did Fran, Patty and I. My mother smiled. 'I suspect, however, that who we wish to dance with will be limited to Englishmen and of course our friends from the home nations and the colonies.' A small murmur of agitation spread around the listening GIs. But Mother wasn't done yet. 'And,' she said. 'No Americans.' The murmur grew louder. Mother laughed. 'Silly me,' she said. 'I should have been more clear. No white Americans.'

A soft cough made her turn and look over to where Waldo stood watching, looking faintly amused.

'Perhaps one or two,' she conceded. She looked back at the colonel. 'We will dance with whomever we choose.'

'You can't do that, Mrs Henry,' the colonel said.

But my mother shook her head. 'I think you'll find that I can do exactly as I please.' She clapped her hands. 'Now who's for a dance?'

The Louisiana GI appeared surrounded by his friends and each one swept one of the local girls into their arms and on to the dance floor. Eugene took Patty's hand and led her away, and Jerome smiled at me.

'I think we should dance, don't you?' he said.

'I do.'

'Because I'm worried if we don't, your mom might shout at me the way she shouted at Colonel Kidd.'

I chuckled. 'Let's go,' I said. 'Teach me how to jitterbug.'

Chapter 29

Gloria

At first, it was funny. All us British women refusing to dance with any of the white GIs. They kept asking and we kept saying no, and instead heading to the dance floor with local lads, or RAF airmen, or the other GIs.

And it was a giggle. A bit of a laugh. Cocking a snook at the Americans who thought they could tell us what to do.

Patty had a whale of time, swirling across the dance floor with Jamaicans, who told her stories about Victor and wished them well. She danced with Englishmen, and Eugene and Stanley. My mother spent most of her time with the Louisiana airman and his friends, who were all jabbering away in their oddly accented and strangely old-fashioned French. But I knew she and Waldo were always aware of one another. I could see them looking at each other across the room.

I stuck with Jerome, because really there was no one else I wanted to dance with.

But it was funny.

At first.

After a few dances, though, when the white GIs realised we

weren't being silly, and we weren't about to relent, the mood began to shift.

After an hour or so, I spotted my mother and Waldo by the door.

'We're off home,' Mother said to me.

'It's early yet.'

She smiled at me. 'The night is young, but we are not,' she said. 'Waldo and I are going to walk home as it's such a beautiful evening.'

She was right about that. The sky was full of stars and the air was soft and warm.

I kissed her goodbye and waved to Waldo, and then went back inside.

As I went into the hall, I saw Perkins in the corner, with a few of his cronies, huddled together like they were in a rugby scrum. The sight of them plotting made me nervous and I nodded in their direction, warning Jerome about them.

'I get that they're annoyed,' he said with a resigned expression. 'I'm not entirely comfortable with this myself. It's only a few of the white GIs that go along with the colour bar so enthusiastically. Most of them just follow the rules because they have to.'

I hated that he was so accepting of a system that treated him as less than others, but I was also very aware that this wasn't my battle, so I kept quiet.

For a minute or two, at least.

'Perkins isn't a good one,' I pointed out as we jitterbugged our way across the floor. I wasn't very accomplished, but Jerome was a strong enough partner to make sure I didn't make a total fool of myself.

'Perkins is an asshole,' Jerome said. 'But it's not fair to blame the others for his shortcomings.'

'One bad apple spoils the barrel,' I said but he just shrugged, and twirled me round.

Out of the corner of my eye, I saw Perkins and his friends separate and make their way across the room, stopping to speak to some of the white GIs. They swerved Taylor and the lads he was with, and a few others.

The warm air hung heavy in the hall, full of sweat and excitement and adrenaline. I felt my stomach turn over with trepidation. What were they going to do?

'Don't look,' Jerome said in my ear as the men all gathered at the end of the hall. 'Don't give them the satisfaction.'

But of course I couldn't resist. I kept half an eye on them, feeling my palms sweating on Jerome's shoulders.

The men – there were a lot of them, perhaps twenty or more – all stood for a moment in a group and then as one, they all turned and left the hall, letting the doors slam shut behind them.

And that should have been that.

We all relaxed a little bit at first, and then more as the evening went on. We had the most wonderful time. Patty kept meeting Jamaicans who knew all about her because Victor had told them all how fabulous she was. I danced my socks off. Everyone drank a bit too much punch and the noise level in the hall increased as we all got a little giddy.

Everyone was there. Clive, and Martin, and Mr Fingal, and all of the Home Guard, bless them. And there were a few local lads home on leave, and some RAF airmen, and everyone shook off the worries of living through a blasted war, and simply had fun.

It was a hoot, all things considered.

And the best bit was when Jerome and I, worn out from dancing and too hot, crept out of the back door and shared some sweaty, breathless kisses under the stars. It was so romantic I thought I'd died and gone to heaven.

'Gloria Henry,' he said, pushing away a strand of hair that had stuck to my face. 'You're the most beautiful girl I've ever met.'

'I'm sure I'm not right now,' I pointed out. 'With my victory rolls unravelling and my mascara sliding down my face.'

'Shh,' he said, planting a kiss on my now-bare lips. 'You don't always have to argue, you know.'

I let him kiss me, enjoying his closeness.

'What I was going to say before you rudely interrupted me,' he said a few minutes later. 'What I was going to say . . .'

'What?' I asked. 'What were you going to say?'

'I was going to say that I'm falling in love with you.'

I stared at him. 'Really?'

'Head over heels, baby.'

I kissed him all over his face. 'I'm falling in love with you too,' I declared.

'Well, that's lucky,' he said. 'Because I'm never letting you go.'

He held me tight and I marvelled at how fortunate we were to have grown up so far from one another and yet to have ended up in the same place.

'Shh,' Jerome said.

'I didn't say anything.'

'Shh,' he said again, putting a finger to my lips and speaking in a whisper. 'I thought I heard voices.'

We both stayed quiet for a moment, listening. But the night was still and all we could hear was the occasional hoot of an owl, and the music drifting from the hall.

'You must have imagined it,' I said. 'Shall we go back inside?'

'I suppose so,' Jerome said.

Hand in hand we went into the hall again. The band were taking a break now and people were standing in small groups, chatting and laughing.

'Having a nice time, Gloria?' Mr Fingal asked me.

'Lovely, thank you,' I said. 'How about you?'

'Oh marvellous,' he said, with a grin. 'I've not felt this energetic since 1935.'

I laughed. Across the hall I spotted a little girl, fast asleep on two chairs pushed together and I tugged at Patty's hand.

'Look,' I said. 'That's what we used to do.'

I glanced round the hall, feeling content.

And then, just as I was congratulating myself on living in a place like Honeyford, where life was good, despite the war, there was a huge thud. The doors to the hall flew open and in came two military police officers in their tin hats.

As one, we all fell silent.

'Now, look here . . .' Mr Fingal began, but the men interrupted him.

'We're looking for Beau Landry,' one of the MPs said. He was a big man, with wide shoulders and a thick neck.

There was a pause and then the Louisiana GI stepped forward. 'I'm Beau Landry,' he said. 'What's the problem?'

'We've had reports that you're not wearing the correct uniform.'

Beau's shoulders slumped. 'You have, huh?'

'You're under arrest.'

'Hang about,' said Mr Fingal. 'You can't arrest him for that.'

It was as though he'd not even spoken. The MP simply took Beau's arm, roughly. Patty gasped. Next to me, Jerome was completely still, but I could tell his senses were on high alert, like a rabbit that was watching a fox.

Beau didn't argue. It was like all the fight had gone out of him and he just let the MP lead him away.

We all watched, stunned, as they took him outside. And then pandemonium broke out.

'We can't let this happen,' I said to Jerome, and then louder, to everyone, I said it again: 'We can't let this happen.'

'I agree,' said George from the pub, who'd appeared from behind the punch table. 'It's not on.'

'It's not bloody cricket,' said Clive.

'Well, perhaps we can have another go at talking them out of it,' Mr Fingal said, sounding somewhat reluctant. 'Come on, they might listen if there are a few of us.'

And so, Jerome and I followed Mr Fingal and George and

Clive, and Patty and the ladies from the Happiness Club, and Eugene, and the rest of the RAF men, outside.

'I say?' Mr Fingal called.

And that's when we saw them. The MPs were there, one on each side of Beau. And behind them, lurking in the darkness, were Perkins and so many others. Their faces set in fury.

'Shit,' breathed Jerome.

'Shit,' agreed Eugene.

I looked at Patty, who'd gone pale. 'Go,' I said. 'Take your mother, and the Happiness ladies and go.'

'Gloria, you should come too,' she said, but I shook my head. 'I'm not leaving Jerome.'

'Gloria,' she said, more urgently this time.

'Go back into the hall and out the back door,' I said. 'Make sure someone's got that little girl. Make sure she's safe. Take everyone you can. Get everyone away. Take them up to Honeyford Hall and tell Waldo what's happened. We'll follow as soon as we can.'

'I'd rather you came with me.'

I looked at Jerome. 'I can't.'

Patty kissed me on the cheek and squeezed my hand and then began to herd the women through the doors into the hall. If the Americans noticed, they didn't care. It was the local men – and the Black GIs – they were interested in.

Once more I was reminded of a cowboy film as the men all looked at each other. The local lads, and Taylor and his pals, and bold Mr Fingal. And Perkins and his hangers-on. I didn't know where the colonel had gone to but I couldn't see him anywhere.

Then the men all advanced on one another. And someone – looking back later I couldn't remember who threw the first punch – but someone launched himself at someone else and suddenly there were fists flying and thuds and shouts.

'Gloria, get the hell out of here,' Jerome yelled. But as he turned to shout at me, Perkins landed a punch right on his jaw, sending him backwards. Furious I grabbed Perkins's arm, slapping and kicking him.

'How dare you,' I screamed. 'Don't you dare.'

'Get away from me, you alley cat,' he hissed. He shoved me hard in the chest and I stumbled into another GI who was throwing a punch in Clive's direction. Clive was flailing around but defending himself rather well.

All around me was a tangle of bodies, the smell of testosterone and sweat coming from every pore. I couldn't see where Jerome was and I couldn't catch my breath to call for him – if he could even hear me. I was winded from Perkins shoving me and my chest ached.

I tried to get out of the group but instead I ended up taking a fist to the cheek. Stars exploded in my vision, and I couldn't even tell who had hit me. It was a mess. An enormous, frightening, awful mess.

I felt panic rise up in me, still not able to get my breath back and now dizzy from the punch in my face too. I couldn't see properly and I thought my eye was swelling, because I was crying now and the tears were stinging so badly.

I felt my way through the crowd, not knowing which direction I was going in and not caring. And then, to my absolute terror, I heard a gunshot and saw a bright flash.

'Oh God, oh God, oh God, oh God,' I said over and over again, as another shot was fired. I tripped over something and fell over, banging both my knees hard. 'Oh God,' I said again.

Another gun fired and this time I saw someone slump to the ground near me. I was properly panicking now, unable to get myself upright.

'Gloria.' Jerome was there, dragging me to my feet. 'Gloria, come on. We need to get out of here.'

'Are you all right?' I gasped. 'Someone's shooting. We need to help.'

'No, we need to get away,' he said. 'Trust me, this is not going to end well.'

He pulled my hand, so hard that I thought he was going to yank my arm from its socket. 'Come on,' he urged.

I was limping and gasping and crying and I kept stumbling. 'I can't walk,' I wailed. 'I'm sorry.'

Jerome held me close. 'The car,' he said in my ear. 'Go to Waldo's car.'

He half dragged, half carried me out of the melee. Propping me up against the car, he felt under the wheel arch and found the key, then he opened the door and pushed me in. He leapt in himself and started the engine. He had to reverse, because the fighting men were right in front of us, but he did it without hesitating, then swung round, and put his foot to the floor, speeding off into the night.

We were halfway up the hill on the way back to Honeyford House, before I'd got enough breath to talk.

'Who was shot?' I gasped. 'Who was shot?'

'One of the guys with Perkins,' Jerome said.

'And is he . . .' I couldn't say the words. 'Is he?'

'He got shot in his foot,' Jerome said. 'He'll be fine. But the rest of us? We're in trouble.' He thumped the steering wheel. 'Stupid, damn idiots,' he said.

'It might not have been an American who shot him,' I began but even as I said the words I realised how silly they were. No one else had a gun.

'What should we do now?' Jerome said, sounding a little panicked. 'I can't take Waldo's car back to the base. I don't know what to do.'

'Come home with me,' I said.

'I can't do that, Gloria. They'll know where to find me.'

'They won't care about you,' I said. 'Will they?'

'Someone was shot,' he said. 'They'll care about everyone who was there. They'll come and find us all.'

I must have looked frightened because he put his hand on my leg gently. 'Not you,' he said. 'You won't be in trouble.'

'I don't give two hoots about myself,' I told him, fear making me speak more sharply than I intended. 'I care about you. Lord, I saw how they treated that airman from Louisiana, just for wearing his uniform wrong. I can't imagine how they'll treat a Black GI who may or may not have shot a white airman.'

'Well, exactly,' Jerome said.

I stared out of the window. We were nearly home now and I had a sudden idea. 'Stop here,' I said. 'I know a place we can go.'

Jerome stopped the car beside the sentry box.

'You need to go home,' he said. 'You're hurt and you need looking after.'

'I'm fine.'

'Really?' He looked at my face, which was throbbing, and I tried to smile.

'I'm fine,' I said. 'Listen, you need to stay out of everyone's way until things calm down.'

'Gloria,' he said. 'I'm not sure . . .'

'You said yourself, they'll try to find you.'

'But . . .' Jerome began.

'Trust me,' I said.

There was a pause and then he nodded. 'Where will we go?'

'Follow me.'

I led him through the trees, slowly and painfully, to my special oak. The little hollow in its roots the perfect hiding place. Jerome took off his jacket and put it down for us to sit on, then we curled up together, cradled and protected, and to my surprise, I went to sleep.

When I woke a few hours later, the sky was beginning to lighten. I was resting on Jerome's chest, and he was looking out over my head.

'I have to go,' he said. 'I'm a witness. I need to go and speak up for Beau, and Eugene and the others.'

'But what if they arrest you?'

'That's a risk I'm going to have to take,' he said. 'I can't abandon the others now.' He gave me a little smile. 'My Grandma Elaine would never forgive me.'

'You're a good man.'

He kissed me deeply and sadly.

'I love you,' he said.

'Stay a while,' I murmured. 'Don't go yet.'

Astonished at my own boldness, I sat up and took off my blouse, then I reached over and began unbuttoning Jerome's shirt.

'Gloria,' he said, catching my fingers in his. 'Are you sure?'

'If you're sure?'

He nodded. 'We might never see each other again,' he said. 'If I'm arrested . . .'

'Don't,' I said. 'Don't say that.'

'It's true.'

'Then we need to take every moment of happiness we can,' I said. 'That's what Patty says.'

'Patty is very wise.' Jerome leaned over and kissed me, and I kissed him back and then we didn't talk any more for a long time.

Much later, when the sun was fully up, I was starting to feel every ache from the night before. My knees were bloodied and bruised from my fall, my cheek was swollen and my eye was puffy.

Jerome looked at me in concern. 'You need to go and get looked after,' he said. He took a breath. 'And I need to go and face the music.'

He stood up and helped me get to my feet too.

'I love you,' I said.

'I love you too.'

He kissed me once more and then, without looking back, he walked away.

Chapter 30

Philippa

'I've been helping local people trace their family trees for a long time,' Jackie said, swigging her coffee. She'd returned with drinks and pastries, Alex had come back with the missing phone, and everyone had looked relieved to see Vanessa and me chatting away like old friends.

Because it turned out, Vanessa was very nice. And of course I knew that really. Of course I did. When I wasn't being irrational and acting like a total weirdo, it was obvious.

'So what have you learned from your years helping people trace their ancestors, then?' I asked Jackie.

She smiled. 'Well, like I said, often you have to think outside the box. What do you know so far?'

'Very little.' I'd brought my laptop along and now I bent down to get it out of my bag. 'I've literally found a birth certificate for Gloria and one for her mother.' I opened my notebook and leafed through the scribbles until I found the name. 'Rose. And that's it. I've got Rose's marriage certificate, too. But no death certificates.' I smiled. 'Alex suggested they might have gone to America. He said he did something at school about all the women who married GIs and went off after the war.'

'They definitely could have done.' Jackie nodded. 'There was obviously a connection, after all, because we found the sweetheart pin. It would make life a bit trickier though, as there's no central site to search for documents in the US. We'd need to know the state. But we could look at passenger lists for ships.'

Vanessa made a face. 'Would that take a while?'

'It could do,' Jackie admitted.

I felt a shiver of nerves. 'Time is really of the essence,' I said. 'I need to work out what this is as soon as I can, so I can tell Marco and get him to come home and open the restaurant.'

'So we're back to thinking outside the box,' said Jackie. 'In the past I've had success in finding out what happened to people by tracing the people round them. And much as it pains me to say this, men are better.'

'Well, that's a matter of opinion,' said Vanessa wryly. She shot an apologetic glance at Alex, but he was absorbed in a game on his phone and not paying us the least bit of attention.

Jackie laughed. 'Men are easier to find,' she explained. 'Because they don't change their names. And because we're looking at World War Two, the men may have been in the military and military record-keeping is excellent.'

'So we could look for the Henry husband?' I said. 'The one who was killed?'

'Yes, absolutely.' Jackie nodded. 'Or for Mrs Henry's father. They might give us a clue about where to go next.'

I cracked my knuckles. 'Right then. Let's get started.'

We found poor Geoffrey Henry without any difficulty whatsoever, but finding out that he'd been killed very early on in the war didn't help us much.

'Let's see if we can find the dad,' Jackie suggested. 'His name should be on Rose's birth or marriage certificate.'

I nodded. I opened up the file and clicked on Rose's birth certificate to enlarge it.

'Her father was called Wilmington,' I told Jackie. 'Edgar Wilmington.'

She typed the name into her own computer and nodded in satisfaction.

'Here we go,' she said. 'Edgar married Delphine Allard in London in 1898. He was born in London, but Delphine was born in Paris.'

'Paris?' I breathed. 'Rose's mother was French.'

'Apparently so.'

'France was occupied in the war though,' I said. 'They couldn't have gone there.'

'Not during the war, but later perhaps?' Jackie suggested. 'If Rose and Gloria went to France, that could be another reason why we can't find any death certificates.'

'Is it easier to search French records than American ones?' Vanessa asked. 'Because if we can, we should do that. If they're not there, then we can think about the US connection.'

Jackie grinned. 'We absolutely can search French records. I've got some logins for those sites. I'll just go and find them. They're in my notepad in the office.'

Flooded with relief, I leaned back in my chair and smiled at Vanessa.

'Feeling happier?' she asked.

'It's complicated,' I said. 'Even if we do find out where Gloria and Rose went, it doesn't necessarily mean we'll find out what the cherub in our garden means.'

'It's worth a try, though.'

'It is.' I rubbed my forehead. 'I just hope we can find out enough to persuade Marco to come home.'

'Here we are,' said Jackie coming back. 'Got them.'

'I'm going to go and root through the files we've got about the GIs coming here,' said Vanessa. 'There's all sorts of info in the archive. I imagine it was terribly exciting when they arrived. There might be something useful in there.'

'Excellent,' said Jackie.

Vanessa went off into the office, and I pulled my chair closer to Jackie's so I could see as she logged on to the French website.

'How's your French?' she said.

'Shaky.' I sighed. 'We need Marco. He's good at French.'

'Well, let's hope we can muddle through without him, eh?' Jackie said. 'This site covers births, marriages and deaths from 1600 until 1912. *Naissances, mariages* and *décès*.'

'*Tres bien*,' I said. 'Search for Gloria Henry.'

Obediently, Jackie typed in the name but nothing came up.

Ridiculously disappointed I sighed loudly. 'Gosh, I really thought that might be it, you know?'

'I know.' She tapped her chin with her finger, thinking. 'How about we try Rose?' She typed in Rose Henry. 'Remind me of her maiden name?'

I scanned the wedding certificate I'd found.

'Wilmington,' I said.

Jackie typed that in too and pressed return. 'Bingo.'

I caught my breath.

'You found Rose?'

'She married someone called Benjamin Waldo in Paris in 1946.'

'Benjamin Waldo doesn't sound very French.'

'No,' Jackie said with a grin. 'He was American.'

'Rose married a GI!' I said in delight. 'So the sweetheart pin could have been hers.' But then I thought about it. 'So then why bury it like a memorial? Or even a dirty secret?'

Jackie made a face. 'Exactly,' she said. 'If their romance was all above board and happy, and Benjamin didn't die, and they got married after the war? Doesn't seem like anything that needs a memorial.'

'I suppose not,' I said, deflated.

'I'll print this out,' Jackie said. She pressed a few keys, snorting in frustration. 'The website's chucked me out, hold on. I need to log in again.' She tutted. 'Honestly, the security is tighter than my bloody bank. Name of first-born child. Pet's name. Mother's maiden name . . .'

I stared at her.

'Mother's maiden name,' I said.

'Yes. But it's annoying because my mother's maiden name was Fox and often that's too short . . .'

'Not yours,' I said with a chuckle. 'I was thinking what if Gloria used her mother's maiden name? Or even her grandmother's maiden name? If she actually was pregnant out of wedlock, there'd be a certain amount of shame, right? And they must have been quite well-to-do if they lived in Honeyford House. Maybe she was going incognito.'

'Right,' said Jackie, looking excited. 'So, Gloria Wilmington?'

She typed it in and pressed return. 'Nothing.'

I was disappointed. 'How about the grandmother's maiden name, then?' I looked down at my scribbled notes. 'Try Allard.'

'Allard . . .' Jackie tapped the keyboard.

'Huh.'

'What?' I tried to see the screen.

'Gloria Allard married someone called Remy Bernard, also in Paris, in 1965.'

'She did?'

'She did.'

'It's definitely our Gloria?'

'Definitely. Parents Rose and Geoffrey.'

'So she'd have been . . .' I frowned, trying to do the maths, 'Thirty-nine? Any kids?'

Jackie shook her head. 'Nothing else is coming up.'

'This is so hard,' I said. 'Just lots of dead ends. Maybe it's nothing to do with Rose or Gloria.'

Jackie sighed. 'We're not done yet,' she said. 'There must be something we're missing.'

'How about looking for Gloria Allard on the British website?' I suggested, not ready to give up yet either.

Jackie opened another tab and typed it in. 'Nope,' she said. 'Nothing.'

I felt a tear trickle down my cheek. 'This is hopeless.'

'Is it bad news?' Vanessa came out of the office and looked at me, concerned.

'Not bad, no.' I wiped away my tears with my sleeve. 'Just no news.'

'I suppose no news is good news,' said Vanessa. 'I still don't think it's a grave.'

'Will Marco think the same, though?'

She gave my hand a sympathetic pat. 'We'll work it out,' she said. 'Somehow.'

'Did you find anything interesting?' I asked her, wanting to change the subject. 'Any photos of GIs who might look like the type to have knocked up a teenager?'

She chuckled. 'I'm afraid not,' she said. 'But I did find lots of accounts of the Americans taking over Honeyford.'

'Maybe Gloria just fell for a GI who died,' Vanessa suggested. 'And the memorial was for him?'

'That could be it.' I nodded. 'Perhaps.'

'I guess we'll never know,' said Jackie.

'I guess not,' I said. 'Poor Gloria.'

Chapter 31

Gloria

The house was quiet when I went home. No American jeeps on the driveway. No sign of my mother, or Fran. Everything was still.

Surprised by the calm because I was expecting a hubbub after the fight at the dance, I walked round the side of the house, wincing with every step, and in through the back door, and found my mother fast asleep on the sofa in the living room. She was still wearing her outfit from the dance and the mascara we'd so carefully applied the night before was smudged across her cheek.

'Mother,' I said, gently touching her shoulder. 'Mother?'

She blinked her eyes open and then scrambled to sit up when she saw it was me.

'Gloria, thank goodness.'

'Where is everyone?'

'Benjamin had to go to the base,' she said, rubbing her eyes. 'What time is it?'

'A few minutes past eight o'clock. Who's Benjamin?'

'Captain Waldo.' She sat up properly now, and looked at me with concern. 'Gloria, your face. Oh my God, darling girl. Who did this?'

'I don't know,' I said, my voice wobbling. 'It was just a mess of bodies and limbs and fists. It could have been anyone.'

'Come and let me clean you up.'

Mother got off the sofa and helped me into the kitchen, where she sat me on one of the chairs and filled a bowl with warm water. Then she gently dabbed my swollen eye with some cotton wool. It was painful, but it felt nice to be looked after, to be safe and cared for after such a frightening time. I wondered if anyone was bathing Jerome's jaw, where Perkins had landed his punch. I doubted it. The thought made me breathe in sharply.

'Sorry,' Mother said.

'It's fine.' I started to cry. 'It's fine.'

Mother was standing in front of me, so I leaned forward and put my forehead on her stomach. She cradled my neck and smoothed down my hair and kissed the crown of my head.

'There, there,' she said. 'Don't be upset, my darling. You're safe now.'

Once I'd sobbed a bit, I felt slightly better. Mother made us both a cup of tea and we went back into the lounge because I needed somewhere comfy to sit.

'Did you know?' I asked. 'Did you hear what was happening?'

She nodded. 'Benjamin and I were having a nightcap together, when one of his men came and told us what was happening.' She took my hand. 'I was so worried. I wanted to come straight down to the village to find you, but Benjamin wouldn't let me.' Her voice wobbled. 'He said it was too dangerous.'

'He was right,' I said, grateful that my mother hadn't turned up in the middle of the fighting. 'It was awful, Mother. Awful.'

'He went back to base as soon as he heard, and then Patty and Fran turned up with most of the Happiness Club and a few others.'

'Where are they all now?'

'Some people went home. Celia and Millicent are in your room. Patty and Fran are in mine. Margery's in the study. They'll all be exhausted. It was late when we all eventually went to sleep.' She hugged herself even though it wasn't cold. 'Where were you?'

'With Jerome,' I said. 'We ran away when the fighting started. He took Waldo's car.'

'Quick thinking,' Mother said.

'I was scared he'd get into trouble, so we stayed in the woods overnight. But he's gone now. Back to the barracks. He said he needed to be with the others.'

'He's a good man.'

I blinked away tears. 'He really is.'

My mother looked at me for a second, then she tucked a strand of my hair behind my ear. 'How about we have a wash and change our clothes, then we can wake the others and we can all go down to the village?' she said. 'See if we can find out what's happening?'

I gripped her fingers. 'Someone was shot,' I said. 'I heard gunshots.'

'Good grief.' Mother tried to make light of it but her voice was thin and wavering. 'They're so trigger-happy, these Americans. I hope Benjamin gets them in line.'

'I'm sure he will.' I tried to smile but it didn't really work.

'We'll go and find out what's happened.' She put her hands on my shoulders. 'Everything's going to be all right, Gloria.'

Everything was not all right. The village was a mess. The hall windows were smashed. The pub's door was splintered, and its windows had been shattered. One of the trees on the green had broken branches.

'Oh, heavens,' I said, putting my hand over my mouth. 'What a mess.'

'Tea?' said Margery. She looked pale and fragile, but underneath I sensed a steely determination to Put Things Right. 'Millicent? A hand, please.'

Obediently, Millicent followed Margery to her cottage, leaving the rest of us surveying the damage.

'Gloria?'

Patty and Victor were coming across the green.

'Isn't it awful?' she said. I turned to face her, and she shrieked. 'Did someone hit you, Gloria?' she said. 'Look, Victor! Look at Gloria's face.'

'Are you in pain?' said Victor, who was still looking a bit battered himself.

'A bit,' I admitted. 'But it's not important. I don't understand how this could have happened. The dance was so much fun and then suddenly things changed.'

'Tempers have been fraying,' said Victor in his deep, lyrical accent. 'Tensions hotting up.'

'That's true enough,' said Patty. 'The Americans were annoyed about George's sign, and they didn't like us dancing with the Black GIs, and the Brits were cross about being told what to do, and everyone was edgy after what happened to Victor . . .'

'Lord,' I said, despairing. 'I just want to know that Jerome's all right. He went back to base, Patty. And someone was shot. Who got shot?'

Celia had found a broom and was sweeping up broken glass.

'Chap called Taylor, apparently?'

'No!' I said. 'Taylor? Is he hurt badly?'

'Lost a toe,' Celia said briskly. 'Not life-threatening. Don't stand there like lemons, girls. There's a lot of clearing up to do. Grab a broom, come on.'

As we swept up glass, and picked up chairs, and boarded up windows, we all shared what we knew about the events of last night.

'Fingal's been arrested,' Martin from the hardware store told me as he handed out planks of wood and nails for people to cover broken windows. 'And Clive.'

'Clive?' I said in disbelief. 'Surely not?'

David the telegram boy took a handful of nails from Martin. 'I saw him giving that Corporal Gordon a proper pummelling.'

242

'Did he?' said Patty, looking impressed. 'He probably deserved it, mind you.'

'Where's George?' I said, glancing at the pub, which was in darkness. 'Is he all right?'

Martin bit his lip. 'I've not seen him. What about you, David?'

David shrugged. 'Not since last night.'

'He'll turn up,' said Margery, handing round mugs of tea from a tray, like we were all at a parish council meeting. 'Don't fret. George is strong as a horse.'

I hoped she was right.

Everyone was chattering nineteen to the dozen, and there was a real buzz around the village as we cleared up the debris. There seemed to be a general belief that we'd shown them. Given them what-for, as David said. But I had a knot of anxiety in my stomach. I felt horribly nervous about what was happening elsewhere. About who'd been arrested. About where George was, and whether Taylor was all right – I'd heard from different people that he'd lost a toe, an ear and a thumb and I wasn't sure who to believe.

There were no Americans to be seen and I wondered where everyone was. And I longed to see Jerome. To find out if he was all right.

A car drove into the village, and everyone fell silent as it approached.

'Police,' said Martin under his breath, and he was right. It stopped beside the pub and Constable Wainwright got out.

'How do?' he said in his Yorkshire accent that he'd never lost despite having moved from Leeds twenty years ago.

He opened the back door of his car and out came Mr Fingal and Clive, looking a little exhilarated.

'I do not want to see you in my cells again,' he said to them sternly. Clive shook his head, but Mr Fingal gave Constable Wainwright a slightly defiant glare.

'I think you'll find we did nothing wrong.'

243

'Aye, this time,' said the constable.

'Excuse me, Constable?' I called. 'What's happening? Where are all the Americans?'

'It were an American gun that discharged,' Wainwright said. 'The Americans are dealing with it.'

'What does that mean?' said Patty. 'Who's dealing with it? What does dealing with it mean?'

'It means, it's nowt to do with you or me, Miss Flynn,' he said.

Patty opened her mouth to argue but the constable raised an eyebrow and she shut it again.

But I wasn't about to give up.

'Is it the US policemen who are investigating?' I said. 'The military police?'

Constable Wainwright opened the car door. 'I imagine so, Miss Henry. But I can't see how that's any of your business.'

Worry made me bold. I pulled my shoulders back and marched over to the car, putting my hand across the door to stop him getting in.

'We all saw what happened last night,' I said firmly. 'We saw awful things. Everyone is worried. Corporal Taylor is in hospital. No one has seen George. And we need to know what's going on.'

Constable Wainwright looked at me sternly and then his face softened.

'George is in the hospital. He took a whack on the head wi' a chair leg,' he said. 'Last I heard he was still out cold.'

I swallowed. 'And Taylor?'

'Lost his thumb.' Wainwright nodded. 'Happen he put his hand up to stop the bullet, the daft lad.'

'Right,' I said.

'I don't know who else has been arrested,' Wainwright said. 'But I reckon that man can help you.' He tilted his head over towards the village hall and I followed his gaze to where Waldo stood, slightly away from the rest of the villagers.

Constable Wainwright got into the car and Waldo walked, so

very slowly, over to where I stood. My mother came to stand on one side of me, Patty on the other.

'What's happened?' I said. 'Is it Jerome?'

Waldo gave a quick nod. 'Sorry, kid,' he said. 'Privates Scott, Silver and Lee have all been arrested. Private Landry, too.' He reeled off some other names, but I wasn't really listening because I was absolutely furious.

'Stanley?' I said. 'He wouldn't say boo to a goose.'

'Story is, he was covered in blood, standing next to Taylor,' Waldo said.

'Stanley is a doctor,' I said slowly. 'If he had blood on his hands, it'll be because he was helping. I don't suppose anyone's asked Taylor, have they? Or are they just sure Stanley's guilty because he's Black?' My voice was shrill but I didn't care.

Waldo took his hat off and wiped his forehead with the back of his hand. He looked very, very tired.

'It's all a big mess,' he said.

'That's an understatement,' I snapped.

'No one's talking,' Waldo said. 'I've got men who are supposed to have each other's backs, at each other's throats. How can we defend this nation if we can't even defend one another? It has to stop. This has to be the end of it.'

'It's not the end of it,' I hissed. 'Because innocent men have been arrested.'

'If they're innocent, then they'll go to trial and they'll be cleared,' Waldo said, his voice weary.

'Really?' I said. 'Will they?'

I stared at him until he dropped his gaze.

'Gloria,' said my mother. 'Let's go home shall we?'

But the thought of Jerome and the others hoping for a fair trial made me want to scream.

'You know Private Scott wasn't even there?' I told Waldo. 'He got thumped by bloody Perkins and then he got me out of there. He was protecting me. He didn't throw a single punch.'

'Folks are saying that it was after Taylor got shot, when it all went south,' Waldo said. 'That's when George got whacked on the head, and when things got smashed up. It was nasty. We can't let it go. People need to be punished.'

'The right people,' said Patty.

'We took your car,' I said, sounding a little desperate. 'As soon as we heard the gunshot, we took your car and drove away. Jerome wasn't involved in this. You have to believe me.'

My mother put her hand on my arm. I thought it was to stop me saying anything else, but knowing she was there with me made me bolder.

'Captain Waldo,' I said. 'Please. I can give Jerome an alibi. He was with me.'

Waldo looked at me, his gaze steady. 'Gloria, this is bigger than you. You could make things a whole lot worse if you get involved. You need to back off.'

'But I have to tell someone,' I begged. 'I have to tell someone that he wasn't involved.'

Across the green, I saw an American jeep pull up. Colonel Kidd was in passenger seat. I saw him, and Waldo saw me see him.

'Gloria, no,' he said.

But I'd taken off, running over the grass, darting past broken branches, to where a bewildered Colonel Kidd stood.

'What on earth . . .?' he began.

'Colonel Kidd,' I said, gasping for breath. 'I have to speak to you.'

He looked at me, bedraggled and frantic, bruised and battered, and went to walk past.

'Stop,' I said. 'Stop. I'm Gloria Henry. I'm Edgar Wilmington's granddaughter.'

Now he did stop and look at me. 'Good God,' he said. 'What happened to you?'

'Last night,' I said, trying to catch my breath. 'I need to tell you about last night.'

Colonel Kidd took my arm and steered me to the jeep. 'Sit down, child,' he said. 'Take a moment.'

But I didn't want to sit down, and I didn't want a moment.

'Private Jerome Scott,' I said. 'He wasn't here in the village when the worst fighting took place.'

Colonel Kidd frowned. 'Scott?'

'He's from the barracks at Burton, sir,' I said.

Kidd's lip curled. 'He wasn't here?'

'No, sir.'

'Where was he?'

'He was with me,' I said. I lifted my chin and looked him straight in the eye, unashamed. 'We spent the night together.'

Colonel Kidd put his forefinger on my jaw and gently turned my face from side to side, looking at my bruises.

'Private Scott?' he said.

'Yes, sir.'

He turned to the GI driving the jeep and said: 'We need to go to Burton immediately.'

'I could come,' I said. 'I could come to Burton and explain.'

'Miss Henry.' His voice was kind. 'You've been very brave in telling me this and let me assure you Scott will be dealt with. I'll telephone your grandfather myself and reassure him that Scott, the man who did this to you will face the most severe punishment.'

Cold fear dripped down my spine. 'You don't understand,' I said. 'Jerome . . . Private Scott . . . he didn't hurt me. We spent the night together. I chose to spend the night with him.'

Colonel Kidd put his hand on my head like I was a little girl.

'How could you choose that?' he said. 'A white woman and a Black man? There's only one way that can happen.'

'No,' I said. 'No.'

'Private Scott forced himself on you,' Colonel Kidd said, speaking slowly as though I was simple. 'He forced himself on you, and now he will be punished.'

Chapter 32

Gloria

One month later

'Anything?' I said.

My mother looked up from her book. 'Not about Jerome. I'm sorry.'

I sat down next to Mother and she put her arm round me. We went through a version of this same conversation every day, and every day I felt a little bit worse.

Jerome was in Shepton Mallet jail, which the Americans had taken over, and he had been accused of rape. But that was all we knew.

Stanley had been accused of attempted murder.

Things were bleak. Waldo was trying to find out more but there had been no news for days and days. It was like everyone was pretending nothing had happened. The fight hadn't even been in the newspapers, which had surprised us all. Grandpa said they wouldn't report anything bad about the GIs. He said any stories that were remotely negative about them would be stopped before the ink was on the page. But when I asked him if it would be the Americans or the British authorities that would shut them down, he didn't answer.

'But . . .' Mother said.

'Yes?'

'There is some news.'

My stomach plummeted into my shoes. 'What is it?' I said. 'Tell me.'

'It's Corporal Taylor.'

'Is he dead?'

Taylor had lost his thumb and everyone had joked about it at first, just as Constable Wainwright had done, saying he'd tried to stop the bullet. But then he'd got an infection and things had been touch and go ever since.

'No,' Mother said. 'He's awake.'

I put my hand to my mouth. 'He's awake?'

'He is. He's sitting up and talking.'

'So now he can tell everyone that Stanley wasn't the one who shot him?'

'That's what Benjamin is hoping.'

I felt dizzy for a second. 'Thank goodness,' I said. 'Thank goodness.'

'Benjamin says the MPs are going to speak to him as soon as they can. They're expecting Stanley to be released after that.'

'There's no evidence against him,' I said. 'Just that he was near Taylor with bloodied hands.'

'Exactly.' Mother smiled at me. 'And now they'll have an explanation for that – one that doesn't come from Stanley himself – and they'll let him go.'

'We told them Stanley wasn't guilty. We told them over and over again.'

'There are people they believe, and people they don't.'

There was a short pause. I knew what we were both thinking – that Jerome was one of the people who was not believed, and I was the opposite. Except no one was really listening to me, either.

I'd begged Colonel Kidd to pay attention when I told him that I'd wanted to be with Jerome. That I was in love with him. But everything I said seemed to be taken as evidence against Jerome rather than in his favour.

'Folks like Kidd can't believe that a white woman would ever consent to be with a Black man,' Waldo explained to me, the day after Jerome had been arrested. 'They think he's manipulated you into believing you love him. That he's fooled you.'

'I should have stayed quiet,' I said. 'I thought I was doing the right thing and now he's in jail and it's all my fault.'

'It's not your fault, honey,' Waldo had said. 'You're a victim of these crazy laws, too.'

But I didn't feel like a victim. I just felt horribly, crushingly guilty, every second of every day. I was desperate to get a message to Jerome, to know he was all right, and to tell him how sorry I was. I wrote him endless letters, but I hadn't received any replies and I had no way of knowing if he'd ever seen them.

My mother rubbed my arm soothingly. 'Grandpa's here,' she said. 'Look.'

'Again?' I rolled my eyes. My grandfather had appeared on our doorstep regularly since the fight at the village hall. He kept finding reasons to talk to me alone, and then quietly reassuring me I could tell him the truth. And every time I would tell him that it was the truth. That I loved Jerome, that he hadn't hurt me, that my bruises came from someone else.

And every time he looked at me with tears in his eyes, kissed my now healed face, and told me he would look after me.

I felt like I was in a nightmare, screaming for help but no one could hear.

'Hello, Gloria,' Grandpa said, falsely jovial as he came into the room. 'Hello, Rose.'

We both offered far more muted greetings to him and he gave us a broad smile.

My mother got up from the sofa and went to give him a hug.

'Is she eating?' I heard Grandpa say in a low voice.

'Barely.'

'Has she been outside?'

'On the terrace, for a few minutes at a time. But she won't see anyone. Only Patty, and now she's gone away again.'

'I can hear you,' I said.

'Darling, Grandpa's just worried about you,' my mother said. 'We're all worried.'

'Gloria, the sun is shining and there is not a cloud in the sky,' Grandpa said in his overly cheerful voice. 'Would you care to join me on a walk to the village?'

'No,' I said. 'Don't you have work to do?'

'Not today.'

'I just want to stay here.' I looked to my mother for back-up, but she let me down.

'Actually, darling, I think it might be good for you to get outside,' she said.

'I don't feel well.'

'You just need some fresh air.'

I looked at them both. They were wearing identical bullish expressions and I realised my own face probably looked the same. Realising I was outnumbered, I sighed. 'Fine. But not for long.'

'How about we go to the library?' Grandpa suggested. 'I'm sure you've read all the books you borrowed now.'

'I have.'

'Well, there we are.'

Dragging myself upright, I went to find my books, and a sweater because I was chilly all the time at the moment, despite the summer weather. I thought it was icy cold guilt making me shiver, and I thought I probably deserved to feel that way.

'Good news about Corporal Taylor,' Grandpa said as we began walking down the hill to the village. 'I've heard that means Private Silver will be released, as long as Taylor confirms his story.'

'Taylor will confirm his story,' I said dully. 'Because it's true.'

251

'Of course it is,' Grandpa soothed. 'Of course.'

'But you know what isn't true? That Jerome forced himself on me.'

'Gloria, let's not argue now,' Grandpa said. 'Let's focus on the positives. Taylor is on the mend, which is a relief.'

'If only we knew George was going to recover.'

George had broken his back in the beating he'd received. His spine had snapped like a twig. He'd been taken to a special hospital in Birmingham, and it looked like he wouldn't walk again.

No one had been arrested for hurting him.

My mother had told me Clive and Martin had taken on the pub, running it with considerable enthusiasm if a lack of expertise, and they'd kept up the signs that said Englishmen and Black Americans only. And Patty had revealed that underneath, Clive had added "and Jamaicans" because there were more airmen arriving every day from the colonies and he wanted to make everyone feel welcome. She'd been pleased about that.

As we approached the village, my steps slowed. I was nervous about seeing anyone, worried they'd blame me for what happened to Jerome – which was fair enough.

'Come on, Gloria,' he said. 'It's taking us forever to get there.'

The village was quiet and still. I paused at the edge of the green, marvelling at how now you'd not know anything awful had happened. The windows had been mended. The debris swept away.

I shivered as a sudden memory of being surrounded by men, punching and kicking, overwhelmed me.

'Grandpa . . .' I began. 'I can't . . .'

Grandpa gave me his arm and I hung on for dear life, as he started walking again, more slowly now, guiding me towards the library.

'Gloria!'

I flinched as someone shouted my name and Grandpa looked at me in concern.

'It's fine,' he said. 'It's fine.'

Victor was walking across the green towards us.

'Gloria!' Victor shouted again.

To my surprise, as he got close, he bundled me into his arms and hugged me hard.

'We've been so worried about you.'

Stunned, I looked up at his face. 'You don't hate me?'

'What for? Why would we hate you?'

'Because Jerome is in jail because of me.'

'Jerome is in jail because Colonel Kidd is using a stupid law against him,' Victor said. He sounded very matter of fact. 'If it wasn't you, it would be something else. It's not your fault.'

I untangled myself from his arms. 'You really think so?'

'I know so.'

I felt a little better suddenly.

'We need to get him out.'

'We'll all do our best,' said Victor. He paused. 'I've just been talking to the police. They came to the base and pulled me out of training. Totally unexpected. Like being bowled a googly.'

'Military police? What about?' Grandpa was standing a little way from where we were, watching us talk. I hoped he wouldn't be rude to Victor.

'About the beating I got.'

'What did they say?'

'They wanted me to identify some airmen from their voices.'

'Did you?'

Victor shrugged. 'I think so. But they didn't give anything away. Maybe they'll say I got it wrong.'

Grandpa gave Victor a long, measured look.

'I believe some bigwigs have been speaking to the Americans,' he said. He tapped the side of his nose like he was revealing a secret. 'Let them know we take a dim view of this sort of behaviour.'

'Some bigwigs?' I said, looking at my grandfather through new eyes. 'Or you?'

253

He didn't answer. Instead, he put his hand on Victor's shoulder.

'Bowled you a googly, eh? Are you a cricket man?'

'From the moment I could walk, sir,' said Victor.

'I was in Kingston in 1935,' Grandpa began. 'West Indies playing England . . .'

I tuned out, squinting at a group of Americans sitting on the grass at the far side of the green. They were talking and laughing and I thought Perkins might be among them. But the sun was in my eyes and I couldn't tell for sure. I most definitely did not want to walk past them though. I'd make Grandpa go to the library the long way.

But before I could interrupt his discussion about being out for a duck, which made no sense to me but which Victor seemed to be enjoying, a Military Police jeep drove into the village, and stopped right beside the Americans.

'Grandpa.' I put my hand on his arm. 'Grandpa, look.'

Cautiously, Victor, Grandpa and I moved closer to the group. Two MPs had got out of their car.

'Corporal Cole Perkins?' one of them was saying.

Perkins – because it was Perkins, I could see him clearly now – got to his feet.

'That's me.' He looked uncertain and nervous, his customary confidence vanished.

'We need to speak to you,' the MP said. 'About an attack on a British airman.'

I looked at Victor, who was watching with his mouth open in shock.

'They believed me,' he muttered.

Grandpa looked quite pleased with himself. 'Well,' he said. 'You're one of us, aren't you?'

Chapter 33

Gloria

'They won't let you in,' said Private Silver a week later. I'd tracked him down at the base as soon as I'd heard he'd been released. 'There's no way they'll let you in.'

'Waldo said they wouldn't let me in here,' I pointed out. We were standing beside the gates of the base. Just inside the gates, despite the protests of the guard on the door. 'But here I am.'

Stanley frowned at me. 'It's a prison, Gloria.'

'I'm very persuasive when I want to be.' I smiled. 'And, I have a plan.'

'It's not a nice place.'

'Even more reason to get Jerome out of there.'

'It's really old, the jail,' Stanley said, with a tiny, sad smile. 'Someone said it was built in the 1600s. That's older than America.'

'I suppose,' I said, uncertainly. I wasn't sure where he was going with this.

'And it's dark. And cold, too, even when the sun's shining. I guess because the walls are so thick. But the noises echo. Folks are in there crying and shouting and groaning. So it's loud. Every wail just goes right through you.'

'Was Jerome one of the people crying?'

'I'd be surprised if he wasn't,' said Stanley matter-of-factly. 'It's a terrible, hopeless place.'

He rubbed his nose with a trembling hand. 'I cried the whole time I was in there. And every time I shut my eyes, I dream I'm back there.'

I felt sick. 'But you saw him? You saw Jerome?'

'From a distance.'

I breathed out slowly. 'I'm still going,' I said.

Stanley sighed. 'I don't understand what it is you want.'

'I want two things,' I said. 'My grandfather always says you should be clear about your aims if you're going to be successful.'

'Right.'

'I want to say sorry to Jerome. In person. And I want to speak to someone in authority to explain what happened.'

'Gloria.' Stanley's voice was full of sympathy. 'Gloria, this isn't going to work.'

'I have to go,' I said with a shrug. 'I have to try.'

'You're not going to change your mind?'

'No.'

'In that case,' said Stanley, 'we're coming too.' He lifted his chin and shouted across the tarmac. 'Hey, Eugene?'

Eugene was standing across the way, leaning against a wall. 'Yeah?'

'You free for the rest of the day?'

Eugene glanced over his shoulder. 'I guess.'

'Gloria has a job for us to do.'

Eugene sorted everything out. He told Corporal Taylor where we were going and he took a jeep and Taylor said he'd cover for us, even though he wasn't officially back on duty yet, as he'd only been out of hospital for a few days.

And then we rattled all the way to Somerset, which took much longer than I'd expected it to. The closer we got to the prison, the quieter Stanley became until we pulled up outside and he shook his head.

'I'm so sorry, Gloria. I can't go in.'

'That's all right. I really wasn't expecting you to.' I pulled my shoulders back, trying to find courage from somewhere. 'It's enough just knowing you're here. I'll go alone.'

Eugene took his hat off and rubbed his forehead. 'Sure?'

'I'm sure.'

I got out of the car and straightened my skirt. I'd sneaked into my mother's bedroom and taken one of her smartest dresses, with a crisp collar. It made me look much older, though it was a little long on me and slightly snug around the waist. I'd swapped my summer pumps for proper shoes that were rather hard to walk in, but I was hoping there wouldn't be much walking to do.

I'd put my hair up and added some lipstick. Then I'd dug around in Mother's notes for the summer fair and gathered together a folder of official-looking paperwork.

I bent down and checked my makeup in the car mirror. Then I picked up my folder, and gave Stanley and Eugene a slightly wonky smile. 'Wish me luck, boys,' I said.

'Good luck,' they chorused.

'Hey,' Eugene added. 'If you see Jerome, tell him . . .' He paused. 'Tell him we miss him.'

I pinched my lips together and looked up to the grey sky to stop the tears that welled up. 'I will.'

Without looking back, and only slightly wobbly on my high heels, I walked right up to the entrance of the prison.

There was a white wooden sentry box at the gate, staffed by a bored-looking white American soldier.

As I approached, he sat up a bit straighter and smiled.

'Well, hello there,' he said. 'Can I help you?'

'I'm sure you can,' I said in my best, clipped English accent. 'I'm here on behalf of the British Government.' The soldier looked alarmed, as I'd hoped he would, and I gave a little laugh. 'Gosh that sounds terribly official, doesn't it? That's what I was told to say.' I leaned forward over the desk. 'I work for Edgar Wilmington at the War Office. I was down here for a meeting with Colonel Kidd at Eaton, and Edgar wanted me to call in and check everything is in order.'

'You have an appointment?'

I looked at him, disappointed. 'No,' I said. 'If I'd made an appointment, then everyone would have run round like headless chickens making everything look marvellous for me, and that wouldn't give me an accurate idea of what's happening here, would it?'

The soldier looked a little stunned. 'I guess not.'

'And gosh, Edgar can be a frightfully hard task master, you know? I'm sure you know. I'm sure some of your superior officers can be the same?'

He nodded.

'I just want to do as he asked and get back to London, because if I let him down, then I'm pretty sure he's going to give me the sack, and without a job, I'm in real trouble.'

I looked straight at him. 'It'll be a disaster,' I added, wondering if I'd laid it on a bit thick.

'Sounds tough,' he said. 'What do you need?'

'Barely anything,' I said. 'I just need five minutes with . . .' I opened my folder and ran my finger down the list of stalls for the summer fair, hoping the soldier couldn't read my mother's writing. 'Gosh, I had the name right here, and now I've lost it. Lieutenant Colonel . . .'

The soldier's expression cleared. 'Lieutenant Colonel Arthur J Cooper,' he said.

I nodded proudly. 'That's the one,' I said in triumph. 'You've hit the spot there.'

'He's a busy man.'

'Well of course he is.' I smiled. 'We're all busy, aren't we?

Defending our great nations from our common enemy. And that's why we need to make sure the wheels of war are turning smoothly.'

What on earth was that, Gloria? I thought to myself. But the soldier was nodding like I'd said something very profound.

'What's your name?' he asked.

Holy Moses, I'd not thought he might ask for my name. Of course I couldn't give my actual name because it was bound to be in Jerome's file, and I couldn't use Wilmington because, dammit, I'd lied about working for Grandpa. For a horrible second my mind went blank and then inspiration struck.

'Allard,' I said, using my grandmother's maiden name. 'Gloria Allard.'

'Wait here, Miss Allard.'

He left the sentry box and I thought he'd go into the prison himself, while I waited. But no, he gestured for me to follow.

We went through the imposing entranceway, and into the jail and I shivered as the cold air hit me, even though it was warm and muggy outside.

'Horrible, huh?' the soldier said. 'I hate being in this building.' He looked round at me. 'It's haunted you know?'

I shivered again. 'I don't doubt it.'

My heels were clicking on the floor and I felt a bit sick with nerves, but I'd come this far. I wasn't giving up now.

'Where are the prisoners?' I asked, because the corridor we were in was clearly all offices.

'Straight through there,' the soldier said, pointing at a thick metal door at the far end. 'Then the ones accused of capital offences are over the back in the execution block.'

'What's a capital offence?' I asked. 'Murder?'

'Yep,' said the soldier, turning down another corridor. 'Murder mostly. But there's also a fella in there for desertion. And a couple for rape.'

I stopped walking. 'What?'

'Desertion,' the soldier said. 'And rape.'

'Rape's not a capital offence,' I said, my voice shaky.

'Not in England, perhaps. But this is a US jail.'

'Right,' I said, beginning to tremble. 'But it must take a long time for the executions to happen. Because you'd have to be sure, wouldn't you? Before putting a man to death.'

The soldier was looking at me in concern. 'Are you okay, Miss Allard? You look a little pale.'

'You'd have to be sure, wouldn't you?' I said again, a little shrill now.

He rolled his eyes. 'You'd think so. But honestly, I'm not sure. Seems we have an execution just about every week.'

My vision blurred and I swayed on my high heels.

'Miss Allard?'

I dropped the folder and the papers scattered across the floor of the corridor.

'Let me get those for you,' the soldier said. He crouched down and I watched as he picked up the list of volunteers to man the coconut shy. 'What's this?' he muttered, reaching for the little hand-drawn map of where the stalls would go on the village green.

I stepped out of my mother's high-heeled shoes. 'I'm sorry,' I mumbled.

And then in my stockinged feet I ran back the way I'd come, tears streaming down my face.

Chapter 34

Philippa

I found Gloria. Well, Alex found her. He'd taken to genealogy like a duck to water, and it turned out while we'd been searching at the museum, he'd been listening to our conversation.

'Jackie said to think outside the box,' he said to me a few days later.' He'd turned up on my doorstep after school one day, his uniform filthy and his hair sticking up.

'Hard day?' I joked.

He looked at me like I was a bit odd, and said: 'Just a normal day. Do you have anything to eat?'

'Does your granny know you're here?'

'I sent her a message.'

'Then yes, I have something to eat. Come in.'

I made him a sandwich and he sat in the kitchen telling me how he was brilliant at thinking outside the box.

'I'm sure you are,' I said, resisting the urge to give him a hug. I was still wary about growing too close to him, no matter how funny and lovable he was proving to be.

'So, I was thinking,' Alex said, through a mouthful of ham and cheese. 'Jackie said men were better.'

'You heard that?'

'Yep.' He looked pleased with himself. 'Every word. Can I have a drink? Do you have Coke?'

'Please?' I said.

'Please.' He gave me a disarming smile and I got a can from the fridge. 'So we should look up Gloria's husband.'

'What husband?'

'Remember you found that she got married in France?'

'Oh yes,' I said. 'I'd actually forgotten that because it didn't seem important.'

'We won't know unless we look him up, though, will we?' Alex said.

'I suppose not.'

I went to get my laptop and Alex inhaled his sandwich and polished off the Coke and then I found Gloria's wedding certificate that Jackie had downloaded.

'Remy Bernard,' I said. 'That was his name.'

Alex adopted a comedy French accent. 'Bonjour, Remy Bernard,' he said, waggling his eyebrows. '*Plat du jour.*'

'That means dish of the day,' I pointed out.

He shrugged. 'I do Spanish.'

I laughed. 'Let's google Monsieur Bernard, shall we?'

I typed in the name, pressed return and sat back in astonishment as my screen filled with results.

'Alex,' I said. 'Look at this.'

'He was an artist?' he said, peering at the screen. 'What does that mean?' He pointed at the words "*nouveau réalisme*".

'New realism, perhaps?' I said. 'I don't know exactly. It looks a bit like pop art.'

Alex frowned. 'Looks a bit rubbish,' he said.

'I quite like it.'

'I like that one.' He pointed to a canvas covered in blue splodges.

'Me too.'

We admired the art for a few minutes, then I remembered what we were supposed to be doing.

'If Remy Bernard was a famous artist then surely Gloria will get a mention in articles or books about him?' I said.

Alex fixed me with a hard stare. 'Wives are often overlooked,' he said.

'Are they now?'

He grinned at me. 'I heard Jackie saying that, too.'

I shook my head and searched for Remy Bernard and wife.

'Here,' I said. 'Something from *The Guardian* about a Bernard exhibition in . . .' I checked the date '. . . 2017.'

'What does it say?'

I scanned the feature as fast as I could.

'Here!' I read aloud. 'Bernard was one of the older members of the *nouveau réalisme* movement, and continued painting until he passed away suddenly in 1979 at the home he shared in Paris with wife Gloria.'

'Well, that's not very helpful,' said Alex. 'Find something else.'

We spent the whole evening reading about Remy Bernard. By the time we'd finished, Alex and I were quite the experts on *nouveau réalisme* and Alex had planned a whole art project in homage to the Yves Klein paintings that used bodies as paint-brushes. I hoped his art teacher would be impressed rather than alarmed.

We'd discovered that Remy had been married before he married Gloria and had two daughters called Angelique and Sylvie, who were in their sixties themselves now. He'd been 55 when he and Gloria got married – more than fifteen years her senior.

'He sounds like a kind man,' Alex said and I had to agree. Remy had founded an art prize, and scholarships, and a high school in Paris focusing on creative arts that still existed today. And I'd read two features about his younger daughter Sylvie, who rather thrillingly was a costume designer for Hollywood films and who'd won an actual Oscar. In both features she'd talked about her dad very fondly.

Alex had given up looking at my laptop and was instead using his own phone to search. Now he yelled: 'FOUND HER!' making me jump about a foot in the air.

'Gloria?' I said. 'You found bloody Gloria?'

'I bloody did,' he said with glee. 'SHE IS ALIVE!'

'What?'

He thrust his phone in my face. 'LOOK!'

I pulled away because I couldn't read the tiny font that close-up. Frustrated, Alex sighed.

'I'll read it,' he said. 'It's about Sylvie. Well, it's not about her. It's about that new Anne Frank thing on Amazon.' He made a face. 'YAWN.'

'Anne Frank's an amazing story,' I said.

He rolled his eyes. 'Whatever. But it says something about it being authentic and, look, it's literally one line, but it says: "costume designer Sylvie Bernard ran her ideas past her stepmother Gloria Bernard, who lived through World War Two". She's alive!'

'What's the date on that article?' I said.

'Last Tuesday.'

My jaw dropped. 'She's alive?'

'That's what I said.'

'She must be almost 100.'

Alex shrugged. 'The queen was almost 100.' Then he frowned. 'I suppose we should be quick, though. Because Gloria is very old.'

'She is,' I said. I was thinking hard. 'I wonder if we could contact Sylvie, perhaps?'

And that's exactly what we did. We contacted Sylvie via her LinkedIn page. I spent ages on the email, trying to explain exactly what we wanted and that I didn't want to unsettle or upset her stepmother, but I was desperate to know what the memorial was and whether it was anything to do with her.

I really didn't expect her to reply but she got back to me within twenty-four hours, the email dropping into my in-box as I watched *EastEnders* listlessly the next day.

"*Gloria is very frail now, but her mind is still sharp,*" Sylvie wrote. "*I called her and asked if she would like to talk to you and she was keen to answer your questions. I live in LA but I am going to France next week to see my sister and Gloria. So, perhaps we could FaceTime when I am there? I don't want to promise you'll get answers. She sometimes gets upset when she talks about the war, and she's not been back to England for a long time.*"

I leaned back against the sofa, watching Phil Mitchell shouting about something I didn't care about, and smiled. We'd found Gloria.

Chapter 35

Gloria

I hadn't left the house since I'd been to the prison, almost a month ago. I'd only spoken to Mother, and Waldo very occasionally and reluctantly.

My grandfather had been working long hours in London, so I'd seen nothing of him. Eugene and Stanley, and Corporal Taylor had all called round, more than once, but I'd refused to see them.

Because Jerome was accused of rape, and he was facing the death penalty, and it was all because of me.

But after three weeks of hiding away, of feeling drained and exhausted, sick as a dog, and crippled with guilt, I realised there was something else going on.

I was pregnant.

At first, I thought I was mistaken. I lay in bed, counting backwards on my fingers and then forwards again. Then I went to find my diary, and checked that too. And however many times I'd checked and double-checked, I got the same result.

Perhaps I was simply worn out, I wondered. Maybe the possibility of Jerome being sentenced to death was so very awful that my body had shut down. I remembered once when

I was at school and worrying myself sick over an exam that I'd been late.

But not this late.

And back then I'd felt completely well. Now I had a terrible dragging sickness that reminded me of how I felt when I'd travelled to France by sea once in a storm. And my waist was, perhaps, a little thicker.

It took me two whole days to realise there was no other explanation for it.

I was expecting Jerome's baby.

And I found to my surprise that I was absolutely delighted.

I was planning to tell my mother today. I hoped she'd be pleased, too. It felt very much like a tiny spark of good news in a very dim, bleak world.

And I even held a little hope that when Waldo heard, he could petition Lieutenant Colonel Cooper at the prison for Jerome's release. Or even for him to be charged with an offence that didn't mean the death penalty. I just wanted him to be moved away from the execution block so that one day he might meet his daughter.

Of course I didn't know the baby would be a girl, but that's what I thought. I would call her Elaine, I'd decided, after Jerome's fierce grandmother. But of course, her middle name would be Rose.

And the Happiness Club would be such proud surrogate grandmothers. I knew Mother and Fran, and all the women in the village would stand by me and support me and help me with bringing up little Elaine, until Jerome came home.

I had it all planned.

I got out of bed, but I sat on the edge for a minute because I'd learned that if I got up too quickly I'd feel light-headed and then terribly nauseous for ages.

So slowly and cautiously, I waited for a second or two – I seemed to feel all right today – before I got to my feet.

I had a wash and got dressed, and then I went downstairs.

The hot weather had broken and we'd had days of thunderstorms and torrential rain. Today was no different. The windows were rattling and raindrops were lashing down.

I found my mother and Waldo in the living room. They were standing together in the middle of the floor and something about the way they were holding themselves made me think suddenly and unexpectedly to the day we'd got the telegram telling us my father had been killed.

The thought made my blood run cold.

'Mother?' I said quietly. 'What's happened?'

She turned to me, her face stricken.

'Darling,' she said. 'Oh, Gloria.'

I felt very calm. I dropped my hand to my abdomen. I had to be strong, for my baby.

'Is it Jerome?'

Waldo glanced at my mother and then at me. 'He's been found guilty,' he said. 'And sentenced to death.'

I closed my eyes, wishing this was a nightmare and that I could wake up. But when I opened them again, my mother and Waldo were still standing in front of me, their faces full of worry.

'Gloria?' Mother said. 'Gloria, darling, say something.'

But as I opened my mouth to speak, a sudden, violent cramp twisted my insides and I doubled over in pain.

'Gloria?' Mother rushed to my side, and I looked up at her.

'I'm bleeding,' I wailed. 'I'm bleeding.'

Chapter 36

Philippa

'Stop pacing,' said Vanessa. 'You're making me nervous.'

'I'm not pacing. I'm walking.'

'You're pacing,' she said. 'Sit down.'

We were in the museum because its Wi-Fi connection was better than the one at Honeyford House, waiting to Zoom Gloria. Sylvie had sent the link after I'd talked to her on the phone and she'd clearly been reassured that we didn't want to upset her stepmother.

'What if Marco can't connect?' I said, sitting down at the table and then immediately getting up again.

'Of course he'll connect. But we'll record the call if you like, just in case.'

I wiped my sweaty palms on my thighs. 'It was a silly idea to send him the link. What if it's bad news and it really is a grave? He'll be devastated.'

'It's not a grave,' said Vanessa mildly. 'I'm almost certain.'

'Almost,' I said, starting pacing again. 'Almost isn't good enough.'

'Well, we'll know for sure very soon,' she said.

'We should rearrange, perhaps? For a time when Jackie and Alex can be here. It's not fair to do it without them.'

'Philippa,' said Vanessa in the same tone she used to tell Alex off for kicking his ball against the wall of the house. 'Calm. Down.'

'Right,' I said. 'Yes.'

'Shall I connect?'

I sat down again. 'Go on then.'

It took a while but suddenly the screen filled with the image of a glamorous woman, with a pixie cut and a broad smile.

'*Bonjour!*' she said. 'Hello! I'm Sylvie.'

Marco's face appeared in a little window at the top and my heart lifted at the sight of him.

'Hello, Sylvie,' I said. 'I'm Philippa – we spoke on the phone. And this is my friend Vanessa, and my husband Marco is here, too.'

Everyone said hello, and then Sylvie moved the screen to show a small woman sitting in a big chair. She had soft white hair and pink-framed glasses, and she was wrapped in an enormous brightly coloured shawl. Gloria.

Sylvie spoke to her in rapid French, and Gloria smiled.

'English now,' she said. 'Sylvie is worried because I don't speak English often. But she forgets I am English.' Her voice was quiet, and Vanessa leaned forward and turned up the volume on the computer.

'Mrs Bernard,' I began.

She snorted. 'My name is Gloria.'

'I'm sorry if this is upsetting to you. But my husband and I have moved into Honeyford House, and we found something in the garden. A statue.'

Gloria nodded.

'Yes,' she said.

I swallowed and in the little thumbnail on the screen, I saw Marco rake his fingers through his hair.

'Gloria, we – Marco and I – we have lost babies, and so we thought . . . we wondered . . . Is it a grave?'

'It's not a grave,' she said.

Relief flooded me.

'But it is a memorial.'

Sylvie took her hand and spoke quietly to her stepmother. Gloria nodded.

'I will tell you,' she said.

Chapter 37

Gloria

Honeyford House, 1969

I was too old to be at this party. There were models swanning around here who were young enough to be my daughters. Models the same age as I'd been the last time I'd seen Honeyford. It made me uncomfortable. I'd sneaked out on to the terrace for some air, and interrupted a beautiful young man having his photograph taken, draped over the stone balustrade.

'Having fun?' My husband Remy came up behind me as I watched the man pose for the camera. He put his arms round my waist and gave me a sympathetic kiss.

'It's so strange being back here,' I said. 'I'm desperate to go and have a look round the house but I'm scared Lucien will have installed mirror ceilings in the bedrooms.'

'I'd be surprised if he hasn't,' Remy said.

'Do not tell my mother we've been here,' I warned him. 'She'll be furious.'

'She'll know,' Remy said in a resigned manner. 'She'll know I'm hiding something as soon as I see her. And she'll drag it out of me.'

I gave him a kiss. 'Stop being such a drama queen. Go and speak to whoever you need to speak to and then let's go home.'

'That sounds like a plan,' he said. 'I'll be an hour at the most. Hold on . . .'

He caught a passing waitress and took a glass from her tray, then he thought again and took a second. He handed them both to me. 'An hour,' he promised.

With a glass in each hand, I wandered to the edge of the terrace. The young man had finished his photo shoot and gone back inside and I didn't blame him. There was a chill in the air.

I looked down towards the woods. It was dark, so I couldn't see much. I didn't like thinking about the war, and everything that had happened. But it was getting less raw now. Less awful. Time was a healer; the cliché was true.

As I leaned over the wall, the music inside went quiet for a second and in the silence, I heard crying. Curious, I listened hard, then followed the sound and found a very beautiful, very thin, very young woman slumped against the wall at the edge of the terrace.

'Are you all right?' I asked.

She lifted her head and looked at me. 'No.'

'Drink?' I handed her one of the glasses and she took it gratefully and drank it down in one mouthful.

I sat down next to her.

'You don't have to tell me what's wrong,' I said. 'But sometimes it helps.'

'You'll think I'm being ridiculous.'

'Try me.'

'I thought I was pregnant.' She sighed. 'But I'm not.'

'And you wanted to be?'

'No,' she said. 'It would be a complete nightmare. Total disaster. I'm a model, for crying out loud. My boyfriend is . . .' she looked up at the sky in despair, at a loss for words '. . . unpredictable.' She pushed her hair away from her face. 'But just for a second I thought it might be nice.'

She gave a little laugh. 'Silly.'

'What's your name?'

'Indigo.' She smiled. 'But my real name is Betty.'

'Well, Indigo,' I said.

'Betty.'

I laughed this time. 'I was pregnant once,' I said. 'I was seventeen. Almost eighteen. And my boyfriend was in jail.'

Betty stared at me in amazement. 'In jail?'

'Yes. So I understand what you mean about the circumstances not being ideal.' I put my hand on her bony knee and gave her what I hoped was a sympathetic rub.

'You wanted the baby?' Betty said.

I shrugged. 'It doesn't matter what I wanted. You're the one who's upset. Shall I fetch someone for you? A friend?'

Betty shook her head adamantly. 'No one knows,' she said. She grabbed my hand. 'Stay here and talk to me. Then I'll go and fix my makeup and pretend this never happened.'

I looked at her, thinking of Remy's daughters, who I adored. I hoped they wouldn't ever end up sad and alone at a party, but if they did, perhaps someone would take care of them too. I smiled at Betty.

'I thought having a baby would be a wonderful thing.'

Betty glared at me through her blotchy makeup. 'Was it a wonderful thing?' she asked, sounding very much like she hoped it hadn't been.

'No,' I said. 'It didn't work out that way.'

'Did you have the baby?'

I shook my head.

'You had an abortion?'

'No, I miscarried.'

'That's sad.'

'Yes.'

'What happened to the boyfriend?'

I swallowed. 'Jerome. He died in jail.'

274

'Huh,' said Betty. 'My mother was right: there really is always someone worse off than you.'

I gave a little laugh, despite myself. 'I guess so.'

'Was it awful?'

'It was awful for a long time,' I admitted. 'I had a breakdown after I lost the baby. I didn't want to live without Jerome, and without my baby.'

'I understand that.' Betty nodded. 'You felt you had nothing to live for.'

I took a breath. 'I tried to kill myself.'

'Shit,' Betty breathed. 'That's heavy.'

'Oh, I don't know if I meant it, or if it was just desperation,' I said. 'I took lots of pills and washed it all down with a bottle of gin. But the gin made me sick and my mother found me.'

'Lucky she cared,' Betty said.

'I was.' I smiled. 'She took me away to a convalescent home in Wales. We stayed there for more than a year. Mother hated it, bless her. But it was the right place for me. Then when the war ended, we moved to France. I've lived in Paris ever since.'

I looked at Betty. She was probably about the same age as my baby would have been, if she'd lived. 'Sweetheart, life is hard and messy and heart-breaking, but it goes on. Make your peace with this.'

'I will,' she said earnestly, nodding her head.

'And find yourself a new boyfriend.'

'Yes.' She got up, all limbs and elbows. 'Have you made peace with it?' she asked.

I thought for a moment. 'Not yet,' I said. 'But I think I know what I need to do.'

Betty blew me a kiss, then she teetered off on her platform shoes. I drained my glass and picked up my handbag. I had a plan.

Next to where Betty and I had been sitting was a pile of debris left over from when Lucien had updated the terrace. A small statue of a cherub was perched on top. It was fairly horrible, but it seemed appropriate. I picked it up, put a few stones from the pile into my bag, took a candle from a table, kicked off my shoes, and set off across the lawn in my bare feet.

It was very dark and the candle didn't cast much light, but I knew the garden at Honeyford better than anywhere else in the world, and my steps were sure and strong. When I reached the trees, I skirted the edge until I got to the hollow in the roots where I'd once sat to read. The ground was hard there so I knelt a little further away. I put the statue down, tipped the stones out of my bag and then felt about inside for something else – something I always carried with me. The sweetheart pin Jerome gave to me.

I wasn't a religious person, but I said a little prayer to whatever entity might have been listening.

'I'm so sorry,' I whispered, to my baby and to my love.

Then I dug a little hole, dropped the pin in, and covered it over. I put the statue on top and surrounded it with the smooth stones.

I got to my feet, brushing the dirt from my knees and blew a kiss towards the little memorial I had made. 'Goodbye,' I said.

Chapter 38

Philippa

When Gloria finished speaking, we were all quiet for a moment. Sylvie kissed her stepmother on the cheek.

'I am tired,' Gloria said.

'We'll not keep you,' I promised. 'Thank you for sharing your story. I'm so sorry about your baby.'

'And I am sorry about yours.' She smiled at me through the screen. 'I have a lot of joy from having Sylvie and Angelique in my life. There are many ways to be a mother.'

Choked, I could only nod.

'Gloria,' Sylvie said. 'Philippa sent me something to give to you and I have it here.'

She opened her palm and there was the sweetheart pin we'd found.

'I thought you should have it,' I said. 'As a memory of Jerome.'

Sylvie gave Gloria the pin, and the older woman regarded it with wonder. 'Thank you,' she said. She smiled. 'I have another part of the story to tell you. Could we talk again tomorrow?'

'Of course.'

* * *

Marco came home.

He borrowed his dad's car and drove overnight, so he'd be with me when we spoke to Gloria again the following day.

'That was nice of your dad to lend you the car,' I said.

'Aye, well, he doesn't know I took it, but he doesn't go in the garage very often,' Marco said, remarkably cheery for someone who'd been driving half the night.

'Marco!' I said.

He laughed. 'I'm kidding. He and Mum are going to come down for the opening and they'll take the car back then.'

'So there is going to be an opening?'

He put his arms round me and I relaxed into his embrace, glad he was home.

'I want to make this restaurant a success,' he said. 'I want to stand on the terrace, with you, and hear people chatting and laughing, and glasses being chinked together, and know that we made it happen.'

'I want that, too.'

'The only trouble is,' he said. 'My little temper tantrum has lost us a lot of time. We're meant to be opening in ten days.'

'First of all, it wasn't a temper tantrum, it was a totally understandable response to everything that's happened.'

'I should have stayed, though,' he said. 'God, we've had enough therapy between us to know that stopping communicating is the worst thing you can do.'

'Maybe. But I didn't help, kicking off about the whole Vanessa and Alex thing.' I screwed my face up. 'I'm really sorry.'

'Me too,' he said.

'Are we okay?' I looked up at him.

'We're okay,' he said.

We stayed there for a minute, holding on to one another. Then I said: 'I've been thinking . . .'

'Uh-oh,' said Marco.

'Yesterday, on the call, Gloria said there was more than one way to be a mother.'

'She did.'

'And I was thinking about Alex, and how much joy both of you have got from getting to know one another, and how I'm getting to know him now, and how much I like that he just turns up when Vanessa's busy . . .'

'Right,' said Marco, looking slightly cautious.

'And then I was thinking about the times my mum couldn't care for me. When I went to Rick and Ellie's, or later when I went to the foster families. How lovely it was, to get into a bed at night, and feel safe. To get up in the morning and have someone ask me how I slept, or if I wanted cornflakes or toast. And I was thinking . . .' I took a deep breath. 'What if we foster?'

'Foster?' Marco put his hands on my shoulders and looked at me. 'Really?'

'It's not easy because we'd have to say goodbye over and over,' I said. 'But in between the goodbyes, we'd have a lot of fun.' I smiled. 'We've got plenty of room.'

'We have more than enough room,' Marco agreed, beginning to smile, too.

'I think we'd be really good at it,' I said.

He pulled me close and kissed me. 'I do too,' he said.

'Shall I call the council?'

Over my shoulder, Marco looked at his watch. 'Well, not now,' he said. 'Because it's four a.m. But yes, let's call the council. I think it's a great idea.'

I leaned against him, relieved. 'Shall we get some sleep before we have to speak to Gloria again?'

'That's also a great idea.'

Today Gloria was joined by her other stepdaughter, Angelique, along with Sylvie. She was very smiley and friendly, though her English wasn't as good as Sylvie's. Still a good deal better than my French, though.

Vanessa had a hospital appointment for her ankle, so Marco

and I had logged on alone. I felt butterflies in my stomach, unsure what else Gloria had to tell us.

'I said there was another part of the story,' Gloria said. 'And there is. Would you like to hear it?'

'Of course we would,' I said.

'Here we go.'

Chapter 39

Gloria

New York, 1980

'I don't want to go,' I said like a sulky child. 'Your father was never honoured while he was alive, so it seems a little late to be giving him an award now he's been gone a year. You know he thought prizes meant nothing.'

Sylvie was on the floor, stitching up the hem of my gown, where it had snagged on my shoe.

'Go, smile, shake some hands, and tomorrow you can go back to Paris,' she said. 'And you know as well as I do that Dad wouldn't mind getting an award for his schools and scholarships. He was very proud of his hard work.'

'I know. I just wish he'd got it when he was alive.' I made a face at myself in the mirror. 'It's going to be so dull,' I said. 'All these worthy people, doing good deeds.'

'Who else is getting an award?'

I rolled my eyes. 'That actress who does the animal rights stuff,' I said, listing them on my fingers. 'The First Lady, some civil rights campaigner, and an Olympian who didn't go to Moscow.'

'I heard,' Sylvie said from her position on the floor, 'that John and Yoko might be coming.'

I snorted. 'If they get out of bed.'

She laughed and got to her feet. 'There, all done.'

I looked at my reflection. I was wearing a long, rose-pink dress made by Sylvie, who was proving to be a very talented designer, even though she was still at college.

'Very lovely,' I said. 'No one else will be wearing a Sylvie Bernard original.'

'Not yet,' she said with a grin. 'Maybe next year . . .'

She pinned the side of my hair back and clipped in a rose bud, then she gave me a hug. 'Let's go,' she said.

The awards were being held at the Plaza. It was terribly fancy and I felt a little awkward, even though I'd got used to being at glitzy parties when Remy was alive. I wished he was there with me, by my side, because I missed him.

Sylvie and I mingled and chatted and when it was my time to accept Remy's award, I got up on stage and said what I wanted to say, without stumbling over my words.

'Thank you very much,' I said.

Off stage there was a bit of a kerfuffle. One of the awards winners had been held up in traffic, so they'd shuffled us all around, but evidently they'd just arrived – I could see one of the organisers, flushed with relief.

I hitched my beautiful gown up as I walked down the stairs and joined Sylvie at the bar.

'You did very well,' she said. 'Dad would be proud.'

'I hope so.' I put the award on the bar and ordered a drink.

On stage, the civil rights campaigner was getting his award. There was a round of applause and then he spoke.

'Thank you,' he said. Two words. That was all. Just two words. But I knew that voice. I'd heard it in my dreams for more than thirty years.

Stunned, I turned round slowly to face the stage.

'Gloria?' Sylvie was saying. 'Gloria, are you all right?'

But I wasn't listening to her. I was staring at the civil rights campaigner. His hair was greying now, and his face was lined, but there was no doubting it. It was Jerome. My Jerome. On stage, right in front of my eyes.

I gasped loudly and staggered backwards, gripping the edge of the bar for support. And somehow, through the audience and the waitresses and the close-up magicians who were in between the two of us, Jerome looked straight at me, and I looked straight at him, and I felt the rest of the room fade away.

'I have to go,' Jerome said into the microphone. 'Thank you.'

And then he was there by my side. I stared into his eyes, and he stared into mine.

'Gloria?' he said, in wonder. 'Gloria?'

I pinched him, hard and he yelped.

'You're real.'

'Yes I'm real. That hurt.'

'You died,' I said, furious with him. 'You died.'

'I didn't.'

'So why did no one tell me?' I wanted to laugh and scream and cry and jump up and down in frustration, all at once.

Jerome looked round at the guests swarming past us to get a drink.

'Shall we get out of here?' he said. 'We've got a lot of catching up to do.'

'Two seconds.'

I found Sylvie, and introduced her to the animal rights actress because she'd admired my dress and I wanted to spread the word about Sylvie's talent. 'I've met an old friend,' I said. 'See you back at the hotel?'

Sylvie looked doubtful, until I gave her my credit card and told her to have fun, then she nodded and gave me a kiss. 'See you there,' she said.

Then I rushed back to Jerome's side.

'Where can we go?' I asked.

He grinned at me – oh, how lovely to see that smile after so long. 'I know a place,' he said.

He took me to the New York Library, just a couple of blocks away. We didn't speak the whole way – just looked at one another in wonder.

The library wasn't open, of course, but Jerome knew the security guard. He let us in, and we sat opposite one another in the reading room, surrounded by books, and I looked at Jerome and he looked at me.

'Tell me everything,' I demanded. 'Everything.'

And so he did.

'I was found guilty of rape,' he began. 'I thought that was it, Gloria. It was an awful place, Shepton Mallet jail. Awful. So cold.'

'I know,' I said, shivering. 'I went there.'

'You did?'

'I wanted to speak to someone, to get you out, but I couldn't. I'm so sorry.'

He took my hand across the table and I let him. His fingers felt familiar in mine.

'You were just one person,' he said.

'How did you get out?'

'It took a village,' he said. 'The whole village.'

'What?'

'Well, it was Eugene and Stanley at first – they started it. They went to Mr Fingal. Remember Mr Fingal?'

'Yes, of course.'

'And they asked him to help.'

I was bewildered. 'What could he do? He wasn't military.'

'But he gathered an army just the same,' Jerome said. 'An army of local people – Clive and Martin and George. Taylor got involved. And Victor and Patty. They were in on it. It was a huge campaign – I still have the press cuttings; Clive kept them all for me. They called in every favour, phoned anyone they could think of, exploited every connection however weak. They got politicians involved, and journalists and some local aristocrat. It was an amazing effort.'

I was speechless.

'At first, they just got a stay of execution, but then Fingal managed to get my conviction thrown out. I never quite got to the bottom of how he did it.'

'He was always very determined,' I muttered, still astonished.

'I was dishonourably discharged, but I didn't care about that,' Jerome said with a shrug. 'I'd had enough of the war by then. I came home to New York and I worked in dead-end jobs for a few years, but on the side, I was making contacts, building a network.' He gave a thoughtful smile. 'I guess I learned a lot from what those folk did back in Honeyford.'

'Seems so,' I said.

'I'm based in DC now. I lobby the government on behalf of the NAACP, working for racial equality.'

'You always wanted to be in politics.'

'You remember that, huh?'

'I remember everything.' I was still completely astonished.

'I tried to find you,' Jerome said. 'I tried to track you down, but no one knew where you were – not even Patty and Victor. I went to their wedding, you know? I thought you might be there.'

I took a deep breath. 'I tried to kill myself,' I admitted. 'I had a breakdown – I don't remember much about the last years of the war. My mother was terrified. She took me to Wales, to a convalescent hospital, and when I came out, I was still fragile. We stayed close to the hospital until the war ended and then we went to Paris. Mother cut all ties with our old friends – she didn't tell anyone where we'd gone. She didn't want any links to our life in Honeyford in case it triggered another breakdown.'

'I wrote to your grandfather,' Jerome said.

'You did?'

He nodded. 'He didn't reply.'

'He died,' I said. 'Before the end of the war. Heart attack. He might not have got your letter.'

'And I wrote to Waldo,' he said. 'At least, I tried. But I couldn't find him.'

'He was transferred to the Pacific,' I told him. 'I think he asked to be moved, though he never admitted it. But he and my mother kept in touch, and they married after the war. They lived in Paris for a while and then they moved to Boston.' I took a breath. 'Waldo passed away about five years ago, and my mother a year later.'

'All this time,' Jerome said in wonder. 'All this time we've been apart.'

'I got married,' I said in a rush.

'You're married?'

'Widowed.'

'I'm sorry to hear that.' He smiled at me. 'Was he good to you?'

'He was.' I squeezed his hand. 'And you? Are you married?'

'Nope,' Jerome said. 'Never found anyone willing to take me on.'

'I'm willing,' I said.

We smiled at one another.

'There's something else I need to tell you,' I said.

Chapter 40

Philippa

'I told him about the baby,' Gloria said, her gaze steady through the screen. 'And we cried a little and he laughed when I told him I'd planned to name her Elaine, after his grandmother. Then we left the library together and we were barely apart from that moment on. We divided our time between Washington DC and Paris.'

I wiped my eyes. Marco was holding my hand tightly and he looked just as emotional.

On the screen, Angelique reached to her side and showed us a photograph of a younger Gloria with a handsome man, dressed in a smart suit. They were gazing at one another and laughing, and they looked very happy.

'That was my sixtieth birthday,' Gloria told us. 'We threw a huge party. I had so much to celebrate.'

'And now?' I asked, not wanting to know. 'Is Jerome . . .?'

'He died in 2015,' she said. 'He was 90 years old.' She looked proud. 'You know, the Obamas came to his funeral.'

I was impressed. 'They did?'

'I'm so pleased you found one another again,' Marco said, dabbing his eyes with a tissue. 'So pleased.'

'Me too,' said Gloria.

We promised to keep in touch, then we said our goodbyes. And when we'd shut the laptop, Marco turned to me.

'The whole village worked to get Jerome out of prison,' he said. 'It's amazing, isn't it?'

He nodded. 'I've got an idea about how to open the restaurant on time.' He took my hand. 'We just have to ask for help.'

And so that's what we did. We asked for help. And Vanessa – now fully recovered – and Alex, and Jackie and her daughter Lauren, and Harvey, and Mick from the shop, and Marco's parents, and his old business partner, Jonny, and Alex's friend Arjan, and Arjan's mum and dad, all answered our cries for assistance and somehow, between all of us, we managed to get everything ready for our opening night.

And now it was a year later. We were on an even keel, finally, and we'd decided to throw a party to say thank you to everyone who'd helped us.

Marco and I stood on the terrace, glasses of fizz in our hands and looked down the garden towards the wood where the bluebells had all grown and were putting on a glorious display of colour. All around me I could hear chatter and laughter, and glasses chinking – just as Marco had dreamed it would be.

'Philippa?'

I turned to see Alex – taller than me now but still funny and sweet – with Maddy, our new foster child, and her little brother, Troy. 'Are you all okay?' I said. Maddy and Troy had only just arrived, which wasn't great timing, but we'd not wanted to say no and our social worker, Gretchen, had assured us we could still hold the party.

'Can I show them the woods?' Alex asked. 'Maddy, you've got

to see what they've done. It's sick. You'll love the treehouse. And there's a swing, Troy. You'll like that.'

He led them off down the garden and I smiled. Alex had appointed himself tour guide for all the children who came to stay and he was very proud of the woods, which we – well, Harvey really – had made into a bit of a play area with a wooden treehouse, and a rope swing tied to one of the trees. And of course there was a hammock – the perfect place to lie and read on a summer's day. I'd even put the cherub back where I'd found it, where it now nestled among the bluebells. I just wished Gloria could have seen it.

'I wish Gloria could have been here,' said Marco.

'I was just thinking that exact thing,' I said. 'Maybe she's watching us from somewhere.'

'I'm not sure if that's a nice idea or really spooky,' Marco said. 'But I know what you mean.'

We watched as the children made their way across the lawn, Alex and Maddy in deep conversation, and Troy running ahead.

'The party is going well,' Sylvie said, coming up behind me and putting her hand on my arm. 'You've done a marvellous job.'

'We had a lot of help.'

I gestured to all our guests. 'Everyone pitched in.' Across the terrace, I saw Vanessa – looking amazing, obviously, in leather trousers – standing close to Harvey, who was just as smitten with her as she was with him. She caught my eye and raised her glass. I raised mine in return.

'I brought you something,' Sylvie said. 'Gloria wanted you to have it.'

Gloria had passed away a few months earlier. Marco and I had gone to Paris for her funeral, and Sylvie and Angelique had scattered some of her ashes with Jerome's in Washington DC, and some with their father's in France.

Now Sylvie held out her hand to show me the little sweetheart pin.

'For me?' I said. 'Really?'

'I think it belongs here, don't you?'

I was absurdly pleased.

'I do,' I said. I showed Marco and he grinned.

'We can put it in a frame and put it up next to the Bowie photograph,' he said. 'Celebrate the history of the house.'

'Perfect,' said Sylvie. 'The perfect ending.'

'Oh it's not the end,' said Marco. 'It's only the beginning.'

The Book of Last Letters

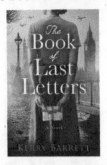

Inspired by an incredible true story, this is an unforgettable novel about love, loss and one impossible choice . . .

London, 1940

When nurse Elsie offers to send a reassuring letter to the family of a patient, she has an idea. She begins a book of last letters: messages to be sent on to wounded soldiers' loved ones should the very worst come to pass, so that no one is left without a final goodbye.

But one message will change Elsie's life forever. When a patient makes a devastating request, can Elsie find the strength to do the unthinkable?

London, present day

Stephanie has a lot of people she'd like to speak to: her estranged brother, to whom her last words were in anger; her nan, whose dementia means she is only occasionally lucid enough to talk.

When she discovers a book of wartime letters, Stephanie realises the importance of our final words – and uncovers the story of a secret love, a desperate choice, and the unimaginable courage of the woman behind it all . . .

The Missing Wife

1933. Hannah Snow is fleeing her unhappy marriage when she finds herself in a small hotel on the banks of Loch Ness. But when a monster is spotted in the depths of the waters, the press descends – and Hannah finds her hiding place is discovered. Someone has been looking for Hannah, and when they find her events will take a devastating turn . . .

Present day. True crime podcaster Scarlett finds herself intrigued by the mystery of Hannah Snow, wife of a promising government minister who disappeared in 1933 – just months before her husband also went missing, presumed dead. As Scarlett works to uncover the truth, she discovers a tragic family secret, and a story as murky as the depths of the loch where Hannah and her husband were last seen . . .

The Secrets of Thistle Cottage

The truth can be dangerous in the wrong hands . . .

1661, North Berwick, Scotland

One stormy night, healer Honor Seton and her daughter Alice
are summoned to save the town lord's wife – but they're too late.
A vengeful crusade against the Seton women leads to whispers
of witchcraft all over town. Honor hopes her connections can
protect them from unproven rumours and dangerous accusations
– but is the truth finally catching up with them?

Present day, North Berwick, Scotland

After an explosive scandal lands her husband in prison, Tess
Blyth flees Edinburgh to start afresh in Thistle Cottage. As she
hides from the media's unforgiving glare, Tess is intrigued by
the shadowy stories of witchcraft surrounding the women who
lived in the cottage centuries ago. But she quickly discovers
modern-day witch hunts can be just as vicious: someone in
town knows her secret – and they won't let Tess forget it . . .

Acknowledgements

This book was really hard to write! And so the first person I need to thank, for her support and patience and good ideas, is my fabulous editor Abigail Fenton. She didn't even flinch when I sent her a half-finished first draft!

One of the things that made this book so tricky was writing about 1940s attitudes in 2023. I chose to use the language that we use today, rather than the language of the time when it came to race and racial issues. It's not strictly accurate but I think we made the right decision, I hope you'll agree.

Thanks as always to my lovely agent Amanda Preston, and you all – my readers. I hope you enjoy this story.

Dear Reader,

We hope you enjoyed reading this book. If you did, we'd be so appreciative if you left a review. It really helps us and the author to bring more books like this to you.

Here at HQ Digital we are dedicated to publishing fiction that will keep you turning the pages into the early hours. Don't want to miss a thing? To find out more about our books, promotions, discover exclusive content and enter competitions you can keep in touch in the following ways: